When a rising country star is found dead in the Missouri Ozarks, sheriff's detective Katrina "Hurricane" Williams must confront the possibility that the man she loves is involved . . .

Called to investigate the theft of valuable timber, Katrina finds the dead body of young singer Sharon Rose lying in the snow, shot execution style. When Sheriff Billy Blevins arrives at the crime scene, his strong reaction to seeing the victim is as baffling as a pretty corpse surrounded by tree stumps . . .

Until Katrina learns that Billy was involved with Rose. The sheriff's refusal to confide in her, coupled with his erratic behavior, not only puts a strain on their already complicated relationship, it hobbles her homicide investigation. With Billy going rogue, Katrina can't rely on anyone but herself. Secrets and suspects abound, even in the singer's own family, and the key to the murder may lie in the lyrics of what is now her swan song . . .

Visit us at www.kensingtonbooks.com

Also by Robert E. Dunn

A Living Grave
A Particular Darkness
A Dark Path

Published by Kensington Publishing Corporation

A Killing Secret

A Katrina Williams Novel

Robert E. Dunn

LYRICAL UNDERGROUND
Kensington Publishing Corp.
www.kensingtonbooks.com

LYRICAL UNDERGROUND BOOKS are published by
Kensington Publishing Corp.
119 West 40th Street
New York, NY 10018

First Electronic Edition: August 2019
eISBN-13: 978-1-5161-0655-4
eISBN-10: 1-5161-0655-5

First Print Edition: August 2019
ISBN-13: 978-1-5161-0657-8
ISBN-10: 1-5161-0657-1

Printed in the United States of America

For Barbara, Beverly, and Betty. My sisters.

Chapter 1

The difference between death and murder is not always obvious. Executions are different. It didn't take an experienced eye to pin a definition on what I faced. The entrance wound in the temple, stippling from hot powder burned into the skin, lack of an exit wound—indicative of a small-caliber weapon—and the bindings on the girl's wrists, make the kind of story we've all seen in a million movies about mobsters. But she was no mobster. That would be the hook this particular drama hung on.

The victim was a girl, maybe in her teens, no more than twenty-five, I guessed. There was no sign of anything personal about the killing. Pretty, young girls, the kind who wore puffy down coats with snow boots and lip gloss all in matching pink, were not usually murdered with such dispassion. I was already thinking that this was a business killing.

I stood no closer than fifteen feet from the body. Bitter flakes, so cold they were almost desiccated, dropped through bare trees. The breeze carried them in streams across the surface of older, crusted-over snow. Creeping white followed the currents and eddied along the crooks of the girl's body. She was being buried slowly by clean, crystalline water.

Watching took me back to a burial in my own life—a moment in Iraq, when I thought myself dead and desert dust piled over me. I came back from that. This girl wouldn't.

I backed away from the body, taking note of my path and the fading footprints leading in. It wasn't until I was another twenty feet back and had reached the first fresh-cut stump that I turned around. Snow and January daylight conspired to make the scene unreadable. I needed help, fast.

Threading my way around the cast-off limbs that littered the snow-covered ground, I waved at the truck idling at the edge of the new clearing.

Hosea Fisher grudgingly came out into the cold. I called dispatch as he trudged over.

"How goes the great tree-rustling case?" Doreen asked as soon as she connected.

"It's a little something more," I answered.

"Did they take shrubbery too?" She laughed.

My call-out had been in response to Fisher's complaint that someone was stealing trees from his property. I thought it was some kind of joke too, until I had arrived to find a newly cut clearing and obvious signs that large trees had been harvested.

"Tell the sheriff we have a body on-site. Definite homicide. Get the crime scene tech out here as quickly as possible. Get me some deputies to secure the scene. Send the coroner out. Tell someone to bring coffee. A lot of it, and hot."

"You got it, Hurricane. Anything else?"

Doreen knew I hated that nickname. Everyone in the department knew. It didn't seem to be the time to remind her. "No," I said. "Just everything quick."

I disconnected and looked at Mr. Fisher, who was staring at me with a gaping mouth.

"You said a body?" he asked.

"Yes." I pointed at his truck. The bed was piled with wood, tools and what looked mostly like junk. Everything was covered with a blue tarp held down by bungees. "Do you have another tarp?"

"Just that one."

"Get it. Bring it up there." I pointed again. This time to where I had found the girl.

"Who?" he asked. His mouth still had trouble staying closed.

"I don't know yet."

"What happened?"

I looked at him. Hosea Fisher was not ancient. It was the best you could say about his age. He had stringy hair and a gold tooth where his upper far-right incisor belonged. The man looked like a perfect suspect. The problem was he also looked stunned. "You and your tarp are going to help me make sure we figure that out."

"I don't like it," he pronounced. "Not one bit."

"I understand, Mr. Fisher. Death gets pretty inconvenient."

"You think I'm some kind of monster? Thinking only about myself?"

I looked into his saggy-lidded eyes. I didn't answer because that was exactly what I was thinking.

"Whoever you got up there is done with troubles. I figure mine are just starting."

"If you don't get moving quickly, you're going to have fresh troubles with me. Bring me the tarp."

He sniffed and wiped at the clear drop of moisture tracking under his drinker's nose. He looked at his truck, then back at me, then up where the body was. Whatever calculations he was doing must have come out on my side. Fisher turned and dragged feet through the snow to his truck.

I knew a little about the man. Everyone in this part of Missouri did. He had gotten into the Branson music business when it was still roadside attractions and hillbilly shtick. It was still that in a lot of ways, but in multimillion-dollar theaters and thousand-dollar sequined suits. Fisher owned one of the biggest. And the Ozarks Star Road Theater had made him a rich man. A few years ago he had married his stage manager. She was much younger and even more talented at the family business. Mostly she worked the show side now and he tended the land that he obsessively acquired.

He was an ugly man with an uglier attitude. But I didn't think he murdered the girl in the snow.

I returned to where I had stood earlier and pulled out the pad and pencil I always had in my pocket. Fisher came through the tangle of cut wood dragging the tarp as soon as I had the basic layout drawn.

"Stop where you are," I ordered.

He stopped but looked as though he didn't like it. "You told me to get the tarp up here."

"I don't want you to drag it." I tucked my pad and pencil away. Then I nodded at the footprints he was about to tramp through. "And I don't want you walking over them."

Fisher stared at the tracks as I approached him.

"What are you looking at?" I asked.

He wiped his nose and snuffed in the remaining drip. "Nothin'."

"Hand me two corners."

He passed the tarp and we pulled it out like a married couple about to fold up the laundry. "Walk it over with me. Stay as far away from the tracks as you can and keep the tarp up off the snow."

Hard flakes of icy snow ticked on the plastic tarp as we carried it along the path. I was watching for the best remaining set of prints. Fisher was watching the ground too.

"You see something," I said.

"Can you tell about someone from tracks like this?"

"We can learn things. Maybe match shoes to the print. Find the right shoe and you might find the person who walked in them."

"What about those?" He looked down.

I didn't need any more indication than that. The smaller set of prints were treaded snow boots. And I was certain they matched the pink camo pair still thirty feet ahead of us. The other set of tracks was larger in size and stride. They were oddly oval and indistinct.

"I don't know," I admitted. "They look like an overshoe or something. Rounded at the bottom like a foot in a sock if the foot had no toes." I stopped over a set that was still unfilled by drift snow. "Here. Lower the tarp straight down and hold it against the ground."

He did as he was told, crouching to keep the forward corner in place.

I scooped up snow and piled it on a corner, then did the same for the other. "Why?"

"Why what?" Without being asked he scooped snow and piled it on his side. He didn't look at me as he worked.

"Why are you so interested in those footprints?"

"Just curious."

"Yeah?"

He stood and looked right at my eyes. "Yeah. Don't believe me?"

"Most people are more curious about that." I nodded my head sideways toward the small body in pink being slowly buried in white.

Fisher turned to look. I kept watching him. I could see his eyes searching for meaning in what he saw. Then I saw the meaning blossom. It settled on him like a weight dragging down his face, then his shoulders. For a moment I thought his knees were going to buckle. They didn't, and he didn't look away, either.

"Rose?" He spoke the question as if he was walking up behind someone he didn't quite recognize.

"Who?"

"Rose."

"You know her, then."

"It's Rose.

I watched the burden of knowledge grow heavier on the old man. He watched the pink-and-blonde mound continue to be buried without making a move to get closer. I glanced at the girl, then back at Fisher. It took me a while but I began to understand. Rose had to be Rosemary Sharon, the young singer they dubbed the Rose of Sharon. She was a star in the local Branson music scene but she shone even brighter than that. Branson had not yet produced the kind of true country music star that its rival Nashville was famous for. The entire community believed Rose would be the first.

"I need you to back away, Mr. Fisher," I said.

He didn't move.

"Mr. Fisher!"

He looked at me and seemed momentarily surprised that I was there.

"Back away," I commanded. As soon as he started moving I told him, "Back to your truck." It was a long, cold walk.

By the time we got back to where his truck sat, still idling, by the fence, a deputy was pulling up to park beside my GMC. He was one of the new guys. I didn't know his name yet.

"Hey, Hurricane." He had a jolly grin and waved as he walked up.

"Don't call me that."

"Sorry." He dropped the grin.

I pointed back along the tracks that I'd left in the snow. "There is a body up there. You can't miss it. Tape the perimeter. Give it fifteen feet on a side. Tape off the tracks leading in from between that pair of trees. Don't walk in the tracks and don't mess up the tarp that's on the ground."

"Got it," he said, then turned to get what he needed from the trunk of his cruiser.

Fisher was in his truck with the door closed. I knocked on the window. He rolled it down.

"I have to ask you questions," I said.

"I figured."

"You didn't know she was out here?"

"I didn't know anyone was out here but tree poachers. And they were long gone by the time I found the damage."

"You didn't know about the trees until you got here?"

"Course not. I found it like this." Fisher wiped at his nose with the back of his hand, then pressed the heel of the same hand into his eyes.

"Why were you out here?'

"It's my land. I got a right to be here."

"That's not an answer."

"What do you want from me?"

"I'm trying to understand things. You came out here, found a crime, then I found a girl who hasn't been dead that long. Sometimes things line up. Most times they don't. Why did you come out to this piece of land on this particularly crappy day, Mr. Fisher?"

"She was part of the reason."

"You were looking for her?"

"Hell no. I was trying to get away from her. Her and my wife, and my stepson and that whole shitstorm I married into. Next time I marry I'll get myself a big dyke like you and be left alone."

I get that a lot. I'm a six-foot tall female cop. Every older man I meet assumes I'm a lesbian, some with more condemnation than others. "It's a new world, Mr. Fisher. It's not okay to say dyke."

"I'm too old to relearn and too old to care. It makes me no never mind if you like the girls. I like 'em too." He almost smiled at the feeble joke. Almost, but not quite. He was talking, but his head was still trying to deal with what he'd seen in the snow.

"If it makes you no never mind, don't talk about it," I said. "Tell me what you mean about getting away from family. Is Rose Sharon family?"

"May as well be. She lives in my house." He stopped and dropped his face. I could see his lips move silently to say "lived."

"Mr. Fisher," I prodded.

He lifted his head and said, "She was one of my wife's projects. That's all she has, projects. They infest my house. It ain't my home anymore. That's why I come out here. Pretty much every day I amble out to check the fences and the land. Trees don't talk back."

I thought about that a second and nothing about it made sense. But on a basic level I understood murder. It was the trees that really confused me. Who would kill a girl to cut down some trees? "Start from the beginning," I told Fisher. He was wiping his nose again. "With the trees. A minute ago you said something about tree poachers. Who does that and why?"

"If I knew who I wouldn't have bothered calling the sheriff. And why do you think? Money."

"I don't understand. What money?"

He looked at me like I was a complete idiot. I didn't mind. It was the first time since Fisher had seen the dead girl that his eyes had any spark at all. "See that stump?" He nodded in the direction of several truncated trees.

"I see a lot of stumps."

He shook his head vigorously, then stuck his arm out the window. "That one. Lowest to the ground and already covering up with snow."

I followed his waggling finger with my eyes. There was a low lump drifting over with blowing snow. It was bigger around than I could have reached. And what was showing was dark as tobacco stain. "Walnut?" I asked.

"You got it, girl." Fisher pulled in his arm. "That tree was about sixty feet tall. The span from the ground to the first limb was at least fifteen feet. The other trees were good wood, but that one was Grade A veneer-quality walnut."

"That's good, I'm guessing."

"$2,000 good at least. Maybe $2,500."

"The other trees?"

"Three prime quality white oak, about $750 each. Another oak—veneer quality—at least $1,000. Over at the edge, the smaller one was walnut but probably not veneer quality, say another $750."

"So we're talking about..." I tried to do the math in my head.

"Somewhere between six and seven grand." Fisher beat me to it.

I looked over at the piles of cast-off branches. It was hard to wrap my head around such a high price tag for trees. If it was true, then the wood theft could definitely have played a part in murder.

"Is there a chance Rose Sharon was involved with the tree poachers?"

The light that was in his eyes when Fisher talked about the trees was gone again. He shook his head and said, "Nah." Then he turned away to stare out his front window again.

He was hiding something. I still didn't think it was murder. I had the feeling it was more about family and shame. "Here," I said, handing over my card. "Call me if you have anything at all to add. And expect to hear from me even if you don't."

I left him to go back and check on the deputy and my victim.

Chapter 2

The new guy had strung tape only halfway around the scene. He was standing back from the girl and putting something away in his pocket when I came out from behind the pile of cast-off limbs. He saw me and looked guilty. I was about to ask him what was going on when I noticed the still-steaming froth of vomit off to the side.

Because he had had the sense not to puke on my crime scene, I cut the guy some slack and didn't say anything about the unfinished job.

"Hey, Hurricane," he said as I got closer.

"Don't call me that," I reminded him.

"Yeah, I'm sorry." He said something more but it was lost in the wind. I assumed it was something I wasn't meant to hear anyway.

"You need to finish the job," I told him. "Get your tape to that tree, then over to there ought to do it, and down the line of tracks."

"You know who she is?" he asked, sounding a little awestruck.

"You recognized her?"

"Yeah. She's the biggest thing in town."

"All the more reason to get to work."

He took the hint and trudged off with his crime scene tape in hand.

"When you finish that, wait down by your cruiser. When the crime scene tech and coroner's van show up, keep them there. I'll let you know when I'm ready for them."

The new guy raised his hand in acknowledgment but kept walking his yellow ribbon to the next tree. I thought he might have said something else, but I didn't hear that, either. My focus was on the dead girl and a circle of ten feet around her. I pulled off my gloves and brought out the pad and pencil I always kept with me.

Crime scenes are always photographed extensively. There was no evidential value to my drawings. But I've always found that photos show all the details of what things are. Sketching helps me see the details between all the *whats*. My first husband was a very successful artist before he died. He helped me improve my sketches and clarify how I looked at the things I drew.

I sketched out how she lay. Then I drew the footprints that showed her killer had stepped over to examine the girl's face. The closest pair of prints were gouged out and irregular. There was an additional divot in the snow a few inches ahead of the left print. The killer had knelt beside the girl. The small forward impression was where the left knee had imprinted the snow. Had the killer just been making sure the job was done or was there an instant of regret?

The girl had been pretty. Her clothing expressed an expensive, manufactured innocence. Pink country chic wasn't unusual for southwest Missouri, but it was on corpses. I couldn't get that in a pencil sketch, but I got the look on her face. It wasn't soft or pleading. Even in death there was a toughness in her pretty features. There were no tears frozen on her cheeks. It could have been that she didn't believe death was imminent. I thought it more likely she understood there are some people and situations who will not be swayed to mercy. I thought she stood, pretty in pink, blond hair flying with the snowflakes, and looked her killer in the eyes. I might have been projecting my own hopes for her brave death.

I understand my own triggers. I'm getting better with therapy. Better isn't well. Some experiences write themselves into us like a devotion carved into tree bark. It becomes of you as much as about you. Some things that happened to me when I was Lieutenant Katrina Williams in Iraq are literally gouged into my skin. There are times in my life that the scars are the only reality. I spent some time trying to smooth them out with whiskey. Other times I used violence and abused my position of power. Violence and intoxication are illusions of control. So before I surrendered to the triggering of my own fear and rage, I walked away from the body. Rose Sharon deserved to be her own tragedy, not mine.

Distance made it easier to drop the veil between the victim and myself. So did concentrating on the smaller elements of the scene. I sketched out the run of foorprints. After that I tried to find some understanding by drawing them in detail. Two sets. One was distinct, the other oddly featureless. The smooth pair seemed to be behind and slightly offset to the left of the other. There was a point when the girl's tracks turned. They stomped down a ragged void in the snow. When they began again it was with a long drag and spraddled steps. I believed she turned to face her killer and was shoved back on track.

I sketched it all out. At that point it was as much about fighting my thoughts as it was about clarifying them.

It wasn't until I heard boots crunching in dry snow behind me that I realized how deeply I had failed at distracting myself. The sound pulled me back from that other place in my mind. I wondered first how long I had stood there with my pencil poised on paper, making no mark. Then how long I had been holding my breath. It never occurred to me to wonder who was coming to my crime scene. I assumed it was the new guy.

I rubbed a fist over my eyes just in case I had been crying. Then I touched a fingertip to the pale ridge of a scar that ran out of my eyebrow and circled down to ring the outer ridge of my orbital bone. It was something I did to hold back the past that went with the wound. "I said I would call when I was ready." I didn't look back as I spoke.

"I'm not here to get in your way," the new sheriff answered.

"Billy?" I still didn't turn.

"Who puked over here?" he asked. Billy was giving me the moment and space he always seemed to be able to sense I needed.

"The new guy." I still didn't look. I didn't need to. I could see in my mind's eye the nod of his head, amplified by the wide-brimmed Silverbelly felt Stetson I had bought him as a present for winning the election. It was an El Patron. If I'd told him how much it cost he wouldn't have accepted it, let alone wear it in the snow.

I continued drawing the scene of violence in front of me. Billy kept out of my field of view. He didn't speak. That didn't mean I was unaware he wanted to have a talk.

We hadn't been getting along lately. A few months ago, I was sure we were headed for wedded bliss. Everything seemed to be pushing that way. Even my dead first husband was telling me in signs and dreams to marry Billy Blevins. The thing is, when I'm pushed, I push back, usually without thought or plan.

"What's under the tarp?" he asked.

"Tracks. I wanted to keep some clear of snow for the tech."

"Anything interesting?"

I used my pencil to point over at the nearest set. "See for yourself," I said.

"The bigger ones," he responded. Billy was always quick to spot the details. "They're smooth and round without tread marks."

I walked away, following my own path in the snow back to the girl's body. "Yes." I started sketching again. It was easier to look at her when I wasn't alone. His presence provided a buffer between the girl's experience and my own. One thing I've learned about PTSD is the value of anything that keeps me from spending too much time in my own head. And if anyone knew the demons in my head, it was Billy. "What kind of shoe leaves prints like that? And who would wear it in the snow?"

"Kids?"

"Why kids?"

"From here she looks like a kid herself. And kids these days seem to think house shoes are reasonable footwear. I see them in the Walmart walking around wearing pajama pants with cartoon character hoodies and weird shoes that look like bear claws, dragon or duck feet. Like their entire life is a cosplay event."

"What's cosplay?" I stopped my pencil over the shading strokes I had been adding to the snow that half covered her jacket.

"Costume play," Billy answered. "Like when they dress up for comic book conventions."

"You sound like you don't approve."

He walked in my trail, moving closer to me and the body. "I don't understand." The stresses in his voice said more than the words. "But there's a lot of things I don't understand."

I started moving my pencil again. This time I was adding the tiny tracks of the crows who had been hopping around and pecking at the dead girl's face. I ignored the tone behind his words and focused on the victim. "I don't think it's a kid. Too deliberate. Someone walked this girl out here. Shot her. They knelt down and checked that the job was done. Then they left."

"They didn't run, either," he added. "Look at the spacing and clear outlines of the prints leading away from the body."

"So not house shoes or kids, I'm betting."

"Galoshes." It wasn't a question. Billy put it out there as a conclusion. He was sure.

"Galoshes? You mean the rubber booties you put over shoes?"

"Sure."

"Who has those anymore? Do they even make them?"

"I have some in my truck."

I didn't have any argument or better ideas. "I'll keep my eyes open for black rubber boots from 1960." I closed my sketch pad, then turned to look at him. Before the election Billy's hair had always been ragged and unruly. After, it was cropped close and all fit under his hat. It made him look older.

"I can't move in," I said. "I've thought about it a lot."

"I thought it was what you wanted."

"Things aren't always about what we want."

"Don't I know it." The acknowledgment managed to sound not quite like an accusation. Billy walked around to the other side of the taped-off scene, crossing behind me like we were players on a stage. He ended up once again at my back.

"Why won't you look at me?" I asked.

"Are you sure it's always about you?"

I turned around. Billy was crouched at the edge of the perimeter peering into the half-closed eyes of the dead girl. "There's only you and me. And I'm the one saying no. Who else is it about?"

He looked up at me with an expression that somehow managed to be sad, disappointed, and angry all at the same time. "Her." Billy canted his head at the girl as he said it.

I felt foolish and looked back at the clouding eyes and blowing wisps of hair. "She's not talking."

"Singing, you mean."

"Singing?" I let the question die as new ones crept into my mind. "You know her."

"Yeah."

"Well..."

"Not that well. Well enough."

"That's not what I meant—"

"I know." Billy turned back to stare at the girl. For a full minute he said nothing, then, "We sang together a few times."

"I didn't know that."

"She's only eighteen." Billy stood, keeping his eyes on the girl. "Was." He turned to look at me. His face, or rather the grief in it, was a shock. "That's why Hosea Fisher is down there in the truck? Did he do this?"

"I don't think so. I found her. He seemed surprised. At first he was just worried about his trees. He might not be innocent, but I don't think he did this."

"No." He took a deep breath and blew out a cloud of vapor. "I don't think it was him, either."

"You have someone in mind?"

Billy didn't answer. He didn't even look at me.

"You knew her more than a little." It wasn't a question. It was me prodding him. I could tell when Billy wanted to talk. Not that he was much of one for holding back. Every once in a while, we all need a push.

He looked at the sky, then he looked back at me, resettled the Stetson on his head, and pushed back. "You stay here. Clear the scene and make sure of every detail. This is going to get ugly."

"Once I release the body the deputies can finish up. I need to get over to the girl's place and start interviewing—"

"You stay. Do all the paperwork. Watch everyone. No souvenir-takers. No selfies. None of that celebrity bullshit. Then you be the last one to leave. Got it?"

There was a hard edge in Billy's voice that I had heard as rarely as I heard him curse. Whatever was going on was more personal than it should have been. "What will you be doing?"

"I'm going to go ask some questions." He backed away from the taped circle with his gaze locked to the dead girl inside. When he reached some secret combination of distance and movement he turned without looking back at either of us and stalked through the crisp snow.

"This isn't the way you want to do things, Billy."

He ignored me.

"Billy!" I took a bracing breath and called again. "Sheriff Blevins! Whatever you're thinking, it's the wrong thing to help the girl."

"There's no helping her." He stopped and hunched his shoulders. I couldn't tell if it was from the cold or some burden he carried until he said, "But I can keep my promise." Billy walked on without reacting further to my calls.

I stood in the snow in front of a dead girl feeling vaguely jealous and guilty for it. What else could I do but put my head down and do the job?

The process was quick despite, or possibly because of, the cold and snow. The sheriff's department, EMTs, coroner's office, fire and rescue—all of us society's carrion eaters—cleared the scene in another hour. Rather than bones we left behind crime scene tape. Like bones and forgetting, the tape would fade, tatter and blow away. Eventually nothing would be left to mark the passing of young life. At least, so I thought.

I was in my truck with the engine running and heater blowing on my numb toes, logging everything in my notes, when the first car arrived. It was a small import that looked out of place on the farm road. It passed my truck and stopped without pulling off the road next to where the tape declared *TANEY COUNTY SHERIFF – CRIME SCENE – DO NOT CROSS.*

Four kids, boys and girls, piled out. The driver hesitated, looking back at my truck, but soon followed his friends. They all held flowers and stuffed animals. One had a glass-jar saint candle she plunked down in dirty snow and lit.

As I approached, I could feel them trying to ignore me.

"Hi," I said.

"We're not going to mess anything up," the girl with the candle said. "We just want to show our respect."

"I can't believe we're the first ones." The driver shifted his convenience-store bouquet of blue-dyed daises from hand to hand.

"You guys know what happened here?" I asked.

"Of course," the driver answered.

"Rose of Sharon was murdered," candle girl added. She was still kneeling in the frozen mud.

"How did you hear about it?"

"The radio." Driver boy placed his flowers, then stared out at the footprints that led into the trees. "Is that where it happened?"

"Where what happened?" I asked.

"Where she was shot," he said.

"Who told you that?"

He shrugged in a way that suggested to me I was stupid and uninformed for asking. The other kids were tying teddy bears to the barbed wire with pink ribbons.

"We're the first," the girl said as she fluffed her ribbon.

"This place is going to be huge," the boy with her said. He stepped back into the road and held up his phone to take a picture. "A shrine." The girl grinned at the camera.

Another car was approaching. I returned to my truck and called out deputies to post at the scene. The first to arrive was the new guy.

He pulled up beside my truck with his window down and said, "Hurricane."

"I told you not to call me that."

"Sorry, it's just…you know."

"What?"

"Cool."

I imagined that every woman named Katrina was called Hurricane after 2005. I never imagined that any of us liked it. "It's not," I told him. "What's your name?"

"Tom."

"Tom what?"

"Dugan. Tom Dugan."

"Deputy Dugan, do you have any idea how the identity of our victim got to the radio station before the girl's body even made its way to the pathologist?"

"No, Detective." He answered quickly, but looked away when he did. His fingers flexed on his steering wheel, both hands gripping it at the top. That was where his eyes seemed to settle.

"Keep people from going over the fence. Control traffic. If reporters show up and ask you questions, the only answer is, 'Talk to the sheriff.' Understand?"

"Got it."

I dropped my truck into gear and threaded past the kids in the road and the next car approaching. As I did I called into dispatch. I had already called in for the victim's address while I was warming my toes. The second call was to log myself as departing the scene and in transit to her home. If I was going to ignore what Billy ordered, I was at least going to do it with the good recordkeeping he wanted.

"You need to get back to the station, Katrina," Doreen responded from dispatch. She sounded frazzled.

"What's going on, Doreen? I have an investigation I need to get onto."

"Sheriff Blevins has a suspect in interview and things are not going well."

"A suspect? In my case?"

"I think it's his case now. You better hurry."

I did. Dropping the mic onto the seat, I hit the gas, then my lights. The county road at that point was little more than a series of blacktop humps. If I went too fast my truck would fly off one of the peaks. On the down sides, wispy snakes of snow crawled, filling the small valleys. I threaded the needle between haste and care.

I was at the bottom of a trough when another car, a beat-up Ford full of kids, topped the hill in front of me. It was going too fast and the tired suspension was no match for the terrain. The car didn't quite fly so much as hop off the road crest. I could see the front tires wag back and forth as the driver tried to find some control. When the wheels hit, the steering was pointed the wrong way. The car veered my direction and whipped its trunk toward the ditch on the other side.

I braced for an impact even as I went off the shoulder on my side of the road.

The car skidded, then righted and passed me so close there would have been contact if the old car still had all its paint.

My truck was in the ditch and stopped dead. In my rearview mirror I saw one working brake light brighten on the Ford before it disappeared over the top of the next hill. I didn't waste time trying to fool myself that they were coming back. I did think a moment on the value of trying to catch them. I decided it would be wasted effort. By the time I got myself out of the ditch and turned around, they could have taken any of three cut-offs or simply gone off-road to hide.

I put the big GMC truck into four-wheel drive and slithered out of the muddy drift. Driving even more carefully, it took me half an hour to get back to the sheriff's office in Forsyth.

Chapter 3

By the time I got to the office the crisis was over. But that's like saying you have a broken sewer pipe and you turned off the flow. You still have to deal with the mess. Sheriff Billy Blevins, the calmest, most thoughtful and careful man I'd ever known, had ignored Hosea Fisher waiting in his truck. Instead, Billy had gone straight to Fisher's Ozarks Star Road Theater. There he had intruded on a circle of prayer for Rose Sharon and arrested Donny Fisher. According to witnesses, many of whom were still at the station complaining, the sheriff was rough and unnecessarily aggressive. When the boy's mother stepped in it turned into a melee. Billy didn't stop after arresting the son for the murder of Rose Sharon. For good measure, he brought in the boy's mother, Sissy Fisher, and their pastor for obstruction and interference.

When I arrived, Doreen was waiting with the story, and phone messages from our district attorney and a friend of mine, Landis Tau. None of it was good news.

"Why are you giving them to me?" I asked.

"Because you can talk to him," she said. "No one else can."

"What are you talking about? Billy is—"

"Something's wrong, Hurricane." Doreen pointed to the closed door of the sheriff's office. "I don't know what happened, but the man in there isn't the same one who started the day."

I took the pink message slips and walked down the hall. The other people in the station made it a point not to look at me. I wondered how open the secret of our relationship had become. I stopped, facing the door and looking at the squares of paper. The DA, Billy could handle. At least the man I thought I knew could. But the other lawyer—Landis Tau—he worried me. He was a friend. Tau ran a not-for-profit called the Midwest Center for Civil Rights. A significant part of that foundation's funds came from Tau's successful efforts for private clients. The man was not a game-player. If your department became involved with him, someone had really screwed up.

The door wasn't locked, at least. And I didn't bother knocking.

His predecessor had always put his muddy boots right on the desktop. Billy sat behind the desk with his feet propped on the lip of an open drawer. In his lap was a pint bottle. It was unopened.

"What's that for?" I asked.

"You oughta know."

My cheeks burned with the flush that bloomed in them. "I know what it is for me. And does to me. You know it too. You were there for some of my worst."

"What is it about the temptation?" He examined the bottle. "You know, I can count the times I've been drunk on one hand. And I've never gotten so drunk—"

"What? Crying drunk? Sick drunk? Blackout?" I sat in the guest chair closest to his line of sight. "Or just as drunk as you've seen me?"

He reached up and set the bottle down on the desk. It hit with a solid thump. "I've never been as drunk as I would like to be right now."

I stared at the bottle until Billy took it away and dropped it into a drawer. It wasn't until it was out of sight that I saw he was looking right at me.

"You're why I don't," he said.

"It's good that someone has learned from my experience."

"You're an idiot."

"What?" I was shocked by the humorless assertion.

"You're an idiot," he repeated. "And you're kind of self-absorbed. But I've told you that before."

"You have."

"You always think it's about you. Even when it is, you think it's about you in the wrong way."

"I don't think either one of us knows what you're talking about at the moment."

"My refraining from getting drunk has nothing to do with your experience, or the lessons of your alcoholism. It's not about you. It's about me, not wanting to make your life harder. I don't want to be your excuse. I do want to be your reason. At least part of the reason you stay sober. That…you stay at the job."

"Billy…"

"That you stay in my life."

"That's not what we need to talk about."

"Yes, it is." Billy leaned back and looked at the ceiling. "Because things get all tied up with other things."

"I don't understand."

"I know."

I waited for more. When it didn't come I asked, "What about the girl?"

"What about her?"

"Okay. What about the kid you arrested?"

"He killed her."

"What's the evidence?"

"I don't have any. I know. And I wanted him to know that at least someone had the truth on him no matter what happens."

"That's not the job."

"As I recall, you never thought I was the right man for the job."

My face flushed again. I loved Billy, but I voted for someone else. "I thought you were too kindhearted for a job that requires a son of a bitch."

"We all have kind hearts and hard ones."

"I guess that's true. What are you going to do about this kid you arrested?"

Billy grinned at me like a gleeful executioner. "I'm going to apologize and let him go. You're going to get the evidence to put him away."

"So today was what? Some kind of show?" I tossed the message slips onto his desk.

He looked at the papers but didn't move. "Some kind, yeah."

"What was your relationship to the girl?"

"It looks like I have some calls to return." Billy finally reached for the notes.

I didn't need a goodbye to tell me when I was being dismissed. On my way out of the station I stopped at my office long enough to print Rose Sharon's driver's license info and call the jail.

"Hurricane!" Donald Duques greeted me. "How's it hanging?"

"Have you ever heard of political correctness, Duck?"

"I'm an old, fat white man with a high school education. Who do you think they invented it for?"

I let it go. "You have people down there. Two the sheriff brought in."

"The Fishers? Yep."

"Cut them loose."

"Even the ballbuster?"

"What do you mean?"

"The kid's mother. She's a two-dollar bitch stuffed into a hundred-dollar dress and pinned up with a thousand dollars' worth of silver."

"What's that supposed to mean?"

"They say she hit Billy. Pulled his hair and tried to kick him in the crotch."

"*Sheriff Blevins…*" I put a lot of emphasis on the title. "Probably deserved it."

"I should ask him about the release."

"Let them out. Let them use the phone to call for a ride or anyone they want. And apologize. If they ask why it happened—you don't know anything."

"Story of my life."

"You got that right." I hung up, then went right for my truck.

Rose Sharon's listed address was the same as the Fishers'. It was a big fieldstone house built into a steep hillside. It shared the same back-door view of the lake as my own home. We were neighbors, two miles away by road, about a thousand yards by the crow's path.

That wasn't nearly as surprising as the little person standing on the front porch waving at me as I parked.

Landis Tau scraped the lower edge of four feet in his shoes. But those shoes cost as much as most people's house payments. His tailored suits and bright bow ties had the kind of elegance that dared you to judge them by size.

I had met him while working a case dealing with white supremacists. Since then he'd asked me to serve on the board of his not-for-profit legal center. In turn, I asked him to serve on the board of a nonprofit I founded to help provide for some refugee girls. I had a feeling our relationship was about to get much more tangled.

"Katrina! My favorite hurricane." He held out a hand as I approached.

I stayed on the walkway level and barely had to bend to shake. "Landis. Why are you at my victim's house?"

Landis laughed like he knew something I didn't. "That's the thing about working for someone you are romantic with."

"Am I supposed to understand what you're saying?"

"Some secrets keep and some don't. Everyone knows you and he are a thing, Hurricane."

"That's not what we're here to talk about."

"Your sheriff beau didn't tell you that Rose Sharon resided with the Fisher family?"

I tried not to let my discomfort show on my face. "He didn't need to. Hosea Fisher told me. But that's not the issue. I'm here to conduct a homicide investigation. I need access to the victim's home."

"See, that's the thing." Landis was no longer smiling. "She was a guest in their home. And even though I got a call saying my clients have been released, I am still going to insist on a warrant for any examination of their home."

"I'm trying to find a killer."

"Your sheriff already declared Donny Fisher a suspect. Arrested him even. Without cause. Given the sheriff's relationship with Miss Sharon, that smacks of vendetta."

That time something must have shown on my face. I saw it reflected in the lawyer's expression.

"You didn't know?" It was a question but it wasn't.

I didn't answer. Instead I asked, "How long?"

"You would have to ask him."

I shook my head. "How long was she a guest here?"

It was his turn to work his face. He was better at it than I was. "I don't know."

"I have a printout of her driver's license issued two years ago. This is her listed address. That doesn't sound like a guest."

"Hosea Fisher owns the home."

"Did Rose Sharon pay rent?"

"No."

"She paid no money? Contributed nothing to the maintenance of the house?"

Landis held his face as if it was cast in concrete. "You're making some good stabs, but you should leave it to a judge."

"Would you stay here guarding the door so ferociously to keep your clients out if I went for one?"

"It's their home."

"It's my investigation."

"Call your DA."

I thought about it. My hand was on the pocket that held my phone. But for some reason I felt like Duck at that moment. He was a man who literally believed that the world was being torn down and rebuilt not just against him, but to spite him. Despite the fact that his was a reaction to losing the good old boy's white privilege, I understood a little bit of it every time I had to face a lawyer. "Where's her room?" I asked.

"Why?"

"Is it a secret?"

"In the basement."

I looked over at the concrete steps leading around the left of the house and down the hill. "Let's go see."

"I will still insist on the warrant," Landis declared, following without trying to keep up.

"Still?" I stopped and looked up the hill at him when I reached the level of the walk-up. "So there's something different?"

He stared down at me from the walk.

I went around the corner and peered into the sliding glass door. Inside was a large room with a couch and TV. The nearest corner was lined with stringed instruments: guitars, banjos, a mandolin and a dulcimer. On the other side was a paneled wall with an open door. Through the door I could see a bed made up all in pink and white.

"Don't think this changes anything," Landis said as he circled the corner.

"It's a separate residence," I said. "And look." The door slid open as I pulled the handle. "It's unlocked." I went through the door and turned around to block Landis. "I can't let you in."

"You know I'll fight you in court."

"Unless you can swear to me right now that Rose Sharon was your client I'll take that chance."

For a moment he hesitated, keeping his gaze hard. After that moment he shrugged and smiled. "It's freezing out here."

"Nothing says you have to wait outside. You can go anywhere else but you can't come in here."

"Think you have the spine to arrest me?"

"Do you think I don't?"

"You don't have cuffs small enough." His joke seemed intended to break the congealing tension. It didn't work. At least not for me.

"I have duct tape in the truck."

"And you wonder why trouble swirls around you like... Well, you know."

I backed into the room and pointed at a spot of floor just inside the door. "You can stand there."

"See?" he asked. "You aren't quite the walking evil people say."

"Who says that?"

"Don't pretend ignorance of your own reputation."

"I'm not ignorant of it. I just never heard I was evil." I walked around the couch and looked through a plastic tray by the TV that held a remote, some keys and loose change. "No dust. No clutter. She was a tidy girl."

"Housekeeper," Landis said.

"There's a lot of money in Branson music."

Landis canted his head like he'd caught me snickering at a funeral. "Judge much?"

"Who says I'm judging anyone?"

"I heard it even if you didn't."

I left him behind and went into the bedroom. There was a stuffed elephant perched on the pillows. Her dresser was stacked with professional music magazines. The mirror was framed by a collage of show tickets, and photos. Two of the pictures stood out. One was Rose with her arm around an older man in the Army battle dress uniform. The name tape on the BDUs was obscured but the sergeant's stripes were clear. They were smiling. Tucked in another corner of the mirror was a grainy print that was obviously a selfie she had taken. It was striking not because of the happy grin on Rose Sharon's face, but because of the smiling man she was leaning up against—Billy Blevins.

"People with money piss you off," Landis continued from the other room. "Even though you have plenty of your own. Plenty hell—your husband's estate left you a rich woman. Why do you even stay on the job?"

I pushed the door aside and stuck my head back into the greater room. "Money doesn't piss me off. Privilege does." Turning back, I crossed the bedroom to the small private bathroom. "I guess *that's* why I'm still on the job." I spoke up loud enough for Landis to hear without really talking to him.

"I hear people lie to themselves all the time," Landis called, and there was no doubt he was speaking to me.

The bathroom was tidy and scrubbed. I left it without touching anything.

"Find anything useful?" he asked as I returned to the main room.

I didn't have an answer. Or, more accurately, I didn't have an answer I wanted to give. So I pulled out my phone and dialed our crime scene tech directly. I gave him the address and asked him to search and secure the rooms. As I spoke I walked into the corner where the instruments were lined up and waiting for hands. The space was defined by sheets of plywood on the floor and two wooden chairs that looked to be garage sale treasures. Littering a half circle around the chairs were lined pages with music notation and lyrics. Penciled in neat script at the head of each page was the title: "You Took What Wasn't Yours."

Before I could even begin to puzzle out the implications of that, my gaze caught on one of the guitars. It was a cheap instrument and looked much the worse for wear. I'd seen it before. It belonged to Billy.

"Find something interesting?" Landis asked.

"Maybe," I answered, putting my attention back on the page in my hand. "If I could read music." I dropped the paper onto the nearest chair. Questions were building up like a dry stack rock wall. Everything was its own thought and nothing stuck to anything else. Still they piled. Worse, I had no idea which side of the wall I was on. Was Billy a suspect? Were the girl and Billy's relationship with her part of the reason for my own personal difficulties with him? Why had Rose Sharon been murdered so dispassionately?

"What's the story here?" I asked Landis.

"The story?"

I looked around the room, then spread my hands to include the entirety of the house. "The girl. The Fisher family."

"Your boyfriend, the sheriff?" He tried to soften the question with a smile. I could tell it didn't work by the way he looked at the floor when his question hit me.

"He's not...We're not..." I shook my head. The gesture served both to say no and to keep from saying it. "Anyway, that's not what I'm asking, and you know it."

"You can't honestly think this girl was killed as part of a family squabble?"

"Are they family?"

"By blood, no. But Rose lived with the Fishers since the death of her mother five years ago. She was part of the family music show."

"Money is a big motivator."

"Everyone knows the girl was breaking out. She was going to be a star. If it was about money they would have done everything to keep her safe."

"Maybe stardom was going to leave the family behind."

"Sissy Fisher was the girl's manager. If money is your motive, the family's not your target. Any way you look at it, they wanted her safe."

"We'll see."

We both looked up at the ceiling at the same time. Someone had come into the house upstairs. There were multiple voices and footsteps.

"I guess we will," Landis said. He pointed at the ceiling. "Because, speak of the devil."

He walked to the stairs at the far end of the room. I didn't object.

Once alone, I felt like an intruder. The feeling intensified when I wandered back to the bedroom. Even when I was her age, my room had never been so girly. I went to college on a basketball scholarship. That was a given for a girl who had reached six feet tall by her sophomore year of high school. And I went straight from my college ROTC program into the family business. We were a military family. My father was army, his brother, a marine. There was a lot more olive drab in my life than pink.

I couldn't help but wonder if that kind of femininity was something that attracted Billy. Maybe it was simply youth and talent. Billy was one of those men who seemed to be good at everything. He had an aura of competence. But more than anything, when you heard him, you knew he was a musician at heart. He could have made a career of it.

The glass patio door slid open and I heard boots stomping snow off on the concrete pad outside. Deputy Bobbi Rantz had arrived.

Taney is a big county, but rural. The only city of consequence is Branson and they have a municipal police force. The sheriff's department handles pretty much everything else. Because of the economies of population density, most rural sheriff's departments are make-do operations. Bobbi was our make-do crime scene unit, a deputy with some extra training and a willingness to do the dirtiest jobs for a little extra pay. I couldn't function without her.

When I didn't hear the patio door slide closed I went out to the main room. Bob was at the open door removing her boots.

"It's not a crime scene," I said. "Contamination isn't an issue."

"It's a good habit to be in," she said, looking at my boots. Bobbi stepped in on stocking feet, then closed the door behind her. "What are we looking for?" She pulled house shoes from her pocket and slipped them on.

"Anything," I answered. "I had a quick look around."

"And?"

I turned and went to stand by the bedroom door. I looked in rather than at Bob. "There is a laptop in there. Take it. Look for social media threats, anyone too close or pushy. She's a girl. Look for a diary or journal. There are scraps of paper all around. Most of it's music, but take and check it all."

"What else?"

I didn't mention the photos tucked inside my pocket. I did step into the bedroom. Bob followed as I pulled back the comforter and top sheet from the bed.

"Got it," Bob said. She set her case down and started unpacking.

When she was ready I turned off the room light and stepped out. Her UV lights flickered on as I closed the door. Bob was looking for evidence of sexual contact on the sheets. I wasn't exactly afraid of what was there to be found. Still, as she worked, I dropped Billy's guitar into a large evidence bag and took it out to my truck.

Chapter 4

The Fisher family was still as mad as a cat in a bubble bath. Landis did his best to smooth out the meeting when I came to the front door. I would have been fine if it weren't for the matriarch, Sissy Fisher. She was a spray-tanned, country music stage mother. She dressed the part with a weird mix of hillbilly and southwest Native American appropriation. Her feet were bare, but she wore a tattered and patched denim jacket over a white skirt with a factory-shredded hem. Overlaying everything was silver and turquoise jewelry. At her neck were squash blossoms and beads. Her waist was draped with a concha belt inlaid with sky-blue crosses. Six of her fingers and two of her toes were ringed. Each ear shimmered with silver, stones, and feathers. Sissy Fisher was one of those people who put on a display of love for a culture but showed it no respect. I disliked her instantly.

"You're the one rummaging around my basement," she said when Landis introduced me.

"I'm the detective investigating the murder of Rose Sharon. The victim's home is a good place to start." I kept my voice even and my gaze straight. She was almost as tall as me.

"Start?" She chirped the word like a bird poked with a stick. "The start was with my son and that bullying sheriff. It won't be the end. I can promise you that."

I looked at the young man standing a few paces behind Sissy and trying not to look embarrassed. "You're Donny?"

"Yes, ma'am," he answered.

"Why did Sheriff Blevins want to arrest you?"

"You know better than to ask that, Hurricane," Landis warned. "And I hope you know better than to answer it, Donny."

"I'm asking his opinion."

"You're fishing for self-incrimination," the lawyer countered. "It's not going to happen."

"You're all the same," Sissy chimed in. "Pointing fingers at innocent young men. You should be looking at drug dealers. Real criminals."

"Are there a lot of real criminals in your life?"

"Katrina," Landis cautioned, with both my name and his tone.

Sissy's eyes hardened and she leaned forward. "Look at the sheriff. He knew Rose. He knew her well. Arresting my son was just a cover-up for his own guilt."

I leaned forward too. If we were cats, we would have already been spitting and scratching. "I'm going to find the truth here." I turned and looked at Donny Fisher. It was a good, hard look. Then I looked back at his mother. "You should be careful when you talk about guilt."

"He was here, you know." Sissy's voice narrowed and quieted. Her lips curled into a smirk with her words. "So many nights. The floor lets a lot of sound through. We could hear the music and the laughing. Was he supposed to be with you?"

Both of us were angry but neither one was stupid enough to take the other's bait.

I kept staring at the mother as I asked, "When was the last time you saw Rose, Donny?" Then I turned to look at him.

Donny opened his mouth. He never got the chance to speak.

"I don't think we'll be answering these questions here," Landis jumped in. "You can call me and we'll make an appointment for a formal interview. But you should probably go now, Detective Williams."

I nodded and stepped back. Landis was right. I was only stirring already muddy waters.

"You're the one they call Hurricane," Sissy said, with venom in her eyes and her tone. "Is it true what they say? You have millions. You own that big bar and an art store in Branson—but you stay a cop so you can beat people down?"

"Part of it's true." Once I spoke I realized that my hand was clenched.

"Which part?"

I focused on opening my hand while I honestly thought about an answer. But if the answer was honest, I might have said—it depended on the day. So I said nothing.

Sissy wasn't interested in letting me disengage. When I turned to leave she said, "It's not very ladylike, is it?"

"Let's let Detective Williams go do her job, Sissy," Landis said.

I told myself not to turn around. I kept repeating it in my head as my body turned. "Ladylike?" I asked when my eyes were again set on hers. "What's not ladylike?"

"Look at you. You dress like a man. You do a man's job. What does that say about you?"

"That I earn my living on my feet and not on my back," I answered. Walking out, I didn't pay any attention to the noise and profanity thrown at my back.

The gray sky had slammed shut, leaving night behind at 6:00 p.m. Snow still spit through the beams of my headlights as I drove. Cops often don't have the luxury of regular hours. In any other case, that wouldn't bother me. I would go back to HQ and start on my paperwork. I would put my feet up and talk things over with my boss. But that was too screwed up to even consider. I called dispatch and logged myself off duty but available. I told Doreen I would be at Moonshines.

Sissy Fisher was right. I was a rich woman. And my snarky comeback to her was not entirely accurate. I didn't earn any of it. I married Nelson Solomon, a man with surprising talents. One of them was investing the money he made as a star artist. Everyone who doesn't know me focuses on the bank account. Those people are as ignorant of money as I was when it was dumped on me. When he died, Nelson left me more responsibility than riches.

Moonshines, a distillery bar and restaurant, was one of my burdens. The last thing an alcoholic needs is ownership of a bar that makes an unending supply of her favorite poison. But the best thing she can have is a friend behind the counter who knows her.

I came in through the kitchen entrance. A couple of people said hello. Even more grabbed me to ask about Rose Sharon. By the time I got into the bar, a mug of hot chocolate with little marshmallows was waiting for me on the counter.

"That's a nice surprise," I said to the man behind the bar.

"Too cold a day for soda or iced tea," he said. "I know you won't drink hot tea and it's too ugly a day for coffee. So…" Clare extended his hands toward the steaming mug in a kind of presentation. "There you go."

That Clarence Bolin had become such a close friend was one of the great surprises of my life. He was a man the age my father would have been, who looked like a hillbilly poster boy with long silver hair and beard. Overalls that barely contained his round gut didn't help the cliché appearance. But appearances only go so far. Clare was a retired history teacher, an ordained Assembly of God minister, a semireformed bootlegger and closet Democrat. Moonshines couldn't remain in business without him.

I put my hands around the mug. The liquid inside was way too hot to put to my lips. "It is an ugly day," I confessed. "I think they are going to stay that way for a while."

"No kidding. I heard there are news trucks parked around the sheriff's office."

"I don't get it." I leaned over the cocoa and let the heat rise to warm my face. "What?"

"Was Rose Sharon that much of a celebrity?"

"It doesn't seem like it takes too much celebrity to be a celebrity these days."

"Maybe." I kept my head down and eyes closed as the hot drink warmed me.

"But she was a real-deal kind of girl. This whole town, and all the country music business outside of Nashville, was watching her do it. She was making it and showing you didn't need to do it the big-business way. America loves a maverick. Especially if she's a pretty young girl."

"I guess."

"Put all the national stuff to the side, and she's still a Branson big deal. This town is going to react like we just lost Dolly Parton."

"They didn't know her. I bet nine out of ten of the anguished crowd have never even heard her sing."

"Maybe not. But people around here are used to music stars moving from the big stage to Branson. It always seemed like a step down. Rose Sharon was the first to be making the move up. She was taking the dreams of a lot of people with her."

I raised my head and watched Clare work behind the counter until he turned. "What's wrong?" he asked as soon as he caught the look in my eyes.

"Billy was involved with the girl."

"Involved? What does that mean?"

"I don't know. They knew each other. They spent time together."

"Is that all?"

"They *sang* together."

"The bastard."

"It's not a joke."

"Isn't it?"

"What's that supposed to mean?"

"What are you worried about? That you're going to lose something you don't want?"

"You think you know what I want?" I put the cocoa to my lips without drinking. It was still too hot but I wanted to focus on another kind of pain.

"I can't claim to. But I can see what you don't want."

"I don't want to talk about it."

"And there's the problem."

"I already have a therapist," I said before finally sipping a bit of the cocoa. It scalded my tongue.

"You want some food?" Clare could always be counted on to drop things that needed dropping.

"Yes. I haven't had a bite all day."

"So I bit her." Clare walked out of the bar laughing at the old punch line. He came back a moment later still chuckling. "Dinner will be just a minute."

"You could have waited for me to tell you what I wanted."

"Do you even know?" He laughed again.

"Funny man."

"Have I ever steered you wrong?"

I pushed the hot chocolate away. "Yes. You tried to boil me from the inside out with this cocoa."

Clare reached into the special ice bin. He kept two ice bins. One with regular machine ice, and one with ice he made in spherical molds from distilled water. They were crystal clear and he usually served them only with the best whisky. He dropped one of the glistening spheres into my mug. "Anything else?"

"Do you know anything about stealing trees?"

"First you get a chain saw—"

"Who." I poked the dwindling ice sphere with my finger. "Who does that? Until today I'd never heard of stealing trees."

"Maybe you've led too sheltered a life. The lands around here are full of thousand-dollar walnut trees. Good cherry goes for the same."

"I don't need a lesson, I need a person."

"Well…" Clare held on to the words.

I could tell it wasn't because he was thinking what to say next. "What?"

"You're not going to like it."

"Since when has liking it had anything to do with my job?"

With that, Clare left. One of the waitresses brought me dinner. She wanted to talk about Rose Sharon, but I told her I couldn't talk about an investigation. Truth was I was too hungry when I saw the plate. Clare had ordered me our new Delmonico steak seared in cast iron. It was still sizzling from the hot skillet with a dollop of herb butter melting over it. The sides were roasted red potatoes and a mix of slightly blackened broccoli and carrots.

After my first bite I pulled out the two photos I had taken from Rose's mirror and set them on the bar. I ate everything on my plate with my gaze fixed to the pictures.

The food went quickly and it was a good thing. The man who walked into the bar and sat beside me would have killed my appetite.

"Katrina," Clare said, "meet E."

"E?" I asked.

"Evens Edward Lawson," the man said.

"That's a mouthful of a name."

"Those that use it call me Double E, some Big E or just E. Most just call me Lawson, and a few E Lawson. I ain't particular." He offered his huge hand. It was hard and callused. Like shaking hands with a shedding snake.

It was the cologne that was the appetite-killer. Not that the rest of him was pretty. Lawson looked like he had dressed and doused himself for a meeting with the law. He wore boots with two-inch heels that kicked him up past six feet eight. His snap-front Western shirt barely contained him. It was covered, not by a coat, but a sheepskin vest. His long hair draped over wide shoulders to the middle of his back. And in all that was still something more striking than anything else. His right eye was a color somewhere between green and brown. His left was blind and mottled in shades of white, as if filled with a terrible storm.

When he released my hand, he waved two fingers at Clare, who already had a glass waiting. As the whiskey was being poured Lawson said, "So you're the big girl cop everyone talks about."

"Well…" I grabbed my cocoa mug and suddenly felt silly about it. I took a drink and let the cooled chocolate slide down slow. When I set it down I didn't feel foolish at all. "I'm a cop and I'm a woman. I'm no little girl."

"I ain't talkin' down. Don't mean to, anyway."

That caught me completely off guard. So much for assumptions. "Thank you," I said.

"You took down Johnson Rath."

He was talking about a white separatist who dealt in drugs and guns to finance his dream of a racially pure enclave in the Ozarks. He had been murdered in prison.

"Yeah," I answered. His face gave me no clue to his feelings. I rested my hand on the telescoping baton clipped to my belt. "I did. Is that a problem?"

"Not for me. He was a son of a bitch."

I relaxed my hand. Then I let the rest of me unwind a bit. "Yeah. He was that."

"Clare said you wanted to talk about…" Lawson worked his mouth a little as he tried to find the words he wanted. "Illegal activities. He said it wasn't about me, though. That true?" He sipped his whiskey.

"I'm not promising. I don't know who it's about."

"You tell me what and I'll tell you if I want to talk."

"Fair enough," I said. "Some trees were taken from land owned by Hosea Fisher."

Lawson nodded and sipped. I couldn't tell if he was agreeing or considering. "When?" he asked, setting the glass on the bar.

"Today."

The big man's broad shoulders relaxed. He took another sip of whiskey. When he lowered the glass this time, Lawson was looking at me and smiling. "I'll talk."

"I know an alibi grin when I see it."

"I was in Springfield last night and all day today."

"Not alone, I guess."

"I was in the hospital watching my daddy die. Last night. Doctors saw me. Nurses. One real pretty one. Till a couple hours ago I was making arrangements and lettin' the pretty one help me feel better about things."

"You don't sound exactly broken up," I said.

"He wasn't much of a daddy." He took another drink.

I was struck by how much I didn't want a taste of whiskey. Usually it was a struggle. I'd found the one person I didn't want to drink with.

"What's a two-thousand-dollar tree?" I asked.

"Around here, probably walnut. It'll be one grown in amongst other trees in a woods. Field trees get damage. Cattle mess with the bark or you hit it with a tractor. The damage shows in the wood, dark spots or burls. You want a mature tree with no low limbs."

"Why?"

"Limbs make knots or tracks in the grain. You want it clear for about twelve feet. Fifteen is better. You take a tree like that to the mill and cut it down thin."

"Grade A veneer?"

"Yep."

"And there's an illegal traffic in trees like that?"

"You know anything of value there ain't an illegal traffic in?"

"Seems like a lot of work."

"I look like someone afraid of work?" He took the last swallow of his drink and set the glass down loudly. "Not that I'm admittin' anything. But I can cut a big tree down, top it, and have the log ready to go in half an hour. Less if I bring help to get it on the trailer. Any way you cut it, that's good money."

"Just to let you know, I'm a cop. Not a reporter. Saying that you admit nothing while admitting a crime is no protection."

"I talk ignorant, but I ain't. I admit what I already been convicted of." Lawson gave me a hard, one-eyed appraisal. "Still, I take comfort in knowing I'm not the lumberman you're lookin' for."

"Maybe," I said. "You know a lot of people who do this sort of thing?"

He looked away and appeared to consider his empty glass.

"Okay. Let me put it this way." I waited for him to turn back, then asked, "You know anyone who would kill for this sort of thing?"

The brow over E's milky eye twitched and his good eye focused sharper. "People who do this sort of thing, do it so they don't have to work hard. Most folks I know loggin' like that, live by hunting and fishing. They barter for most everything else they want."

"What's that supposed to mean?"

"It means they want things easy. Nothin' easy about killing a man for his lumber."

"A girl's dead."

E straightened his back and reached for his glass but didn't lift it. "I didn't know. I thought we were just talking about trees and cash." He tapped the side of the glass with a meaty finger. "What girl?"

"Her name was Rose Sharon."

"That singer girl?" He reached over and tapped the girl's face in the photo of Rose and Billy. "The one gettin' all comfy with the sheriff?"

I nodded.

Lawson raised his glass and sucked the remaining ice into his mouth and crunched it loudly between his teeth. "Then I'd imagine you got some problems headed your way."

"Why's that?"

He put the glass down with a hard thump and pushed it away. Reaching in front of me he swept the two photos up and laid them out between us. "That's your dead girl." He pointed. "That's your boss." He moved his finger to the other picture and thrust it under the unknown sergeant's face. "There's your lumberman. A genuine asshole. But he's her brother and his buddy."

Lawson stood.

I kept my gaze fixed on the photos. Without looking at him, I could still feel the presence of the big man. His cologne lingered with the stink of his revelation. "Thanks for your help," I said.

"Keep your thanks," he answered, walking away. "Just remember you owe me one."

"What's that supposed to mean?" I asked, finally raising my head.

Lawson was gone.

Clare cleared the glass and wiped the bar without looking at me. "E's a horse trader," he said.

"What's that supposed to mean?"

"He trades. Favors. Information. Even actual horses sometimes."

"Why did you call him?"

"You wanted to know about tree poaching."

"He's the only guy you know?"

"E's the only man to ask. There's not a tree, horse, or heifer that gets stolen between Springfield and Harrison, Arkansas that E Lawson doesn't have a finger on or take a cut of."

"And I owe him a favor?"

Clare shrugged.

Chapter 5

I left Moonshines and went to HQ. Billy wasn't there and he wasn't picking up his phone. Billy wasn't the kind to ignore the job, so I had to assume it was me he was ignoring.

The station was still a madhouse. There were news vans from every station in a two-hundred-mile radius filling the parking lot and street around the building. The inside was like an ant farm, all activity and little meaning.

I refused to be sucked into the chaos. At my desk I ignored all the flashing phone lines and worked the computer long enough to get a little information on Levi Sharon. Rose's older brother was an E-5 sergeant. He had been arrested for logging trees on army land while a drill instructor at Fort Leonard Wood. No jail time, but he'd been given a dishonorable discharge. A little more digging showed he had been with the Third Infantry Division in Iraq at the same time I was there as an MP. Billy had been a medic in the Third.

As I worked the official databases, I checked some unofficial sources. The first link to show after typing Rose Sharon into the search engine took me to a picture of her body in the snow. Along with the photo were speculations about the killing. All of them foolish. The most lurid were in large type, and all suggested a sexual element to the murder. Things only got worse from there. A respected local reporter, Riley Yates, posted a story that connected Sheriff Billy Blevins to Rose Sharon. It quoted Sissy Fisher. Riley had written a clear, restrained presentation of facts. But there was no escaping the riptide under the logic. The suggestion that Billy had been romantically involved with the dead girl was obvious.

Despite the late hour, Doreen was still on the job. I went to see her.

"Where's Billy?" I asked.

"He's not here, and the phone calls from reporters are only getting ruder. I don't know what to do."

"Have you talked to him?"

"He's been calling in. He said he's working but won't say on what."

"Call him," I said, trying to sound as decisive and sure as possible. "Tell him I said to authorize overtime and add as many deputies as we can call up. Tell him we need more crowd control at the crime scene and someone outside the HQ. And tell him I'm calling in extra help."

"Extra help?"

"Chuck."

Doreen nodded and punched the speed dial for Billy. I use my cell to call my friend, and the previous boss, Charles Benson.

"Sounds like you have troubles over there," the former sheriff said as soon as the phone connected.

"We do," I said. "Wanna help?"

"Already on it."

"What?" My surprise was doubled when I watched the main door open and the man I was on the phone with walk through. "How?"

Chuck grinned and shook snow from his shoulders as he put his old flip phone away. "The look on your face makes me wonder if I might be a ghost. I hope I didn't pass and no one told me."

"What are you doing here?"

"The sheriff called me and asked me to take a job."

"A job? What are you talking about?"

"I'm the new assistant sheriff."

Doreen stood, then dashed around her desk with open arms. "Welcome home." They hugged each other tightly.

"You don't look near as happy," Chuck said, grinning over Doreen's shoulder at me.

"I don't know what I am."

"Don't try to tell me it was a job you wanted." He disentangled himself from Doreen, then said to her, "I'll be settin' up in the sheriff's office. Send me all the media calls. How are we on the duty roster?"

Doreen quick-stepped to her desk, repeating the orders I had given just a moment before.

Chuck looked back at me. "That's a good start. You gonna stay here and work the phones or do you have other things to do?"

Chuck walked back to his old office and I followed. "What do you know about what's going on?"

"That girl was murdered. The news got wind. Here I am."

"You know what I'm talking about. Billy. Rose Sharon."

Chuck went straight in and sat behind his old desk. He ignored the hat rack by the door and placed his hat, crown up, beside the blotter. "What about them?"

"Where is Billy?"

"Don't you figure if he wanted you to know, he would have told you?" That hit me like a slap. "What did he say?"

"He said he had some things to do." Two lines of the desk phone flashed. Chuck looked from it to me and picked up the handset. "He said you had plenty to do yourself."

"Are we working on the same things?"

"I wouldn't know."

"Why isn't he talking to me?"

"The two of you have a difficult relationship at the best of times."

"Is that you talking or him?" I asked.

My old friend shrugged. It was an exaggerated gesture that for some reason made him look even older than he was. It reminded me there were reasons he'd wanted to retire.

"Trust issues," he said. "Tell me I'm wrong."

"Billy doesn't trust me?"

"It isn't that he doesn't trust you. It's that he knows you don't trust anyone."

"But—"

"There come times in relationships when trust is all you have and is everything you need." Before I could say anything else, he punched a button on the phone and said, "Taney County Sheriff's Office, Assistant Sheriff Benson speaking."

I knew when I was dismissed.

With Chuck helping to smooth things over at HQ, I felt free to follow my thoughts. The problem with that was my thinking was along two different paths. I tried to concentrate on the murder that set everything in motion. But my head kept getting hijacked by more personal concerns. I realized that both sets of thoughts were on the same track. They were leading me straight to Billy's place. The sheriff's office is in Forsyth. Between getting through the news vehicles and the falling snow, it took most of an hour to get to the town of Hollister where he lived.

Lights were on and a car was in the drive, but the sheriff's official vehicle was missing. The car was a newer Dodge but it had been down some tough roads. Its sides were frozen with slush and mud. There was a deep crumple on the left front fender. In the wrinkled metal around the wheel well were brown weeds and packed snow. Someone had run into a ditch, and probably that night. The hot metal of the engine was still ticking as it cooled.

Standing beside the car, I watched the windows of the house for any movement. There was no reason to delay or spy other than my fear of finding out things I didn't want to know. I took a deep breath of frigid air and went for the door.

I didn't knock. I had a key, but the door was unlocked. When I pushed it open a blast of heat rolled out, almost wilting me. The wood stove against the living room wall was radiating enough heat for three houses the same size. It was bigger than necessary, and Billy never built the fire that high.

As I moved into the room I reached for and loosened the seating of my service weapon. "Billy?" I called, even though I was sure he wasn't there. "Hello?"

The house was a ranch. The front door opened to the main living room that spilled to the kitchen on the far end. The main room was clear, but I had to pass the hallway to the bedrooms before I could come around the far wall that divided the living room from the dining room and kitchen.

The hall was dark.

Before I glanced around the corner I pulled my weapon and said in my command voice, "Sheriff's Department. Who's there?"

I darted my head forward for a quick glance down the gloomy hallway. It was clear. I stepped forward, facing into the hall with a wide stance and my pistol raised. "Sheriff's Department," I announced again.

Nothing.

I didn't linger. But I didn't want to go down that hall without clearing the front rooms first. I turned back into the entry and stepped toward the dining room.

That was when I was struck from behind.

Something broad and rough and hard hit the back of my head. It wasn't forceful enough to put me down or out. Not by itself. But it bounced me forward and I struck the wall with my temple. As stars and pulsing purple-red tunneled my vision, I realized that someone had waited behind the wall, then circled around through the kitchen to come up behind me.

I still had my weapon and might have been able to right myself and bring it around if that someone had not slammed me in the kidney. My knees buckled. All the words I wanted to say froze in my throat.

Then a foot hit my back and pushed.

I fell forward onto my hands. My hand still gripped my weapon but it seemed a million miles away and too heavy to lift. The club struck my back again, low and close to the spine. With an odd sense of satisfaction I recognized that it was a piece of firewood. Then I was on the floor.

I don't think I ever quite went out. But the searing pain locked my body. My mouth was a silent rictus. Whoever had ambushed me took the gun from my limp grip. Once I was disarmed, they put their hands under my arms and dragged me back into the blazing hot living room.

"I remember you," a man's voice said as I was dropped.

I reached with trembling and uncoordinated fingers for the baton on my belt. My head was spinning. My gut was roiling. The real fight was to remain in the present. My mind was close to retreating into the dirt and hot wind of Iraq. I could feel the grit of sand in my teeth and on the bloody wounds that tracked my body. Over the years since I had been raped and left for dead by two of my superior officers, that time and place had been a terrible refuge. As if I could hide from new pain in the violence and terror of old pain.

Just like every moment of every day when I struggled to reject my desire to be drunk, I rejected the need to hide in my deepest moment of fear. I came back to the hot room and the man standing over me. But my baton was gone.

I was lying facedown. The man was straddling me at the waist. My reaction was to fight.

As soon as I started to flail my arms and try to roll my body over, the man dropped. He knelt, settling his ass on my back. His knees pinned my arms.

"Settle down," he said. "I ain't gonna hurt you no more if I don't have to."

"You've already assaulted a cop," I managed to say. "Don't make it worse."

"Believe me. Things can't get much worse."

Then I asked the one question that was clear in my swirling brain. "Why is it so hot?"

"What?"

"Why do you have it so hot in here?"

I could feel his confusion communicated through the lessening tension in his body on mine. He shifted and I imagined it was a shrug.

"I was cold," he said. "I crashed my car getting here. It took a long, cold hour to get it out. And I didn't have no coat."

"Who are you?"

"You don't know?" He laughed. It was a high, tittering giggle. "I thought you were here looking for me."

"I was looking for Sheriff Billy Blevins."

"And he's out looking for me." He laughed again. "Looks like we got a big old daisy chain, don't it?"

"What's your name?"

"Why should I tell you?"

"Are you going to kill me?"

Tension came back into his body. It was different. Surprise, not anger. Not violence. "I don't want to kill you."

"If you don't kill me, I'll ask Billy your name."

He was quiet and still for several seconds. I was grateful for his thinking. My mind was clearing.

"Levi," he said finally.

"Rose's brother."

I felt movement again. I interpreted it as a nod. I tried turning my head to see if I could get a look at Levi Sharon. It didn't work. If I turned to the right, my hair fell in my face. When I turned to the left, the raw, rising lump on my temple was on the rough carpet. So I stared at the fire behind the stove's glass.

"Why is Billy looking for you?" I asked.

"I gotta do what I gotta do."

"You're not making sense."

"I have business to take care of." He spoke slowly and enunciated carefully, like he thought the problem was me. "Billy wants to stop me. You get it now?"

"Clear as smoke," I said.

"Do you remember me?"

I recalled what he'd said when he dragged me in the room and dropped me to the floor. He remembered me. "No," I answered.

"I'm not surprised. It was a bad time."

"What was?"

"You were naked. Too beat up—too cut up and bloody to be pretty."

I didn't say anything, but I knew exactly the moment he was talking about. After being left to bleed out behind a mud wall, I had gathered pants and a T-shirt, then staggered out to the road. I was found first by locals in a pickup truck, who wanted to kill me. There was nothing I could do. I was in a ditch saying my goodbyes to the world when a patrol ran them off. I was hustled into the back of a Humvee as a medic cut off my rags. As much as the cuts deep in my skin, I could feel the eyes on my body. The medic was kind and competent.

"You were there?" I asked.

"I was the first one to see you in the ditch. I called for the stretcher."

"Thank you," I said and I meant it.

Levi laughed again. "You're a strange one," he said. "I whack you on the head and you say thank you for something that wasn't nothin' years ago."

"It saved my life."

"Billy did that. I just rode along."

I froze. My face was up, with my chin on the scratchy carpet. My chest was pinned to the floor by a man who could have killed me if he had been trying. The only thing I could see clearly were the flames in the stove. And the only thought in my head was that Billy had lied to me.

I had suspected that Billy Blevins was the corporal medic who had given me plasma and packed the worst of my wounds in the back of a rolling Humvee. In my dreams I saw his face. Over the roar of hard rubber tires on a crumbling desert road the only sound I heard—the one thing I could grasp without terror—was his voice telling me it would be okay.

For a couple of years I doubted the memory. It was a secret I kept, afraid it would turn out to be a dream born in pain and alcoholism. When I finally got the courage to share the memory with him, Billy said he wasn't the man in the Humvee.

"Billy saved me?" I asked the question, almost forgetting that a man was sitting on my back with the answer.

"Course he did. He's the medic."

"I didn't know."

Levi laughed. His shaking body rocked my ribs, grinding my chest to the floor. "He didn't tell you?" Then he laughed again like he just got the joke. "He wouldn't. Mr. Straight. Mr. Reliable. Good old Mr. Tell the Truth and Damn the Consequences. He couldn't tell you he found out who you were and where you were and showed up to get himself in your life. Sounds a little creepy, don't it?" The laughter started again. Levi even wiggled his ass on my spine with his happy dance.

"Get off me," I said.

"Nope," he shot right back. "I don't want to get arrested. And I don't want to hurt you no more to make sure I don't."

"Then stop your stupid donkey braying or I won't worry about hurting you when I get up from here."

"That why they call you Hurricane? All that wind?" He leaned forward, putting more pressure from his knees on my shoulder joints. The pain locked me harder. Trying to roll only threatened to dislocate a shoulder. Levi put his hands on my neck and twisted his right knee down until I gasped. He whispered, "Me 'n' Billy were always like two pages out of the same book. He put things together. I take them apart. I might have seen something in you back then too. But you looked already come-apart to me. You were his kind of girl. Damaged. Maybe now you want to ask yourself what he saw in my sister."

I opened my mouth. Whether it was to scream or answer I wasn't yet sure. I let all the sound die away as Levi lifted his weight from my back. I jerked my arms in despite the pain and pulled them under my body. The moment I pushed up he hit me again. This time it was with the heel of his boot. It struck between my flexed shoulder blades, right in the meat of the muscle to the right of my spine. It was a lightning bolt of pain. I dropped.

Levi Sharon ran out the front door.

I don't know how long I remained face down on the floor, but it was a black and painful time. When I mustered the strength to turn myself over it was in fits and bucks. My joints screamed and my head throbbed. My body felt like a beer left in the car window on a hot day, like it could explode any second. There was blood in the back of my hair and if I moved my neck too far I became nauseated. It was so hot. I kept wondering why.

After a bit I realized I had a phone in my pocket and could call for help. I called Billy. He didn't pick up. I called dispatch. Then I went to sleep.

When I woke I was wrapped in a cotton gown and clean sheets. My first thought was, who had undressed me? My second was, when had the sun come up? Outside my hospital-room window the sky was bright and cloudless.

Behind a partially drawn curtain, someone snorted. It was an aborted snore. The sound of a falling book and a big body trying to resettle in a small chair told me exactly who was there.

"Uncle Orson," I said.

"Yeah," he answered, with sleep in his voice. He pulled the curtain aside and straightened in his chair. "How're you doing?"

"I feel like a bomb went off in my head and a family of skunks slept in my mouth."

"That's good."

"Why is that good?"

"Because that's exactly how you look." He didn't laugh. Uncle Orson did stand and pour me a cup of water from the plastic pitcher beside the bed.

"I want something stronger."

"I brought you an orange soda."

"That's not what I'm talking about."

"I'm not an idiot. I know what you're talking about. I'm just ignoring it."

"As long as we got that settled," I said, reaching out for the cup. "Give me the water."

He handed it over. For some reason my attention fixed on the blurred and faded blue ink of a globe-and-anchor tattoo on his forearm. I took the cup with my left hand and touched the fingers of my right to his tattoo.

"It's gotten old," he said. "Just like me."

"Do you wish it still looked like it did?"

"I got that thing in a dirty, back-alley Saigon shop. It was really just a chair under an umbrella between the back doors of a brothel and a bar. A terrible and wondrous time."

"That's not an answer."

"Sweetheart, wishing time away is like wishing yourself away." He moved his arm. "That's why I brought you orange soda. Want to tell me what happened?"

"First tell me, where are the cops? Someone should be here taking my statement. They need to be out looking for Levi Sharon."

"Old Chuck was here. Billy has the word out on the guy that hit you. I imagine that everything that needs to happen is happenin'."

"Was Billy here?" I didn't look at my uncle when I asked the question. I watched the sun rise higher in the sky.

"Is that the question you wanted to ask in the first place?"

"Things have been difficult." I stared into the infinite blue beyond my window.

"They are talking about him on the news. Saying he had something going on with that girl. Do you believe it?"

I shook my head and winced. The pain made clear to me for the first time how much I didn't believe it. "I don't know what I believe. But I don't believe that."

"What are you going to do?"

"I'm going to get out of here and do my job." Most people would counsel rest and waiting. They would tell me to see the doctor and take any tests. The nice thing about an uncle who is an old marine is that he was never the cautious type. Uncle Orson said, "I had your truck towed to the hospital."

"Did you bring me some clothes?"

"Jeans and shirt."

"Socks? Underwear?"

"I wasn't going to go digging in your delicates."

So much for the toughness of old marines. "What did the doctor say?"

"Slight concussion. You got two stitches in your scalp. Rest and recover."

"Do me a favor and go warm up the truck."

Chapter 6

Getting out of the hospital wasn't as quick as I'd hoped. Dealing with bureaucracy is never an easy or rewarding experience. I caused a stir when I walked into the hall, dressed and not trailing the IV tether they had had attached to my arm. One nurse jumped up from the station and ran right to me. She reached out with both arms as if I might collapse at any moment and she would be able to catch me. The other nurse picked up the phone. Both were professional and courteous but as easy to deal with as a pair of flustered chickens.

They slowed me long enough for the doctor to show up and get involved. He was full of doom and dire consequences that might happen if I left the hospital. If I hadn't been hurt much worse before I might have believed him. In the end he didn't seem to really care once I signed the right forms. I've come by my dim view of the medical profession as one of payment and indemnity honestly.

Refusing to be rolled out in a wheelchair caused another hospital crisis. They were still arguing when the elevator door closed between us.

Uncle Orson was parked in his own truck beside mine. Both were idling and streaming white trails of vapor up into air so crisp a deep breath felt like filling my lungs with icy knives.

"Are you going to come by the dock later?" Orson asked through his open window.

Uncle Orson owned a boat dock with a floating bait shop. He lived above the store and kept a houseboat tied up in the largest slip, close to the gas pumps. That boat was my home away from everything else in the world. I usually ended up there when things in my complicated life got too tangled. It's a safe refuge but not a warm one.

"I might come eat something if you're cooking. But I won't sleep in the houseboat."

"If you're coming, I'm cooking, so let me know." He rolled up his window and drove off without waiting for anything more.

I opened my truck door. The big GMC 2500 was hot. I let the door stand open as I called my old boss.

The new assistant sheriff answered his personal phone on the first ring. "Tell me you're still in the hospital," he said.

"I'm at the hospital."

"What's that supposed to mean?"

"I'm in the parking lot, ready to go."

"Ready? What's keeping you?"

"Where's Billy?"

"Katrina, you don't—"

"I do." I set the words hard, then let them hang. "I have to. He's mixed up in a murder any way you shake it."

"You don't believe—"

"I know." I took a deep breath. Between the cold air and the heat spilling out of the truck it was like inhaling steam and broken glass. "You know too. It doesn't matter that we believe he didn't do it. Billy knows something he's not sharing. And if he isn't in front of it, the real killer will hide behind the mistakes our sheriff is making."

"God dammit," Chuck said. He had a habit of reverting to profanity when he was in a tough spot. But only with those he trusted. I thought of every vulgarity as a vote of confidence. "Everything about this murder is like sitting under the ass end of a bull. You just keep getting buried in shit."

"Has something else happened?"

"The internet happened, that's what."

"It's a new century. Get used to it, old man."

"No. There are pictures on the internet."

"What kind of pictures?"

"The dead girl. In the snow."

"Are they leaked crime scene photos?" I asked, afraid I already knew the answer.

"No. And people are going crazy saying the killer took the pictures."

"It wasn't the killer," I said. "I'm certain of that. Have a talk with the new deputy, Tom Dugan. I saw him putting his phone in his pocket when he was taping off the scene."

"I'll kick his narrow ass if it was him."

"You do that. First tell me where Billy is."

He gave me an address, then explained that Billy wasn't there. He was watching the place.

Driving in the glare of bright sun off a layer of snow exhausted me. It wasn't only the drive. It was the forty minutes of thinking it afforded me. I tried drowning my questions and grievances with the radio. It didn't work. After listening to a moldy chestnut from Hank, Jr., I was treated to my murder victim, Rose Sharon, singing "You Took What Wasn't Yours."

It was modern country pop, produced with strings and piano backed by steel guitar. It wasn't the slick music that chilled me, though. Her voice was raw with truth and hurt. The song, about a girl surrendering herself, without love, seemed to be as much confession as accusation.

I had heard of the girl. It was impossible to live in the Ozarks in the past year and not encounter her name. But I never paid any attention to television and my taste in music was formed by the man who raised me. I knew about Waylon Jennings and Elvis. I had no idea who was on the charts in this century. Hearing Rose Sharon on the radio made me regret that I had never heard her on stage.

Her song ended and I switched off the radio. The last of the drive was made in silence. My own pain didn't seem so sharp anymore.

The address was easy to find. Billy wasn't. It was one of those developments with winding roads and home lots set way back in the woods. Billy, in his Sheriff's Department SUV, was parked in a bit of vacant woods on the high side of the road. He was watching a small house with two expensive cars parked out front.

He didn't say anything or turn to look at me when I climbed in the passenger side.

I let the silence linger a few moments before asking, "You want to talk?"

"No," he answered without turning.

"You need to."

"You think so?"

"I do."

Billy finally shifted around and looked at me. "What exactly do I need to talk about?"

"Well, for starters—"

"How are you feeling?"

"I'm fine."

"You looked tired. The sleep was good for you."

"The sleep?" I searched his expression for meaning. He gave me nothing. "You were at the hospital?"

"Of course I was."

"Why didn't you stay?"

"Why didn't you?"

He had me there. I changed the subject. "Who are you staking out?"

Billy looked back down the hill again and said, "It's probably best you don't know."

"Best for me? Or you?" I put my hand on his shoulder and urged him to turn. It didn't work so I pulled harder. "Is it best for the dead girl? Or the county you're sheriff of?"

He turned around. I'd never seen his face so grim. "You think I was involved in her murder."

"Not her murder." I knew how wrong I was the instant I said it. Billy's face, already hard, went flatter and set like concrete. "I found things at her place. Your things." My voice sounded as feeble to me as the words and reasoning. I tried again, saying, "Billy…" I had nothing to say but his name.

"Get out," he said.

"Billy…"

"Get out of the car and go do your job."

"We need to—"

"No, we don't," he said. The words dropped between us like a mortally wounded animal. Then the animal died.

I pulled the door handle and slid out, keeping my gaze on his frozen eyes.

If I had not opened the door we might have missed the throaty sound of Levi Sharon's Dodge as it swung into the driveway with the two other cars.

At the same time, we turned to look down the hill.

Levi opened his car door and burst out. He left the car running as he charged to the house.

Billy was already out of the SUV and moving forward for a better look when I stepped around the front fender.

Levi didn't stop to knock at the front door. It must have been unlocked. He went straight inside.

Billy dashed forward. He sprinted into the bare trees and went headlong down the steep hill.

I didn't follow. I had my keys in my hand and was planning on driving down until I heard the two gunshots. Then I ran, trying to keep to Billy's blazed path.

Billy pulled his weapon as he ran. He went down the hill without fear or hesitation. I was about fifty yards behind him and falling back. His feet found solid purchase under snow and never once turned on a stone or tripped on a root. I didn't run so much as fast-hop from spot to spot. The exertion was already making my legs burn. The spot between my shoulder blades where Levi had stomped his boot heel was throbbing.

When Billy reached the road at the bottom of the hill he jumped the ditch and went faster on the plowed blacktop.

As he was racing across the road I was falling over a buried stump. I tumbled down about twenty feet of snow and frozen leaves before I could stop myself. I was still struggling to get up, using a persimmon tree to pull myself upright, when Billy was approaching the house with his pistol drawn.

"Come out of there, Levi," he shouted.

I wanted to tell him to wait. When he ran right to the door I wanted to scream.

He got to the door at the same time I got to the bottom of the hill. He never made it inside. Two men came charging out, one in front of the other. Levi Sharon was pushing a shirtless and bleeding Donny Fisher ahead of him. Levi used his shoulder to drive Donny straight at Billy, who was too close to stop.

Billy and Donny collided on the porch. Their contact was audible even across the street where I was. Blood sprayed, a thick red fountain that cartwheeled with Donny as he fell over Billy.

Levi didn't stop. He raised a revolver as he ran, firing twice at Billy as he struggled to get to his feet. The first shot went wide. It made snow puff up like a tiny volcano as it struck the ground. The second came as Billy was lifting his weapon to return fire. That bullet entered the sleeve of Billy's jacket below the elbow. It burst out the shoulder.

Billy sagged away from the impact and dropped his pistol.

I pulled my service weapon as Levi jumped back into his waiting car. I let him reverse the vehicle until he cut the wheels and Levi was presented to me in profile.

"Stop!" I shouted the order more out of habit than expectation. His window was up. Not that it mattered. I didn't believe Levi would stop and I didn't wait for it, either. I fired. The shot shattered the window, but missed the intended target.

Levi jumped as the bits of window exploded inward. He didn't stay surprised very long. He raised his right hand, crossing his body, then fired two rounds at me without aiming. They went wild.

My next shot cratered the metal of the car door.

Levi dropped his weapon. I didn't know how badly he was hit but I knew it hurt. I could hear him cursing over the roar of the Dodge.

Levi jerked the gearshift and stomped the gas. The car slid side to side as it sent rooster tails of slush and snow into the air.

I kept Levi sighted as he fled. There was no chance to take another shot. At least not a clear one. I had to assume that there was another house behind the trees once the angle shifted. It wasn't until he was gone I noticed Billy shouting. It was the sound of his voice I turned toward. I couldn't understand the words.

Billy knelt over Donny Fisher. He had both hands pressed into the boy's neck. He shouted to me again, "Call EMTs."

That time I understood.

"And get my kit," he added.

I was already running back up the hill to get it and shouting into the phone as I went. At the top of the hill I staggered, exhausted and in pain. The cold air I sucked into my lungs hurt more when I coughed it back out.

There was no running back. I drove the sheriff's SUV out of the clearing and back to the road. When I got to the house I backed up through the yard to where Billy still held Donny.

Since Billy was a qualified medic, he always kept a large first aid kit in his vehicle. I pulled it from the back of the SUV along with blankets.

I put the kit beside Billy. The blankets I threw over Donny. He was pale. His breath was shallow and it seemed like each inhalation was an effort. Billy had rolled him on his side and a constant bubbling of blood was coming from his mouth.

"Put your hands here," Billy said, nodding down at his own hands covered in blood. They were pressed to the right side of Donny's throat.

He lifted his hands away and I saw the bullet hole they were covering. I put my hands on the wound. Billy gripped my wrists, moving my palms where he wanted them, then positioning my fingers. Once he was satisfied, he opened his kit and pulled out the things he needed.

Billy worked quickly. Once things were ready he signaled for me to take my hands away. There was a pulse of blood, then he had his fingers in the wound feeling for the open vein. He shoved a clamp in behind his finger, then the bleeding stopped.

"I've got this now," he said. "Go in the house and check on the other guy. I think he's dead. Make sure."

I went, watching Billy work as I did. He put a hand under Donny's neck and tilted the head back. I turned away and stepped into the house as a tube went down Donny's throat.

No search was required. The other man was on the floor of the main room. He felt almost as cold as the air at the open door. Between that and the hole in his chest I didn't have any doubt that he was dead.

A look back out the door, where Billy was pumping air into Donny's chest using a bag attached to the throat tube, told me we had to hurry before we lost another one. I pulled out my phone and had to wipe my bloody hands on my jeans before I could work it. Doreen told me that due to the snow the ambulance was still fifteen to twenty minutes away. Nothing was happening fast. I told her to call off the EMTs. Then asked her to give me Chuck. I walked to Billy as I was transferred.

"Don't talk," I said. I spoke loudly so Billy would hear too. "I've canceled the ambulance. We're taking Donny Fisher to Regional ourselves." I raised my eyebrows to communicate a question mark to Billy.

He nodded.

"We have one dead body at this location," I continued. "We need units to close and protect the scene. As many as we can spare. If a connection to Rose Sharon gets out, this place will be surrounded by press."

"On their way," Chuck said.

"BOLO," Billy said.

"Issue a be-on-the-lookout for Levi Sharon. Last seen in a black, late-model Dodge Charger with a broken driver's side window and a bullet hole in the door. Suspect is wounded. He's armed and extremely dangerous."

I broke the connection without saying anything else.

"Help me lift Donny," Billy said.

We got him into the back of the SUV. Billy climbed in beside him and kept pumping the bag.

I got behind the wheel and eased the vehicle out of the rutted yard and into the road. It was the only slow part of the journey.

Billy and I didn't talk the entire trip. Not to each other. I watched the road on the hills and twists, being careful in the snow. When we got to the county highway and had a few stretches of smooth, plowed asphalt, I watched Billy in the rearview mirror.

He kept his head down and his attention on his patient. Every few seconds I heard the bag in Billy's hands pumping air into Donny's lungs. After it I heard the wheezing exhalation.

Billy said, "It's going to be okay. Stick with me. It will all be okay."

I had to fight hard to keep my mind focused on the here and now. It would have been so easy to let the snow melt into desert sand, to slip back in time, and once more be the patient Billy worked on in the back of a speeding Humvee.

Chapter 7

A trauma team was waiting for us when I pulled up to the hospital's emergency entrance. There was a doctor and two nurses. They hovered over Donny, shining lights in his eyes, asking questions, and pumping air into his chest even as two orderlies pulled him from the vehicle and onto a gurney. Practiced hands strapped him down and got him moving in seemingly one motion. They talked to each other in sharp half sentences, the code of trauma. Billy and I stayed out of the way and were ignored.

Even though we were outside near a busy parking lot, when Donny and his team went through the sliding doors the world turned eerily quiet. I tried to fill the void with some care. Tugging at Billy's sleeve where Levi's bullet had entered, I said, "You need to see a doctor too." Fresh blood rolled out under the cuff. "You need to get your arm looked at."

He looked down at the hole and pulled away from me. "The bullet went up the back side of my arm. It feels like someone painted me with gas from my elbow to my shoulder then lit it. Hurts, but it isn't bad."

"You can't know that without even seeing it."

"If it was bad, I couldn't do this." He raised his arm straight up, then brought it down and flapped it like a chicken wing. It would have been funny if not for the hard set of his face. He walked toward the trauma room doors. "I'll stay here with Donny and call the family. You get back to the scene. Get on top of finding Levi."

"How do you suggest I do that?" I tried not to sound hurt. I ended up just sounding pissed off.

"He's not going to want to keep driving that car. There's a shady guy Levi works for sometimes. I'd check with E. Lawson." The double doors whooshed open. Billy walked through without looking back.

"Wait," I called.

The doors closed.

I closed the tailgate on the SUV, then drove off without worrying about how Billy would get it back. I drove slowly. It wasn't caution that kept my foot off the gas. It was the feeling of being behind on everything. There had not been any real investigation of Rose Sharon's murder. There had been only reaction after reaction to shifting situations. The Sheriff's Department was basically occupied by dealing with the press and ugly publicity, and controlling crime scenes. Billy was running his own thing and he wasn't sharing. I had the feeling that I was in the woods holding a bag waiting for a snipe to show up. I needed to get proactive.

I pulled the vehicle off the road and dialed my cell.

"You know I can't talk to you about my clients," Landis Tau said by way of greeting. "Don't even try."

"I have news you might need to know."

"Helping the other side? That's not like you. Not like any cop that I know."

"Donny Fisher has been shot. He's in the trauma center, but it's a dicey situation at best."

For several moments there was silence from the other end of the line. I used the time to get back on the road.

"What happened?" Landis asked. The tone of his voice had changed. I imagined him tucking the handset under his ear and writing on a yellow legal pad. "Do you know who did it?"

"You know I can't comment on an open investigation," I said.

"You didn't call simply to tell me about Donny." He let the statement sit there, waiting for me to fill the space.

I didn't.

"What do you want?" he asked when he gave up.

"Rose Sharon is not your client. Is that correct?"

"Correct—as far as it goes."

"Can you be more of a lawyer?"

"She is not my client. But she can be considered part of the Fisher family where certain things overlap."

"And the Fisher family wants them overlapping as much as possible," I said. Then I corrected myself. "Sissy Fisher wants them overlapping."

"Get to your point, Hurricane."

"Is there any overlap with Levi Sharon?" I could almost hear gears turning in the quiet on the line.

"Sharon's brother?" Landis finally asked. "Is he your suspect in Donny's shooting?"

"I can't comment on that," I said, clearly and carefully.

"In the murder of Rose Sharon?"

"I can't comment on that."

"I understand." His voice brightened. I thought for a moment Landis was going to chuckle. "So—neither of us can comment on our spheres of responsibility. What do you want from me?"

"Background. A little understanding."

"So you called a lawyer? You must be desperate."

"If I was desperate I'd be in a bar, not calling you. I'm more at a crossroads. I figure you can help me choose a path."

"Why do you think I will?"

"Because you want me on a road that leads away from your clients. I want a few paths closed off."

"Fair enough."

"How did this happen?" I asked. "The girl being with the Fishers. The boy in the army."

"Is that all?"

"There's a conflict in there somewhere. Who's mad at whom and where's the money?"

"What money?"

"There's always money," I said. "And the girl was poised to make it big. Someone had to be left out in the cold."

"I hate to disappoint you, but there's no big secret."

"Then there's no problem with you sharing the story." I took a sweeping turn. The back end of the truck slid just enough to remind me the roads were still slick in places.

"He was seventeen; she was ten. Their parents had been performers in Branson shows since they were kids themselves. They worked for Hosea Fisher."

"What about Sissy?"

"What about her?"

"How did they know her?" I asked. "Hosea doesn't strike me as the kind to take in strays without a little prodding."

"Sissy was front-of-house manager for the same show. Donny and Rose were already performing together."

"Let me guess. They were star attractions."

"You probably saw the billboards," Landis said. "They were all over Missouri and Arkansas. I hear there were even a few in Oklahoma."

"You wouldn't want to break that up."

"Your cynicism is showing," he said, sounding a bit of the same. "Right after Sissy married Hosea, the parents of Rose and Levi Sharon were killed in a hit-and-run."

"What kind of hit-and-run?"

"They were on 160 just after the 176 cutoff, coming home late."

"Drinking?"

He hesitated. When he spoke again it was a sad admission. "A little. It was their date night. Matthew Sharon was driving. There was no indication that drinking was a big part of the accident."

"Why?"

"Because someone came out of a dirt road and slammed into their car. It flew off the road and through the fence and gate on the far side. There were no skid marks. Not from their car or the truck that hit them."

"How do you know it was a truck?"

"The accident report said they were hit high up by something big. Their conclusion was a commercial truck."

"And then?" I asked.

"Then the Fishers took the girl in."

"Why not Levi?"

"See?" Landis asked. "You're getting that judgy sound to your voice again. Probably it was because he was a seventeen-year-old boy who already had an attitude and the problems to go with it."

"Foster family?"

"Yes. If you consider Uncle Sam family."

"He went right into the army? At seventeen?"

"He got caught logging someone else's land. They worked out a plea deal where Levi was declared emancipated and allowed to join up."

"Allowed?" I asked. I made sure my judgment came through in my voice that time.

"I understand it was his choice."

"Choice requires options," I said.

I got off the phone and concentrated on driving.

* * * *

The first thing I saw when I pulled up to the house where Levi had shot Donny was a flash of light. There were sheriff's department cruisers and the coroner's van there, so I wasn't surprised. But it was a single flash, not the strobing of emergency lights, that had caught my eye. It took a moment for that fact to sink in and I started looking for the source as I parked on the road with my own lights on for safety.

Deputy Tom Dugan was standing by the taped-off patch of bloody snow. I saw him looking down at his phone. He pocketed it as I walked up the drive.

"Hey, Hurricane," he called, then corrected himself. "Detective Williams."

"Did Chuck Benson have a talk with you?"

"What about?"

"Give me your phone." I put out my hand. For the first time I saw something more than simple inexperience in his eyes.

"Why?"

I shook my hand in answer. I kept my gaze on his eyes.

Tom smiled. It was an off-balance look, like he knew what muscles were involved but not the feelings behind the expression. "What if I say no?"

"Do you like your job?"

His smile melted into a straight line. His eyes flared, though. They challenged. When I didn't look away or give in, Tom broke eye contact and looked at the ground. His foot dug into the snow and for a moment I thought he was either going to run or throw a tantrum. He raised his head and pulled out the phone at the same time. The wound was obvious in his eyes even though he didn't look right at me. "Whatever," he said, slapping the phone into my hand.

"Unlock it," I said. "And open up the picture gallery."

He took it back and punched the code onto the screen. When it was open he showed it to me.

The gallery was empty. I grabbed the phone from him and tapped my way through the file system looking for pictures. There were none that I could find.

"Satisfied?" Tom asked. His tone suggested he was the only one satisfied, and pleased with the feeling.

"No," I answered. I handed the phone back. "Keep it in your pocket. If I see it again, it won't matter that the pictures aren't there."

"I see why they make you go to a shrink."

I leaned in close and spoke low. "Keep that up. You'll find out why I really go to therapy."

A news van drove past my truck and stopped right in front of the house. It blocked the street. I pointed at the vehicle and said, "Get out there. Keep the street clear and people behind the tape."

Deputy Dugan shoved his phone back into his pocket, then turned and walked. "Whatever you say, Hurricane," he said, just loud enough for me to hear.

I didn't call him on it. I was already walking around the house to go in the back door.

The house wasn't much warmer inside than out.

There were trails of butcher paper laid down leading through the kitchen to the front room. Beside the kitchen door was a pair of boots I recognized as belonging to Bobbi Rantz.

"Bob!" I called.

"Living room!" She shouted her answer. "Stay on the paper."

I did. Bob was kneeling beside the body of the young man I had seen before. Standing by the open front door and on a nest of paper was Deputy Calvin Walker. He was using a small digital camera to take photos.

"Not like that," Bob told him. "Don't worry about me or the body. These are for orientation only. Get straight on to the wall and shoot wide then move in and shoot the places I have marked."

On two walls were yellow-and-black ruled strips that marked bullet holes and blood spatter.

"Hey, the Hurricane is here," Calvin said before snapping another photo. Deputy Walker was not my biggest fan.

"Are you helping me or not?" Bob asked Calvin. "If you can't do it quietly, you can go help outside."

"I'm doing it." Calvin took another photo. Then he pushed a button extending the camera's zoom lens all the way out.

"Not like that," Bob repeated.

I got the impression she had been saying that a lot.

"I told you—" Bob pointed at the paper path on the floor, "go around and get closer. Don't just zoom."

"Calvin," I said. "Would you go out and help Dugan, please?"

"I'm helping here."

"Deputy." I gave him a hard look to make sure he understood it wasn't a request. "Give us the room."

He looked out the door, then down at the camera in his hand. "You okay with that, Bob?"

"I'm fine," she answered.

Calvin set the digital camera down on the paper, then shuffled his feet.

I thought he was going to say something. He seemed to decide against it, then zipped his duty jacket all the way and turned up the fur collar. I had to stand to the edge of the butcher-paper path to let him pass as he went out through the kitchen.

As soon as I heard the kitchen door close I asked Bob, "What was that about?"

"Apparently, Dugan likes my ass," she answered.

"He said that to you?"

"Not to me. I guess he likes to talk about women when they're not around."

"Calvin?"

"They had words, I guess. Calvin's the one who told me—*warned* me."

I looked out the door and watched Tom moving to intercept Calvin. He said something that I couldn't hear. I doubted that it was friendly. Calvin pushed the other man away and went to wave down a news crew that was trying to set up a camera in the road.

Those were questions for another time, I decided, and turned back to Bob. "What do you have here?"

"Classic story," Bob answered without irony. "Boy meets boy and another angry boy busts in and shoots them."

"Boy meets boy? You mean…"

"Yep. There was sex going on here. Do you think that was why they were killed?"

"At this point I don't have much of any idea. I was thinking Levi Sharon targeted Donny Fisher because he had a relationship with Rose Sharon. Who's this guy?"

"Clark Beasley, by the ID I found. Apparently a drummer. There are pictures on the refrigerator of him and Donny Fisher and Rose Sharon on stage."

"So, two people dead and one pretty close to it, all connected to the Ozarks Star Road Theater. That's pretty interesting. Collect the pictures with your evidence."

"Speaking of pictures and interesting things…"

"What?"

"When I was looking over Rose Sharon's room I noticed something funny."

The short hairs at the back of my neck stood on end and a knot of guilt tightened in my chest. "Yes?"

"Her mirror was framed by photos and ticket stubs. Personal mementos. But there were two blank spots just the right size for five-by-seven photos."

She waited but I didn't respond. I didn't look at her, though. I wasn't that brazen.

"I wouldn't have thought much of it…" Bob stood up. She stepped in front of me. "But when I came out of the bedroom I noticed that a guitar was missing from the array of instruments lined up in the corner."

"I have it," I admitted without looking away.

"I know." Bob turned, letting me off the hook. She appeared sad rather than angry. "You can't protect him that easily."

"I'm not trying—"

"Save it. You should know that there were more pictures. They all look innocent but..."

"But what?"

Bob took a settling breath. "But the sheriff's actions kind of color how the pictures are viewed, don't they?"

"Why are you asking me?"

"Everyone knows—"

"What?"

Bob knelt back down beside her kit and started packing it up.

I turned around and went out the way I had come, sticking to the paper trail.

The drive back to the hospital took a lot longer than the last one. I drove slowly. I was hurt, and angry at feeling that way. I didn't believe that Billy had betrayed me with that girl. I didn't know what I did believe, though. Bob was right. His actions would be like guilt-colored glasses that everyone would see him through. He wasn't talking to me and that was the worst thing. That was the real betrayal.

In Forsyth, I stopped at the sheriff's office. I wanted to sit down with Chuck Benson and talk things through. I needed a cooler head and a more restrained perspective. When I parked the truck, though, I was spotted by the throng of press filling the lot and street around the station. They moved toward me in a wave of cameras and microphones. I didn't know why I was suddenly a target but I didn't wait to find out. I put the truck back into gear and bolted.

My intended destination was still the hospital, but I ended up driving to my Uncle Orson's place in Rockaway Beach without really thinking about it. The boat dock was a refuge. This time of year it was usually deserted. Only the most die-hard fishermen got out on the lake in the bald chill of winter.

It turned out that fishermen were not the problem. The parking lot was jammed with cars and trucks, most of which were plastered with bright vinyl stickers that proudly declared call letters or news slogans like *Eyewitness* and *Action*.

I stopped on the road and observed the activity. Uncle Orson seemed to be making the most of the attention. He had fired up the split 55-gallon drums he used as grills and was selling hot meals to the waiting reporters.

I called his cell and watched as he wrestled the phone out of his military-surplus down coat.

"I see you up there," he said, as soon as he connected.

"How can you see me? You have your back turned."

"No sneaking up on this old man."

"I believe it. What's going on down there?"

"I'm cooking chicken for the vultures."

"I can see that," I said, already getting annoyed. "Why are the vultures there?"

"You don't know?"

"If I knew I wouldn't be asking, would I?" Trying to get some people to the point is like trying to race turtles.

"Two words," Uncle Orson said. He sounded much too happy to ease my mind. "Love triangle."

"What?"

"Billy. The dead girl, Rose Sharon. And you." He brayed a windy laugh. Even from where I was I could see him bounce in front of the grill.

"What's so funny?"

"You. In a love triangle."

"How is that funny?"

"Oh, sweetheart…" He sounded suddenly serious and careful. "You know you're my favorite girl in the world…"

"Say what you think you need to say."

"Katrina, anyone who knows you knows you're a fighter, not a lover."

A strong hand squeezed my heart. "That's not true."

"You haven't spent the last couple of years in therapy because of your proclivity for romance, have you?"

"Therapy was a condition for keeping my job."

"Because of your tendency to break the bones of people who get in your way."

"Why are you saying that?"

Down at the grill, Uncle Orson turned around. I couldn't see his face with any detail but I knew he was looking right up the bank to where I was watching him.

"Maybe this is a sign," he said.

"A sign of what?"

"If not a sign, maybe it's just the right time to admit that you were never going anyplace with Billy Blevins."

"That's none of your business," I said, letting my voice get as cold as the frost on my windshield.

"Sure it is. We're each other's business. That's what family is."

I closed the connection on my phone and dropped it onto the passenger seat. Uncle Orson waved as I drove away.

Chapter 8

I was angry. How much of my anger was because of Uncle Orson's words and how much was my need to latch on to anger was a question. It wasn't that he was wrong. It wasn't that he was right, either. It was Billy Blevins and secrets and my feeling of betrayal that had me primed like a miner's borehole and ready to blow when I walked into the hospital.

Reporters were there, too. They made a gauntlet of intrusion that I had to fight through in welded-lip silence to reach the doors. When the doors swooshed closed behind me, I stood a moment in the warmth and quiet. I took off my coat for the first time in what seemed like ages.

I followed the wide halls. Walking in warmth reminded me how much pain I was still in. My back burned as muscles tried to unknot. The throbbing I had ignored from my head all day became like a marching band wearing cleats doing a Sousa march over my skull.

Of course the first person I ran into was Sissy Fisher.

"What are you doing here?" she demanded, stepping forward to block my path to her son's room.

"My job." I answered her with equal force. I caught myself and stopped my march. "I'm sorry about your son, Mrs. Fisher," I said, making an effort to be professional.

Chuck Benson and Hosea Fisher came out of Donny's room.

"Where's the sheriff?" I asked.

"He left," Chuck said.

"He ran, you mean," Sissy blurted. She looked me in the eye, putting her rage on display. "You should too."

"Ma'am, I'm investigating—"

"Investigating?" She made the word sound like a curse. "Investigate yourself. You did this. You and him."

"Ma'am, I assure you—"

"Your assurances are like sheer curtains at a whorehouse, pretense that hides nothing."

"Now, Sissy…" Hosea put a hand on his wife's shoulder. It was a feeble gesture.

Sissy ignored the hand and lunged forward with her finger pointed like a painted arrow. She poked me right below the collarbone. Her nail jabbed into the raised bed of scar tissue that tracked my chest. "You are in this. Right past your big ass and up to your bottle-red hair."

My first impulse was to twist that hand back and leverage her down with a wrenched elbow. I resisted. I kept my calm and took a step back. When I had a bit of distance, I raised my hand to massage the ridge of scar around my eye. "Ma'am, we're doing everything we can to find who's harming your family."

"Look in the mirror, bitch." Sissy struck at me with those turquoise-painted talons.

"Katrina!" Chuck shouted. It was a warning, not about the blow, but my reaction.

Chuck knows me pretty well.

I didn't know until her nails raked my face that I had wanted exactly that, an excuse. Sissy had swiped hard with her right hand. She had the pampered, pretty girl idea of what a fight was. She didn't want to disable me so much as she wanted to mark me. She also had the privileged rich woman idea of consequences.

I turned with the blow across my face. Her hand passed, taking three furrows of skin from my cheek. My right hand was already rising and I caught her by the wrist, turning it over and putting torque on her elbow and shoulder. As she turned, following the force of my hold, I reached up with my left hand and grabbed a handful of hair. It was a perfect handle with which to put her face into the wall. It bounced once. The silver jewelry she wore clattered against the drywall. I rolled my body over hers and locked the bent arm between us.

I was pulling out my cuffs when Chuck put a hand on my arm.

"Don't," he said.

"She assaulted an officer."

Chuck leaned up close. "She's a grieving mother with accusations that a lot of people will listen to." He whispered into my ear but his words remained full force.

I let her go. When she turned back on me I was pleased to see that she would at least be wearing a black eye.

"Get out of here." Chuck pushed me down the hall and kept me walking away from Sissy Fisher. "Go someplace and cool down. Have a talk with Billy while you're at it."

I wished I could.

* * * *

There was no real sunset that day. Gray faded into black in an imperceptible transition. Most of the vans with the bold graphics and the bland white reporters who went with them were gone when I got back to the boat dock. Those who remained were holed up in their vehicles with the heaters on. I thought I could get in unscathed.

I would have made it too, but Uncle Orson had locked the gangway gate. I had a key. It was on the ring I had already stuffed into my coat pocket. The gate is never locked.

The first reporter to reach me was a familiar face. Riley Yates was an old friend to whom I owed a lot. He was probably first because he was a newspaper man. His only tool was the same cassette recorder he had probably used for thirty years.

"Howdy, Hurricane," Riley said as I kept shaking at the gate with one hand and digging in my pocket with the other.

"You know I don't like that name, Riley."

"I don't like being called Love Machine by Mrs. Yates, but sometimes there is no escaping who we are."

"You're a funny man. I'm not going to talk." I found the key.

"You should." He turned on his recorder then used it to point at the crews approaching with lights and video cameras. "Or they will do it for you."

Someone shouted, "Detective!"

We were caught in the glare of tungsten lighting.

"Just you," I said. I opened the gate and pulled Riley through.

The reporters pushed microphones and camera lenses into the gaps in the gate.

"Get away from the gate!" Uncle Orson bellowed. He was at the door to the shop holding a shotgun at port arms. The reporters got back.

Inside, the shop smelled of wet wood, old tobacco, and fish. The live-bait wells gurgled and the ancient soda cooler chugged. It was all a comfort. It wasn't very warm, though. Or bright.

"Why's it so cold in here?" I asked Uncle Orson.

"Off-season. I always cut back on the luxuries in the winter."

"Heat's a luxury now?"

Orson ignored my question. He flipped on the lights and twisted the dial on a thermostat. After that he stuck out his hand. "Riley, good to see you." They shook and my uncle nodded to the recorder that Riley still held ready. "I take it this is an official visit of the fourth estate."

"Yes." Riley looked at me as he spoke. "Katrina has agreed to give me an exclusive."

"But she didn't promise to answer anything she didn't want to," I said. I walked around the counter. Uncle Orson always kept a stock of fruit sodas in the chiller for me, orange and strawberry. I wasn't a huge fan of strawberry. "You want a drink?" I asked. "I need one."

I noticed the change in the men's expressions but made no connection. "Katrina."

Orson said my name with such sadness that I stopped what I was doing. Instead of pulling soda from the cooler I had lifted a bottle of whiskey from under the counter. The seal was broken and the lid lying beside the open bottle.

"Some things the hands never forget," I said.

Orson stepped around the counter and pulled me away. He didn't make any fuss or say anything more, he simply put the bottle away and pulled three from the soda machine. He gave me a strawberry.

I took it and I was grateful.

"I'll understand if you're not up to an interview," Riley said. He took a swallow from his bottle.

I was envious of his orange soda. "I don't even know what's being said. It's been a busy day. But if you think I need to say something, I will."

Riley nodded then took another drink before saying, "This won't be a private conversation, Katrina. I'm your friend. I'm a reporter, too. And there is a lot in your life that's impacting the community."

"And you have a responsibility to ask about those things." I took a long drink of the strawberry soda. It tasted pretty good.

Riley hit record on his tape machine.

Uncle Orson pointed to the little corner nook with the table and benches, then said, "Talk there. I'll get the grill heated back up and make something."

When we were seated and alone I asked, "What are they saying?"

"Which part?" Riley shrugged. "Last I heard you bulled your way into Donny Fisher's hospital room and gave his mother a black eye."

"That's not how it happened. And how did you even hear about it? That was no more than an hour ago."

"Sissy Fisher called the paper. She called the television stations too. You can bet she'll be on the ten o'clock news talking about it tonight."

I thought about that. "Late this afternoon, in performance of my duties, I attempted to visit Donny Fisher to follow up on the investigation into the assault against him and the shooting. It was also my intent to report the information I had learned to Sheriff Billy Blevins, believing him to be on scene at the hospital room. I never entered the room. I was assaulted by a grieving Mrs. Fisher in the hallway in the presence of her husband Hosea Fisher and Assistant Sheriff Chuck Benson. I restrained Mrs. Fisher, but she was not arrested. It was the judgment of both Assistant Sheriff Benson and myself that she acted out of emotional distress, and no charges were warranted. I regret the facial bruise Mrs. Fisher received as the result of her restraint."

"Wow." Riley saluted with his orange soda. "That's a heck of a press release."

"It's the truth."

"That how you got the scratches?"

I touched the side of my face and felt the raised welts where her nails had gotten me. It was just another bit of pain left by that day. "Yes."

"Forgive me, Hurricane, but you're not known for your restraint. Don't you have a history of violence in performance of your duties?"

"I've never been officially reprimanded for excessive use of force. I've never been officially suspended or investigated by the Sheriff's Department or in my previous capacity as a military police officer in the US Army."

Riley held his gaze on me, waiting for more. When I said nothing he asked, "Weren't you required by Charles Benson, when he was sheriff, to attend therapy as a condition of keeping your job?"

"You know I was."

"Has the current sheriff, Bill Blevins, removed that requirement?"

"Bill?"

"Is something wrong?"

"You called him Bill. I've never heard anyone call him anything other than Billy."

"Sheriff Blevins has asked local media to use 'Bill' when referring to him."

"When?" The news made my head spin. It was a small thing, but there seemed to be a lot of them piling up. How much had I missed or ignored? Had I ever really known Billy at all? "I don't want to do this anymore."

"Katrina, you know I have to ask you about your relationship with Billy."

"You know as much about it as anyone."

"Can you describe it? Make a statement. Officially?"

"No."

"There seems to be a lot of turmoil in the Taney County Sheriff's Department since Bill Blevins took office. Do you have anything to say about that?"

"No." I shook my head. "Billy's doing a great job."

"Do you think your romantic involvement with the sheriff has caused a problem for you or for the department?"

The question had a weight I didn't expect. It hung on me like a new layer of concrete skin. "There isn't a romantic relationship," I admitted. "Not since before the election. I don't think I realized that until now."

Riley frowned and looked down at his recorder. He was a good man and a friend. I wasn't afraid he would use that in his reporting. "What about the personal aspects of your investigation into the murder of Rose Sharon?"

"Personal aspects?"

"It's being reported that you might be compromised by your relationship with the sheriff and his relationship with the victim."

"Compromised?" I heard my question and realized that I was just repeating words—echoing—I felt vacant from my own life. "I don't know anything about their relationship. If there is a relationship."

"Sissy Fisher claims to have photos of them. She also claims, and it's been confirmed by the music publisher, that Sheriff Blevins shares writing credit on the song 'You Took What Wasn't Yours.'" Riley took a breath. He leaned forward.

For a moment I thought he was going to reach for my hand.

Hesitation was written in his body language. He took another breath and said, "Sissy says the song is about her young daughter losing her virginity to Sheriff Blevins."

It didn't matter how much care Riley took in saying it. And it didn't matter at all that I had thought the same thing. The statement was a physical blow that I felt in my stomach. "I don't believe that," I said. Then I wondered if I was lying or if Riley could tell.

Uncle Orson burst through the door holding tongs in one gloved hand and a plate of steaming rib eyes in the other. "I had some thin-cut steaks," he announced. "They didn't take long."

"I should go." Riley hit the button on his recorder.

"No," I said. "Stay and have a hot meal."

"Are you sure?"

I gave that question a lot of thought. I gave it a little more as I drained my strawberry soda. Suddenly the pain and fatigue of the day, the biting cold that sucked the energy out of my body, and the darkness all seemed like the dirt of my grave closing in. I needed life around me. "I'm sure," I said. "But I want another soda. This time I get the orange." I smiled and tried to feel the expression. My face seemed like something a million miles away controlled by remote, a drone mask.

Later, when Riley had gone, I was alone with Uncle Orson. I say alone, but the bait shop was also a liquor store. Fishermen like to drink. I felt the presence of each bottle on the shelves like judges who knew my crimes. Taking a drink would be confessing. Confession is always a temptation.

"Why are you still a cop?" Orson asked.

"What else would I be?"

"Why be anything?"

"I don't know what that means."

He settled deeper into the bench behind the cleared table. Orson had a beer. "You have all the money a person could want." He used the open bottle to point over at the calendar hanging on the far wall. It was years old and open to the wrong month. The image was signed by my dead husband, Nelson Solomon, who had painted the scene of golden light on a green river valley. "Your hands could be full just handling the estate and licensing of Nelson's art."

I could smell the beer. It was like the cologne of a lost lover you experience by accident. It hurt and drew me at the same time. "Why are you talking about this now?"

"Because I can see how you're looking at my beer."

I jerked my gaze from the bottle to his face. His eyes were as serious as pointed guns. "I'm not drinking." Even I heard the weakness in my argument.

"Could you say that if I wasn't here?"

"What do you want me to say?"

He tilted his head as if the gesture were both an answer and a question, then took a drink. After wiping his lips with the back of his hand Uncle Orson asked, "What are you going to do about Billy?"

"What am I supposed to do?"

"I'm not asking the plans of Detective Hurricane Williams." He let that sit a moment. When I didn't say anything, he pushed his half-full beer across the table at me. "I'm asking what Katrina, my brother's daughter, the girl I helped raise, the woman who went to war, is going to do about the man she loves."

"Who says I love him?" I looked at the bottle, not my uncle.

"Lies come in a lot of shapes."

"You sound like my therapist."

"She's done you some good."

"I know." We sat in silence for a long while. He looked at me. I stared at the open beer. Finally, I pushed the bottle away and looked up. "I don't know what I'm going to do. I don't know if I have any business doing anything. I just don't…know."

"Stop," he said.

"Stop what?"

"Everything. Stop."

"I don't—"

"Stop talking. Stop thinking. Stop fighting and drinking and running."

"Who's running?"

"Ask yourself why you jumped on that." He took the bottle back and drained it. When he set it down he did it hard, making the glass thump on the wood table. "Just like that. Everything in your life changed in Iraq. The army didn't treat you right because it had its own problems, so you fought. Then—" He thumped the bottle down again. "Your life changed again." Another thump. "And again." Thump. "And again." He pointed his bearded chin at me. "At some point you gotta ask yourself if you're running from the fights or to them."

"That's not fair."

"Nothing's fair. It just is."

"You don't know what you're talking about."

"Katrina. There have been two serious men in your life. Nelson Solomon and Billy Blevins. Nelson was a tough man by any measure. But you married him when you both knew there was no future."

"In spite of his illness."

"If you believe that—have a beer. Or a whiskey. Or any other lie you want to drink."

"Stop."

"It was easy to marry a dying man. It was a fight and a chance to run all wrapped up in one, wasn't it?"

"What's this all about? Why are you butting in? And what makes you think you know anything about me and Billy?"

"Because it's all about you and nothing about him. He made it clear how he feels. It's obvious to everyone but you how you feel. But Billy just isn't the level of turmoil you need, is he?"

"Look around. There were reporters outside. Riley wasn't here for your overcooked steaks. I'm dealing with nothing but turmoil. And all because of Billy. And there's no reason for any of it."

"How do you know?"

"Know what?"

"That there is no reason. Seems to me that's more your signature."

You can search a graveyard at night, going from marker to marker by flashlight. When the sun comes out you realize you never even knew the name you were looking for. Uncle Orson's comment was sunlight on my confusion. Billy was never as much a mess as everything seemed the last couple of days. I was busy being hurt and worried about how it affected me rather than looking for his reason.

"I'm going home," I said.

"You can sleep here." Uncle Orson could always be counted on to put the hard truth aside and make an easy place to land after he said his piece. His rough edges were burnished by life's grind, leaving the core of heartwood and kindness behind.

I, on the other hand...

He lifted the empty beer bottle and reached beyond the end of the bench to drop it in the recycle bin. The clatter was jarring to me but he smiled at the sound. "I have all the soda a girl could want."

He sounded the same as he had when I was a little girl sitting in the same spot. Soda is no longer the all-purpose answer it was back then. I smiled anyway. "Thanks." I stood, then stepped away. "For everything."

"You're not staying?"

"I need a hot shower and my own bed. I'm going to be up early."

"You want to be alone." He didn't frame it as a question.

"No." As soon as I said it, the small word seemed like a big confession. "I think I need to be right now."

He nodded without saying anything.

I appreciated the lack of argument. Still, I didn't go for the door right away. "I'll take an orange soda for the road."

He pulled the frosted bottle from the cooler. "You want it opened?"

I shook my head. "Thank you, Uncle Orson." I thought both of us knew the thanks were not for the bottle of soda. I hoped.

Chapter 9

I arrived home to a cold and dark house. I woke in the morning to the same. The sun was rising to little effect. A thick grime of clouds diffused the light into a depressing gray shadow. It was a day born in sorrow.

The night before, my thoughts were muddled. They got squeezed and twisted by passing through the bottleneck of my own concerns. Sleep helped. Things seem to sort themselves out when I stop pulling on the ends.

My assumptions about what was going on had been jumping on the obvious. Rose was dead and Billy went directly to arrest Donny without evidence or investigation. It had to be because Billy knew the boy was the killer. Unless it wasn't.

The thought I had woken up with was: Billy was protecting Donny. Billy either wanted Donny in jail to keep him safe, or Billy simply wanted to make the kid the conspicuous suspect. It didn't matter which. The real question was, who was Billy trying to fool?

Levi Sharon.

I had the feeling that, for whatever reason, Billy knew Levi would target Donny.

Why?

I believed that Levi didn't want to kill Billy. Or me, for that matter. He wanted to stop anyone who was in his way.

So where was Billy now—chasing Levi, or Rose's killer? The last thing he had said to me was to find Levi and to start with E. Lawson. So that's what I was going to do.

I didn't walk so much as shamble out to my truck. The morning half-light made the pain in my body feel deeper in my muscle and bone. There was one bright spot in my thinking. The supposition that Levi didn't want to kill Billy meant that Rose's brother didn't believe Billy had been the man who took what wasn't his.

I didn't know where to find Lawson but I knew where to start. My first stop was the Taneycomo Café.

Because of the kind of man E. Lawson was, an Ozarks loner, I had a lot of sources to call on. Few of them would be up and around this early in the morning. But our jailer started his shift at 6:30 and he liked a good breakfast.

Duck was right where I expected him to be. "Hurricane!" He greeted me with a raised cup of coffee when I walked in the café door. A few of the other regulars raised their hands or nodded. Most of them wouldn't use my nickname to my face.

"I need to hit you with a couple of questions, Duck." I settled into the seat opposite him without being asked.

"Can't you ever just come say good morning?"

The waitress came and laid down a plate of pancakes, another of eggs and bacon, and a bowl of grits.

"No, I get a heart attack just watching you eat." To the waitress I said, "Toast and coffee, please."

"See?" Duck pointed at me, this time with a fork. "That's why you're so skinny."

"Only you think I'm skinny."

"A woman should have a little meat on her."

"Do you mind not discussing my—*anything*?"

"You brought it up." He slathered syrup onto his pancakes.

"No. I didn't. But I wanted to bring something else up. Do you know a man, goes by E. Lawson?"

Duck put down the syrup and raised a fat finger to his lips. "Don't." The waitress arrived and placed my coffee and toast in front of me. Duck shoved a huge wedge of carbs and dripping sugar into his mouth.

I buttered my toast and waited for him.

"See that guy over there?" Duck indicated which man with his eyes. "He works for Lawson. They're a rough bunch."

The man seated at the far end of the counter looked like anyone else in the café, a workman or a farmer.

"How come I never heard of Lawson until recently?" I kept my voice low then took a bite.

"There is still a lot of the old Ozarks out there in the hills and behind the trees," Duck said. "They hold grudges and they don't call the cops. If you're not in you're out. Know what I mean?"

I did know. It was a lesson that I kept learning. "What can you tell me?"

"There are at least three unmarked graves in this county that he dug and filled."

"He wasn't convicted?"

"He wasn't investigated. The dead men were never reported by anyone."

"But everyone knows."

"Everyone who matters." He gulped down some eggs and then some coffee.

I chewed a bit of toast then asked, "So he's the king of some kind of redneck mafia. Why? Is there enough money in poaching trees and rustling cattle to make it worthwhile?"

"Ask your bartender."

"Clare? He told me about the man. Clare introduced me to Lawson."

"Yep. I'd bet he didn't tell you everything."

"Like what?"

"Whether you know it or not, a piece of the action at Moonshines is going to E. Lawson."

"Extortion?"

"Old-school, pay-us-so-nothing-bad-happens kind of stuff."

"I don't believe it," I said.

"Ask him."

"Clare wouldn't betray me like that."

"Betray? He's protecting you."

"I'm a cop. I don't pay extortion."

"That's why he would. You never know. You're never involved. But no mysterious fires."

"Who else pays?"

"Not the big corporations. You can't muscle teams of lawyers and the cash for private security. Everyone else..." Duck wiped his mouth with a wadded napkin and shrugged. His plates were clean. He started digging into the bowl of grits.

"Where can I find him?"

"He likes wives."

"Wives?"

"Other men's wives."

That reminded me of something Lawson had said about being with a pretty nurse the night before Rose Sharon was killed. He had all but dared me to check his alibi. I hadn't because he had pointed me at Levi and Billy.

"When he's not with someone else's wife, where would I find Lawson?"

* * * *

When I bought the big GMC 2500 I felt a little silly. It was a work vehicle with a luxury interior. That morning, as I put it into four-wheel drive and powered through muddy snow on a barely visible path, I was grateful for my truck.

The trail wound through a break in barbed wire fencing and up a long, wooded hill. It ended in a clearing that was bare only of trees. The ground was strewn with piles of wood and even deeper hillocks of sawdust. Everywhere there were rusting hulks of heavy equipment. In places the snow was stained red with the oxidation of machines that looked like beasts slaughtered and left to rot.

In the center of it all was a long, low shack bellowing noise and smoke.

The sounds of the sawmill dropped away to a hollow silence as I approached. The high-hang roller door at the end of the shack was wide open. Even though the sun was up, the lights inside were on. Four dim bulbs looked like trapped stars in the gloom.

"E. Lawson!" I shouted.

"What do you want?" was the instant response.

"I want to talk."

Lawson stepped from the shadows into the day's frail light. He was not wearing a shirt. His sweating body was shedding smoky wisps of vapor. He had a club of crooked wood that looked to have seen some use slung over his shoulder. "No one's stopping you."

"Tell me about the woman."

His one good eye narrowed. The milky one seemed to get brighter. "What woman?"

"The pretty nurse."

"I don't need to tell you shit."

"What are you afraid of?"

He seemed to consider that for a moment. When he reached whatever conclusion he was working on, Lawson tossed the club aside. Then he pointed at the jagged white-worm scar that split his eye and said, "Nails in trees. Hit 'em with a chainsaw and it kicks back."

"That can mess up a guy's good looks."

"Naw. Ladies like scars." He looked me up and down in the way that communicates to every woman in the world that she's meat for hungry wolves. "Some men like 'em too."

"*Excuse* me?"

"I heard you got a body like Frankenstein's bride."

Heat crept up my skin. I felt it flushing my chest and burning its way into my face. "You need to back the conversation up some. I'm not some pretty target you can run at and come away safe."

"You're not, huh?" His grin was both a dismissal and a challenge. "Just what is it you think you are?"

"I'm the nail in the tree. And I'm the chainsaw you can't handle."

Lawson's answer was to back away. He faded into the mill's gloom. Like a demented Cheshire cat, the last of him to disappear were his sneer and the milky eye.

I put my hand on my service weapon and sidled over to get a better look into the dark interior. "Lawson!"

As soon as I shouted the mill saw started up again.

I couldn't see him. If I stayed where I was, perfectly framed in the doorway by the snow and pale daylight, I was as clear as a bullseye. So I darted forward and right, into the murk. I hoped that Lawson had been watching me. If he had, then his eyes were taking time to adjust too.

I crouched. Waiting.

"I didn't kill that girl," Lawson called over the sound of the saw.

I didn't answer.

"Do you hear me? I didn't kill the girl."

"Did I say you did?" I called back. Then I moved.

"If I was you I would be looking at that cop."

"You're definitely not me."

Something clattered against the old wood and tin sheeting that made up the shack walls. I glanced and saw about four feet of logging chain snaking to the floor. My eyes were opening up. So were Lawson's.

"What are you here for, if it ain't the girl?" Lawson had moved too. His voice came from closer to the door. I peered under the saw's feeder track. I didn't see him, but I noticed that the club he had dropped a minute ago was gone.

"What are you planning on doing with that big stick?" I asked.

He answered by bolting from the shadows and slamming the club into a support beam. The entire building shook. I thought the roof would come down.

Before he could take another swing, I stood. My weapon was held in a two-handed grip. My feet were spread and body balanced. I was prepared to shoot. "Drop it," I commanded.

A saner man or a slower one would have complied. Lawson swung the big stick again. It was just long enough to reach across the saw feed.

I fired at the moment of contact. The bullet went wide. The pistol went flying. I was lucky the wood struck the weapon instead of my clenched hands. As it was, the impact felt like a bomb going off in my fingers. They bent open with the brutal shock then went dead and useless.

I was reaching for the telescoping baton on my belt, my pained fingers scrabbling without closing, when Lawson leapt over the track. He hit me with his shoulder in the center of my chest.

I went down, gasping.

Lawson pulled me up as easily as I would lift a kitten.

"Now—"

Before he could finish his thought, I reared back and planted my forehead against his nose. The crunch of cartilage was satisfying. The gush of blood was a bonus.

"Now what?" I managed to ask before he lifted me even higher and threw me. I hit the same roof support he had clubbed a moment earlier.

My body struck the beam at an angle, leading with my right shoulder. I rolled helplessly into it. My spine and the ribs on my left side hit next. My back bent, sending my arms and legs flailing. I must have blacked out then. The next thing I knew I was being held up again.

My feet dangled.

Lawson grinned. "Feisty," he said.

There were few diminutions I hated more. I tried to say so.

When I opened my mouth to speak, Lawson pulled me to him and pressed his lips to mine. He pushed his thick tongue in. I felt it like a roiling lie made flesh trying to demean me with its intrusion.

I bared my teeth and bit. My incisors and the canines on the right caught the side of his tongue and dug deep.

Lawson released his grip in surprise. It was the worst thing he could have done.

I dropped.

All my weight hung from his tongue. I didn't release him. He jerked away but I clamped my jaws harder and held on. Blood spurted between our pressed faces. I felt the heat of it on my skin. The coppery tang crept up my nose.

Lawson began to make a sound halfway between a scream and a growl. His tongue was tearing away.

He must have realized that my weight was making his situation much worse. Lawson grabbed me again. This time he used one hand at the back of my hair.

I almost screamed. But I kept my mouth clamped and gutted out my own snarl of rage and pain.

Lawson pulled back his huge right fist.

I twisted my head, shaking his tongue like a dog shaking a snake. It tore off in a bloody spray just as his fist struck me in the abdomen. The last thing I saw before the world went black again was a pink bullet of flesh arching away. It trailed red droplets.

* * * *

I woke shivering from the cold and confused about why I was on the ground. The reason came back to me as a spasm gripped my stomach. I thought the top of my head was going to blow off as I threw up into the sawdust.

The turmoil in my brain and my gut fought to see which could make me more miserable. I rolled to the side so I could drop back down without wallowing in my vomit. The cold was still shaking me but I didn't care. It wasn't the first time I had been hurt and left alone to die or live. I took the time to examine some of my life choices.

After an uncountable time, I gave up and forced myself to stand. Fortunately, I didn't have to lift my head to see where I wanted to go. On the floor was a bold blood trail leading away and deeper into the back of the shack. I didn't follow. Not right away. I hobbled around the long feeder track and found my weapon.

Bending to pick it up was a challenge, but not as much as working it into my battered hands. I dropped the magazine, then pulled the slide and ejected the chambered round. With it empty I rubbed it clean on my pants. After that I blew into the barrel and behind the hammer. The work was calming. It was also an excuse. I was procrastinating.

As soon as I realized what I was doing I was angry with myself. It was what I needed. I dry-fired my pistol. Satisfied all the parts were functioning, I reloaded and shambled back to the blood trail. This time I didn't stop or hesitate.

The blood was a ragged spatter. Still, it ran in a basically uniform direction. It reached a door where a huge red handprint was stamped on the wood. I took a stance and held my weapon at the ready, then pushed the door open with my foot.

Beyond the door was only snow and more crimson. The trail ended at a set of tire tracks. Lawson had taken off in a truck. I'm not sure I'd ever been so disappointed not to shoot someone in my life.

Out past the tracks was an outbuilding even more dilapidated than the mill. It was an open shed not quite deep enough to hide the front end of Levi Sharon Charger. I checked the car. It was empty and long cold. The second stall of the shed was taken up by an old International Harvester one-ton truck. It was crumpled up front and covered by a rotting tarp. It hadn't moved in years.

On the far side of the shelter was a trailer stacked with five big logs. The truck that had towed the trailer was gone. There was a set of tracks partially covered by blown snow leading away around the back of the shed. Two trucks had been here. Both gone. E. Lawson was definitely one driver. The only other one I could think of was Levi Sharon.

I turned away from the tracks and examined the logs on the trailer. They were all walnut. Probably the ones taken from Hosea Fisher. It was odd to see hunks of wood and imagine they were worth thousands each. I should have had them taken in as evidence. I didn't. I had more anger in me than responsibility, and if I couldn't shoot Lawson I could still hit him in a way to send a message.

I went back to the mill and found a can of premixed chainsaw fuel. I emptied it on the stolen logs.

Despite the warmth of the flames I didn't linger. I did wonder if Lawson could see the rising column of smoke as I limped back to my truck.

The big GMC fired right up. I didn't drive. I didn't do anything for a while except wait for the heater. When warm air flowed I opened my coat to let it in. I'm not sure, but I may have drifted off again. After a bit I had the presence of mind to use the radio. I called dispatch and issued a BOLO for Lawson. Then I put in a 10-7 code and took myself out of service.

Before anyone could respond or tell me to do something else, I switched off the radio. I turned off my cell for good measure.

There are times when all of us experience a lapse into autopilot. We do things by rote and without active thought while the mind works on other things. Usually we experience it in benign ways. A person might do the same commute every day, and one time you get home with no memory of anything since leaving work. I knew a mason once who worked all afternoon and suddenly realized he had no memory of laying out several courses of brick.

A drunk's autopilot can be different. Somehow the demon within can catch you napping and take over. It always follows the path to its own satisfaction.

I was in the liquor store with a bottle of Wild Turkey in my hand when I realized what I was doing.

I knew. I stepped up with the bottle and my cash anyway.

"You sure about this?" the clerk asked me. I had more than one reputation in the county.

"Don't I look old enough?" My question carried a lot more anger than I wanted it to.

"Hurricane—"

"Don't call me that. Just ring it up."

"Your uncle would have my skin nailed to the boathouse wall."

"You know Orson?"

The man behind the counter nodded like it was an important question, then said, "I know you, too."

"I don't remember."

"I'm not surprised. Last time I sold to you, you went on a jag."

"A *jag*?"

He didn't answer. He didn't look away, either. The clerk stood his ground and held my gaze until I threw a twenty and a ten on the counter. I pointed at the cigar box sitting open in front of the register. "Put the change in the charity box so you don't feel guilty." I was ashamed of myself as soon as I said it. Shame didn't stop me from walking out the door with my bottle in hand.

Chapter 10

There is a place I sometimes go to be alone. That's the easy way to say it. Solitude is the last thing the spot offers. I go there to be away from the living. In the last couple of years, the ghosts that come to keep me company have grown in number.

The spot is nothing. It is the bend of a rutted dirt road where I park. On one side is a fallow field and a border of woods along a creek. The other side is just as empty. There, an eroded wall of sandstone gives an illusion of solidity. Junipers, stunted but still green in the snow, dot the crags of rock.

It is a special nowhere. Once, just a couple of years ago, a girl was murdered down by the creek. It was a difficult case. She was killed by another girl, someone she knew. That girl died in my arms at the same spot.

That was my bottom, a place of tears and drinking. Regret is never a smooth road.

Don't be fooled when a drunk tells you they don't choose the bottle. It is always a choice. It is the easiest, come-to-Jesus decision they can make in a world of hard options. I know that if I open the bottle, the pain in my body and my heart will mute down to an amber glow of warmth. It is not forgetting. It is embracing. Taking the drink would be a reaching-out to see my dead husband and my murdered father. I would see dead girls living. My own life would be resurrected if only for a short time. It is that time, that illusion, drunks like me reach for when they take the bottle.

All illusions are cages. They lock us in and keep us separate from the truth.

That's what I was thinking in the hot cab of my truck, staring at the unopened bottle on my dash when Billy pulled up alongside me.

It wasn't a surprise. Billy knew me pretty well. He had sat with me in this spot and coaxed me through the bars of my cage before.

I didn't want him there. I couldn't have borne it if he didn't come.

Billy opened the passenger door and got into my truck without saying anything. His gaze fixed on the Wild Turkey said everything.

I looked away and wiped my eyes. When I turned back his hat was tilted down over his eyes and his arms crossed as if he was settling in for a nap.

"You're not going to say anything?" I asked.

"Like what?" he answered from under the brim of his Stetson.

"You don't want to talk?"

"I figure if you want to talk you will. If you don't…" He did something that I assumed was a shrug.

"That guy call you? The one from the liquor store?"

"He called your uncle. Your uncle called me."

"You take Orson's calls but not mine?"

"Your uncle is a lot easier to talk to these days."

Billy made an exaggerated point of keeping his face down. At least I thought it was exaggerated—and a point. "You should take better care of your hat," I said. "You let the snow melt on it."

"See now?" Billy asked. He took off the hat and sat up in the seat. For a moment he turned the hat like he was examining each spot. "That's why we're here."

"Why?"

"Because you're always choosing the wrong thing to talk about." He hung the Stetson on his knee then looked up, right into my eyes. He held his gaze there as he moved closer.

When he leaned forward I thought for an instant that he was going to kiss me.

He didn't. Instead he took the bottle from my dash and opened it. Instantly the scent filled the truck. At least in my imagination.

Billy put his nose to the bottle and smelled it.

My mouth watered and my stomach churned. Even without the drink I felt the sensation of the warm liquid bloom. I could have gotten intoxicated just off the need and thought. I wanted to be drunk.

"I haven't had a drink since Nelson died," Billy said.

That stopped my slide into the dry drunk. "Why would you do that? You never even knew him that well."

"You needed someone in your life to be sober with, not just for." Billy put his window down and poured the bottle out onto the snowy ground.

I watched the liquid gurgle away, feeling angry. "Why don't you pour your own drinks out?"

"I have." He put the window up and capped the empty bottle before dropping it onto the floorboard. "When was the last time you saw me with a soda cup?"

He was right. Billy had a habit of carrying around one of those huge thermal mugs from the convenience store. Caffeine and sugar always seemed to be in his hand. I didn't answer his question. I couldn't remember the last time I had seen the cup.

"Ask the questions you really want to ask," he said.

"Were you involved with the girl?" I didn't plan to ask it. Not so soon. Not so bluntly. The thought wasn't even in my mind. But once I asked it, I had to know. "Were you in a relationship with Rose Sharon?"

"I knew Levi from the service. When I came here he asked me to watch over his sister."

"And?"

"And I taught her guitar. And I wrote songs with her. And I told you all about it more than once."

That surprised me. "I would remember—"

"When did I stop drinking soda?"

"That's not the same thing."

"I had a big, sugary drink in my hand all day, every day for how long? Not carrying it around because the voters thought it was a sign of youth and frivolity was a big change."

"Riley Yates called you Bill."

"People who had known me for years couldn't vote for a Billy."

"I didn't know..."

"Knowing takes effort. Engagement."

"Things are complicated."

"You do your job," he said. "You wrap yourself up in it, complications and all."

"That's not fair." I said. Then I hated the word and having said it.

"Was that bottle going to be fair to you?" He waited.

Every second of silence that passed was like a stone placed in my chest.

"I keep running from..."

"I know you keep running." Billy spread his hands out in front of him as if the nothing between them were a gift. "I just don't think you know what from."

I shook my head.

"You know how I feel about you," he said, without making it a question. "I think you tell yourself that's one of the things you run from. I think it's easier to back away from me and ignore my feelings than it is to admit that what you really run from are *your* feelings."

"How can you say that?"

"You married a man you knew was dying after knowing him only a few weeks." He let that sit for a moment, then asked, "How many women are in your life? The therapist doesn't count."

I shook my head, but I couldn't say what exactly I was denying.

Billy ignored the gesture and said, "You surround yourself with men. Strong men, but old ones. I'm the one who wants more from you. And I'm the one you simply can't manage to keep a sane relationship with."

"You were there," I said. I didn't mean it as an accusation, but it was. "Levi told me. You were the medic who stitched me up in the Humvee. You saw it all. You told me it wasn't you."

"It wasn't me." His eyes flashed but his voice remained soft. "It wasn't you, either. We were different people."

"Now who's running away from things?"

"That may be. But I wanted to be the man you chose out of love, or desire—even friendship. Anything but gratitude."

"Why?"

"Love is the worst way to pay a debt."

I thought about that. For a long time I stared through the windshield at the snow and stubby evergreen spikes of the junipers. All the other trees were bare. Against the dirty gray sky their limbs looked like cracks in glass.

Before I could think of anything to say, Billy asked, "How did you get hurt?"

I must have looked confused. He pointed at his face then at me. "You have blood on your face. Your clothes are a mess."

"I found E. Lawson."

"He did that?"

"He almost killed me."

Billy nodded thoughtfully but he wasn't looking at me anymore.

"I need to ask you…" I paused. Wondering if I really wanted to hear more about Rose Sharon.

"Yes?"

"Why have you been hiding?"

"Who said I was hiding?"

"Why have you been out of touch? When you found out about Rose you shut down and closed me out."

"I needed space to feel bad. Rose and I were close."

"Close?"

"Like family. She called me her 'better brother.'"

"Did you ever tell me that?"

"No. You're not very good with other people's complications." Billy shook his head. It was a sad kind of gesture, and regretful. He still didn't look at me. "Maybe I should have tried harder."

I shook my head so vigorously it hurt. "No one tries as hard as you. You're right about me. Sometimes I would rather fight than love."

"Sometimes?" He laughed.

I laughed once, then winced at the pain in my back and ribs.

Billy stopped laughing. "I thought you were exaggerating when you said he almost killed you."

"He hurt me. I hurt him right back. We need to keep an eye on the hospitals. He'll be looking for help."

"We should get you into one too."

"No. I don't think anything is broken but my spirit. You were the best medicine for that."

"I didn't do anything."

"You showed up."

* * * *

Despite my protests, Billy didn't let me drive home. He called Uncle Orson to come get my truck for the second time, then helped me into his SUV. I fell asleep on the drive and woke up once more in the hospital with taped ribs and a bandage around my head.

This time Billy was sitting in the chair.

"What happened?" I asked. As I said it I knew it was a foolish question.

"I couldn't tell if you passed out or fell asleep. Either way it let me bring you here without having to fight about it."

"My left eye is blurry."

"You got another concussion. But I think you knew that. The stitches in your head were popped. There is a place on the back of your scalp, too, that had to be stitched. The doctor said it looked like your hair had almost been pulled off your head."

Reflexively I reached and touched the back of my head. I could feel the lump and a sharp bite of pain under the bandage.

"And, on top of that, you have a vitreous hemorrhage."

"What's that?"

"Bleeding in your left eye. Your vision should be back to normal in a few days."

"Get my clothes."

"Nope. You're off duty. Medical leave for at least a week."

"You can't."

Billy pointed at himself. "Sheriff, remember?" Then he settled his Stetson down on his head and stood. "I have a lot to do. You don't. I'll be back, but it'll be late."

"Late?"

"There's a memorial for Rose at the Star Road Theater tonight. I'm going to play her a song."

I found that hard to believe. "*You* were invited to sing at her memorial?" I made my doubt clear in my tone.

"No." Billy didn't look back or say anything else as he walked out.

I kept thinking of what he said in the truck—other people's complications. Funny how we always seem so eager to make them our own.

After half an hour I was tired of lying in bed stewing in my own mind. Work is almost always the best way for me to get past the fences that circle my life. I pulled the oxygen sensor off my finger and the IV needle from my arm. The nurse came in and we went through the same you-can't-do-this dance as before. This time I dressed without arguing and ignored the demands for signatures.

I didn't leave the hospital. I took the elevator down one floor and went to Donny Fisher's room. He was alone.

Donny didn't look like the strong young man I had first seen. Lying in the hospital bed with his neck misshapen and bandaged he looked like a damaged boy. The bandage wasn't the only sign of the trauma Levi's bullet had done. Donny was intubated. I assumed it was to protect his throat after surgery. It didn't matter for what I wanted. I hadn't expected he would be able to talk.

I walked up to the foot of his bed.

Donny opened his eyes.

We stared at each other. The airy hissing of the machine that fed him oxygen was the only sound.

I was about to apologize and leave when Donny lifted his hand and gestured me closer. Then he pointed to a scribbled pad and ballpoint pen sitting on the stand beside him.

I handed it over.

He flipped to a clean page and wrote. I expected an angry dismissal. I wasn't actually at all prepared for his question.

Did he kill Sharon?

"I don't think so," I said. "It seems like Levi thought you did."

He wrote again. *Stupid.*

I nodded. "Yeah. There's a lot of that going around."

Donny narrowed his eyes and glared at me, then made one mark on the pad: *?*

"No one wants to talk about Rose in a helpful way," I said.

His face sagged.

"You know what I'm talking about, don't you?"

Donny's nod would have been imperceptible if I hadn't been looking for it. Then he wrote, *Mother.*

"Yes. Do you know why she's fighting the investigation?"

Not supposed to talk without lawyer.

"I understand," I said. "You were a suspect. It's a smart thing not to talk without a lawyer. And I shouldn't even ask you questions without Mr. Tau here. But we both want the same thing, don't we?"

Sharon's killer.

"Yes."

I don't know anything.

"She knew about you, didn't she?"

Gay? When he held up the question, his eyes were at first cast aside. Then he looked at me with defiance.

I wondered if it was the first time he'd faced the world with his true identity in the lead. "Yes. She knew you were gay. She accepted?"

My friend. My sister. Always on my side. Clark was her friend too. Rose helped keep our secret but she always said it would be okay to come out.

I opened my mouth to speak but didn't get the chance.

Donny flipped the page and wrote again, furiously. *Sharon didn't deserve—*

"No, she didn't," I interrupted his writing. "Help me get justice for her."

?

I thought hard in a long silence about what I wanted to say. Finally, I asked, "Who is the song about?"

Donny didn't write; he pulled both shoulders up and spread both hands.

"It wasn't about Sheriff Blevins?"

Just her friend, he wrote. After a moment's more thought he added to the page. *Mother is just mad. She's making all that up.*

"Did Sharon have any boyfriends?"

Not since Tom the asshole.

I almost laughed to see the word written out like that. The sentiment behind it, though, kept me focused. "What's asshole Tom's last name?"

Ask sheriff.

"The sheriff? Why should I ask him?"

Asshole is a deputy.

"Tom Dugan."

Donny winced at the pain, but he nodded clearly.

As stunned as I was, some of the pieces seemed to settle in my mind. It made sense. "Thanks, Donny. It helps."

I would have walked out, but he wrote another note. *You think Dugan did it?*

"I don't know."

The look on his face was a strange mix of disappointment and anger. He wrote, *Kill him. Do it for Clark.*

I didn't have a response to that. I walked away, but stopped at the door and turned. "Do you know a man by the name of E. Lawson?"

Donny's widened eyes answered the question, but for good measure he wrote one word on his pad.

Dangerous.

Chapter 11

In the hallway, while limping to the exit, I made two calls. First to my uncle asking where my truck was. The second was to dispatch. Doreen was on. I asked her where I would find Tom Dugan.

"Aren't you in the hospital?" she asked. "The sheriff said not to let you in the building."

"I'm not trying to get into the building. But I need to find Dugan."

"You're off duty," she repeated. "And it's a good thing. You need a rest, Hurricane."

By habit I almost told her not to call me Hurricane. Instead I said, "Doreen. It's really important. I need to know where Dugan is. And where Billy is if you know."

"Of course. Everyone is at the same place."

"Same place? Where's that?"

"Don't you know about the memorial service for Rose Sharon and that other boy?"

"Clark Beasley," I said. I hadn't thought of the service until she reminded me. Billy said he was going to play a song for Rose Sharon. "It's at the Ozarks Star Road Theater."

"Everyone's there."

"Everyone?"

"It's a mess. There are press trucks and reporters everywhere. Branson City Police called us in to help control the scene. We don't have enough people on tour. They called in the highway patrol and asked for support from Stone and Christian Counties."

"I'm on my way," I said.

"You're off duty," she reminded me.

"Has anyone sighted Levi Sharon or E. Lawson?"

"Nothing about Levi. We have conflicting information about Lawson, though."

"What information?"

"One truck registered to him was found in the parking lot of a Springfield hospital."

"One truck? So there's another?"

"Yes. An '01 Ford F-150 was sighted in Branson. The officer who reported it was called away."

"It got away," I said.

"Yes."

"Thanks, Doreen."

"Are you staying in the hospital?"

I closed the connection. Before me were the automatic doors of the trauma center entrance. It was already full dark outside. I didn't have to wait long before two pairs of headlights swept through the parking lot. My GMC followed by Clare's old Dodge swung up the circle drive and stopped.

Uncle Orson got out of my truck and came to meet me. "Are you all right?" he asked.

I kept walking to where Clare was parked. "Come here," I said.

Clare rolled his window down as we approached.

"Let me ask you both something," I added.

"What's going on?" Clare asked.

"You tell me," I said as an answer.

"What's the question?" Uncle Orson asked.

I looked from one to the other then said, "E. Lawson."

Both of the men looked at me. Neither said anything.

"Who's paying him?"

Both of them stopped looking at me.

"Clare," I said. "You're paying protection on my place?"

"I wanted to keep you out of it. Since you're a sheriff's detective you needed to be able to honestly say you didn't know."

"Since I'm a sheriff's detective I should not, and would not, pay him."

"That's the other reason. You would have been stubborn. You would have lost the place."

"I'd burn it down myself rather than knuckle under to Lawson if I'd known." I turned to my uncle. "And you?"

"You can't be on the lookout every minute," Uncle Orson said.

"What's that mean?"

"It means you only need to look the wrong way once for a fire to break out. You know how slim a living a boat dock and bait shop provides. I don't have any real insurance."

"What?" I barked the word so hard and loud my head throbbed with the effort. "Are you crazy?"

"Sometimes you have to make hard choices," Orson said. He sounded like he believed it as much as I did.

"You sound like a girl I knew in high school who got pregnant. She said her boyfriend didn't like to wear a condom and she *just made a choice.*"

"Look, no one's proud of it," Orson said with a little more fire. "But you stomp one cockroach and another one shows up. Pretty soon the only thing you're doing is killing roaches. Either way you end up with no business and no life."

"It's true," Clare added.

"It's over," I said. "Not another penny from either of you. The man almost killed me today. I'm making sure he never extorts anyone in my county again."

Orson pointed to the bandage still on my head. "He did that?"

"Don't worry about it," I said. "Just don't pay."

Orson and Clare looked at each other then back to me. They nodded but didn't say anything more.

"Good." I went back to the GMC and drove straight to the Ozarks Star Road Theater.

* * * *

Snow was falling again. Fast-blowing fluff streaked through my headlights. It piled in blown drifts. In Branson, roads already crowded turned slick and slow. I put the truck into four-wheel drive and hit my emergency lights.

At the main entrance was a bright white marquee surrounded by neon and chaser bulbs. In the center, black letters said, *FAREWELL TRIBUTE — ROSE SHARON AND CLARK BEASLEY.* I had never known Clark, but I pitied him having to share his death and memorial with a star.

The theater parking lot was stuffed. Cars and trucks were filing up to the entrances only to be turned away by cops who had taken over for parking attendants. Around the building there was a gauntlet of news vans and official vehicles. I pulled up over a curb and parked on top of a sickly looking shrub.

A city cop I didn't know was at the back door. I showed my badge and he waved me through. Backstage it was dark and crowded. Between the black-out drapes I could see the performers on stage. It was one of the big Branson family acts. The music was a glossy kind of bluegrass-inspired country. It was carefully crafted hillbilly, produced with thousand-dollar guitars and clear plastic fiddles with color-changing lights inside.

They finished their set and cleared the stage. As they did, a screen rolled down from the overhead fly system. All the stage lights dimmed as the screen flared into life. From the front of the stage, cameras flashed. Everyone in the packed house stood as the music started. The backstage and wing spaces were filling even more as performers packed in to be part of the moment.

I gave up trying to find Billy and let myself get pushed by the incoming tide of Branson royalty.

It wasn't until Rose Sharon began to sing that I looked up at her on the screen. She was alone in a spotlight that sparked off the sequins of her dress. She was beautiful and sad as she sang "You Took What Wasn't Yours."

I looked around at the faces. They were all lit only by the glow of the girl on the screen. Most were singing along. Many were crying.

The intensity of her performance was stunning. The sense of loss that filled the theater was humbling. One girl and one song had touched so many people. I was suddenly glad I was there watching her and not drunk on a snowy dirt road. Or more likely, dead after getting drunk with a concussion while parked in a bit of Ozarks nowhere with a snowstorm coming in. Every so often life has a way of showing its value in surprising ways.

The song faded and I began to hear other voices. They were arguing in angry whispers that failed at being quiet. Other people heard it too. Some moved toward the conflict. Some moved away. There were others that had reasons to stay and work to do. They held their ground, calling performers to clear the stage.

"No!" Sissy Fisher's full shout rose above everything.

"I wasn't asking permission," Billy answered, just as loudly.

The crowed opened up and I saw them. They were in the wing at the far side of the stage. Billy held a guitar in one hand. With the other he was fending off Sissy, who was alternately dragging him away from the stage and beating at him.

The image on the big screen transitioned from a freeze of Rose to video of the roadside memorial that had built up by the site of her murder. It was the same spot where I had seen kids tying teddy bears with ribbons, but it had become something much more. There were flowers and bows, candles in the snow, and hand-painted signs. It had only been a couple of days but the site had become a shrine.

"I know what you did to her!" Sissy screamed. Her voice was like blasphemy in a quiet church. Voices that had gone quiet, set into stunned silence.

I saw Billy shove her back. He raised his free hand as though he wanted to strike out and hit the woman. Instead, he backed away and onto the stage.

As he entered, the projection on the screen faded to nothing. No lights came up. No stage manager called a cue. Billy was not a part of the scheduled show. He didn't seem to notice or care. He slung his guitar and strummed a couple of licks. It was a calming habit more than a check for tune.

He stood alone in the center of the stage and looked out over the audience. It was dim without stage lights. Under the brim of the Stetson he still wore was only black. Billy was literally speaking from the shadows as he said, "You have heard a lot of things about my friend Rose Sharon. You've heard a lot of things about me lately, too." He strummed. "I'm not here to defend or to plead. I'm not going to tell you any stories—true ones or lies. I'm just here to sing a song. One of her favorites." Again he strummed. This time it was a chord. He let it ring, then placed his hand over the vibrating strings. Billy shuffled his feet.

My heart was breaking for him. I suspect he was reaching the audience, too. They were silent as old bone waiting for the resurrection. A light, a clear white spot, came on, then it centered on Billy.

"You know Rose and her brother lost their parents. The loss broke their lives, then reshaped it. Rose fared better than her brother Levi. Mothers." When he said the word he raised his right hand in a fist again. It looked as if he was going to slam it down against the guitar.

I looked away, not wanting to see him break down or make things worse. That was when I noticed that Sissy was gone.

"Mothers…" Billy said again.

I was reminded of my own difficult relationship with a woman who abandoned me. When she returned, I wasn't the girl she remembered and she wasn't the mother I dreamed of.

"Rose, this is for you and your mother," Billy said. He hit a chord on the guitar, then began to play in earnest. There was a collective release of breath as everyone recognized the Paul Simon tune, "Mother and Child Reunion."

Stage lights crept up with the sound of Billy's voice. It was easy to remember at that moment where his true talent was. He didn't sing alone for very long. First, the audience joined in on the familiar song. Then, slowly, other performers moved out onto the stage. There were more guitars, fiddles, mandolins, an upright bass and an entire chorus of brightly clad backup singers. The song turned into an anthem.

I relaxed. I allowed myself to think Billy had made the perfect moment for Rose.

That was when Sissy Fisher appeared again in the far side wing. She had a pistol in her hand. It was a chrome-plated revolver and obviously heavy in her hand. She shouted and waved aside the stage crew who were blocking her path.

I bolted across the stage behind the throng of musicians. Sissy came out from behind the black curtains, leading with the gun. I caught her by the wrist and forced her hand up. The pistol fired into the distant ceiling. I twisted her wrist and kept pushing Sissy back into the darkness of the wings.

With the gunshot, the music died. I was afraid for an instant that there was going to be a panic. As I forced Sissy to the floor and wrenched the gun from her hand I heard the guitar start up again. Billy started singing the old folk tune "Shenandoah." Immediately, the crowd of musicians joined in and made the song a hymn to a lost friend. The audience settled back into the groove the musicians carved.

Sissy didn't stop fighting or cursing me. That made it easier to take a little joy in forcing her over onto her front to cuff her hands behind her.

When I had her standing again, she flashed bright, hateful eyes at me. "You'll pay for this. I'll make sure of it."

"You sound like a character in a bad TV show."

"How's this sound?" She waited for me to look at her. "Your man took everything from us when he screwed Rose."

"Shut up," I said. I was surprised and grateful when she did. I secured the pistol. It was a .357 with magnum loads. I doubted that she could hit anything she aimed at, but anything she did hit would take a lot of damage.

"Where'd you get this?" I asked.

She stared at me, giving nothing.

The chrome on the gun matched the tone set by what Sissy was wearing. Once again she was doing the mock Native American look. She wore a denim skirt trimmed in suede with silver conchas woven in. Around her neck was a huge squash blossom necklace with an inverted turquoise moon pendant.

Holding the pistol up right in her face I said, "Firing a weapon in a crowded place like this—is insane. You could have hurt a lot of people or caused a panic. Is that what you wanted?"

Once again I underestimated the depth of her anger. Sissy lifted her foot. I was distracted by her moccasins. Even they were trimmed in beads and conchas. As I was paying attention to the silver and turquoise, Sissy's foot surged forward. Her kick landed off-center but hit hard on the bend of my lowest rib.

If my body hadn't been already damaged I might have taken the kick and restrained myself. Or maybe I'm giving myself too much credit. The pain was a jolt of electricity. The impact bent me down and forced the air from my body. I don't know if anyone saw me doubled over and gasping. I do know the singing was over and at least fifty performers walked off the stage to witness what happened next.

It was a reflex. The wrong one. After so much abuse and pain, my body reacted without conscious control. I swung out as I straightened my body, whipping my hand at her face. I didn't realize until too late that the revolver was still in my grip. Sissy Fisher was cuffed and under arrest when the barrel of the .357 fractured her cheekbone. She dropped like a prisoner on a gallows.

Before I fully understood what I'd done, Billy was beside me. He eased the revolver from my hand and backed me away from Sissy. "Call 911!" he shouted out to the crowd.

"I didn't mean to," I said.

"Don't talk," he warned. "Don't say anything. Don't do anything. Stay here and stay quiet." He turned back to address the crowd. "Tell 911 we need an ambulance. And stand back." He knelt beside Sissy and put his hands on her neck, checking for signs of trauma to the vertebrae. When he was satisfied, Billy pulled out his cell phone and punched a number. "Calvin," he said, once connected. "Go to my vehicle and get my med kit. Bring it to the stage."

By the time the ambulance arrived, Billy had a cervical collar on Sissy and the split skin on her cheek covered and taped. As she was taken out on a gurney Billy turned his attention back to me.

"I need your service weapon and your badge." He held out his hand.

"It was an accident."

"It doesn't matter. Half the theater saw you pistol-whip a woman who was cuffed and in your custody. You're relieved until things are straightened out."

"She discharged her weapon. I took it from her and restrained her. She attacked me and I hit back without realizing the gun was in my hand."

"We're not talking about it now." Billy kept his open hand out.

I handed over my credentials and my weapon.

* * * *

Outside, I stood in the falling snow trying to reason through what I had done and how things had gotten so far off reality's track. The night was so black even the city lights didn't reach the clouds. The theater was surrounded by neon and thousands of incandescent bulbs. Their light caught the falling flakes as they dropped, making each one appear as a tiny comet that appeared from nowhere. White stars crashed to Earth and buried everything in their cold fire.

I stood watching the white bloom as my hair and shoulders were dusted. Violence is not just a man's game. It's something women play at too. Deep in all of us is a bit of the old lizard brain that loves the chance to take control. People like me, drunks, are prone to the lizard at the best of times. At the worst, even without drinking, we embrace the reptilian promise of a cleansing rage. Therapy and AA have helped me understand that the anger is never properly aimed. No amount of fury or brutality will ever touch the source of the hurt because it is always in the past. We fight what we can because we can't fight ghosts.

Or maybe I was trying to justify myself to myself.

When I allowed myself to move again, my body was wracked with pain. I imagined the Tin Man, breaking loose rusted joints and moving for the first time in ages. For the first time I noticed I was shivering too.

My truck was still where I had parked it, but it wasn't alone. The shrubs took as much of a beating as I had that night. I was blocked from the back and partially from the front. With some careful cutting of the wheel I could jump the curb and ease back into the parking lot.

As soon as I put the GMC into gear, a set of high beams flared in front of me. A truck rushed forward, blocking me. It stopped with the open driver's side window aligned with mine.

Levi Sharon stared and waited.

I put my window down.

"What happened?" he asked before I could say anything.

"Why don't you come in to the sheriff's station with me and we can talk about it."

"You know that's not going to happen."

"Once you back up, we'll see about that."

He grinned like he was having the time of his life. "You're not even a cop now. Sure you want to take that on?"

I wasn't sure of anything. "What do you want, Levi?"

"Is he dead?"

"You shot two men. One is dead."

"Donny Fisher?"

"He's alive," I said. "Barely."

Levi's smile dissipated. "I think I screwed up."

"In a big way."

"He didn't do it, did he?"

"You're going to have to clarify that for me."

"Donny Fisher. Did he kill my sister?"

I shook my head and snow drifted off my hair. "I don't believe so. In fact, I think he was probably a pretty good friend to her. Like a brother."

"You sayin' I wasn't?"

I didn't answer that.

Levi looked away, then stared up into the sky. He appeared to be looking for something in the falling snow. "Sometimes I…" He shook his head and lowered it back down to face me. I could see the transition in his eyes, sadness replaced by anger. "Billy should have told me."

"Told you what?"

"You know what."

I looked away and stared into the falling stars of white, wondering if I saw the same sky Levi did. I wanted to cry. "I bet he did," I said. "I get the impression that you listen about as well as I do." When I looked back at him I saw only confusion. "You need to come in with me. Take responsibility."

"I'm sorry I hurt you," Levi said. He meant it. "But I ain't doin' that."

"There are a lot of cops looking for you. Most of them know only two things about you, you killed before and it says armed and dangerous on the BOLO. That's a dangerous situation."

"Are you sure Donny didn't do it?"

Talking to some people was like trying to argue with a compass; you can't change the way their needle points. "Pretty sure," I said. "Why did you think he was the one who killed your sister?"

"Some lies are slow, ain't they?"

"I don't understand."

"Lies. They don't have to be words. They can be things people do. Their entire life." Levi drew himself into the cab of his truck and looked down at his hands. "My own life."

He worked something around in his lap. My thought was it had to be a gun. He was desperate and depressed. I didn't think he was thinking straight, either. It was impossible to tell if he was more of a danger to himself or me.

"Levi?" I waited. "Levi!"

"You know why they didn't want me?" He looked up and brought a wadded paper towel to his eyes. "I couldn't sing for shit."

I realized I had been holding my breath. My long exhalation made a plume of white vapor.

"They used her. They ignored me. Until they couldn't anymore. Then I got sent away to the army. It was like she was waiting to get her hands on Rose. A plan came together. I was in the way."

I nodded. His pain was palpable, as if it was part of the cold between us. "You mean Sissy Fisher."

"The queen." His words came out like spitting bile—a man expressing a boy's pain. "She was the one who put me in with Lawson. Like she knew what would happen."

"Sissy Fisher knows E. Lawson?" The information was like a new kick in my stomach.

Levi wasn't hearing me or he was ignoring me. He kept talking. "You know, she thinks she's some kind of Indian. She talks about family and heritage and it's all an act." His head bobbed with the derisive snort of air that huffed from his nose. "Bitch." Then Levi dabbed with the paper towel. "She took one of those DNA tests. You know, the kind you spit in and mail off. Rose told me about it. There wasn't anything Indian that showed up. We had a laugh at that. Even Donny made a crack. She got all pissy and said he wouldn't be happy with any results he got, either. How screwed up is that? Or that I always felt left out of a family like that?"

"Levi…"

He kept ignoring me. He lifted a pint bottle of cheap rum and took a swallow.

"That's not going to help anything." It was truth that felt like a lie in my mouth. It was strange to be on the other side of the lecture and wanting to take the bottle for myself at the same time.

Levi took another drink and lowered his head. After a moment he closed his eyes. I recognized the look of someone trying not to look, but unable not to see the past.

People always seem to expect clarity from looking back. If they're lucky maybe they get a little understanding. Probably just enough to regret what they didn't do or say in the moment. Drunks get regret and guilt and the insistent whisper of alcohol telling them this time things will be different.

I was tempted—desperately wanted—to ask Levi to pass the bottle. I might have given in. I was already hating my rationalizations and the sound of shame I would hear in my voice.

Levi raised a revolver to his mouth and pulled the hammer back.

"Don't," I said. My voice was so quiet I wasn't sure he could hear me.

He drew the barrel away but kept it pointing right into his lips. "Why not?" he asked. His voice was quiet too. As if we were both suddenly in some sacred place where every word would be either prayer or lament. "Give me a reason."

I could hear the plea in his words. But I had no good answer to give. No matter what, everything sounded like another lie to pile onto his life. Finally I admitted, "It would kill me too."

Levi cast his eyes my direction without turning his head. The hand that held the gun eased forward. He closed his lips over the steel as if it was the last kiss he would ever feel.

"Not the bullet. The shooting," I said. "If you do it, I'll be dead just the same. Not tonight. But I wouldn't last long."

He lowered the weapon and said, "I see them. I see them all and I can't stop seeing them."

We weren't talking about the Fisher family or recent crimes anymore. I said, "I know. But there are other ways."

"This would be my choice. My own choice. My own way to go out."

"You don't have to go out. There are ways to go through it. I can get you help."

"In prison?"

"There's no avoiding that, Levi."

He shook his head and raised the revolver again. Pressing it to his face, he breathed slow and deep, then said, "There's my way. My terms."

"No." I reached through the window trying to push the gun away as it tilted. But I misunderstood.

I jerked my hand back. Then I threw myself down across my seat, reaching into the far floorboard as he turned the weapon toward me. The concussion of the shot was amplified by the confines of the truck cab. One bullet shattered my back window. I heard his engine rev and Levi backed his truck away. It roared as tires spun on snow before finding enough traction to whip through the parking lot.

I didn't chase him. I didn't even consider it. My day and night had been brutal and I was suspended. I called into dispatch and reported what had happened. Then I went home.

Chapter 12

The house had a chill in it that was more than winter cold. It was dark and it was lonely. Worse, it had never felt completely mine. The rich man's log cabin perched on the edge of a cliff had been my late husband's. His work space with easel and paints and my favorite piece of his—a painting of him and I as empty, drifting boats—still took up a corner by the fireplace.

I didn't turn any lights on. Instead I built a fire in the huge river rock fireplace. Once it caught I piled on dry oak until it was blazing with heat and light. I undressed in the middle of the room and tried to take stock of the abuses my body had suffered the past couple of days.

My hair was still sticky with blood where the stitches were. I had tossed the bandage as soon as I had left the hospital. My shoulder was darkened by bruises. All down my side were contusions and scrapes. I didn't bother to go to my upstairs mirror. Without looking I could count the wounds on my back by the ache in each breath. I had been running on adrenaline and that was all gone, leaving me vulnerable to the pain and prone to the depression and fatigue it always leaves behind.

Still in my underwear, I dropped onto the leather couch. It was cold on my skin. The roaring fireplace was radiating a soothing warmth. I told myself I would only lie there a minute as I pulled the afghan over myself.

At some point in the night, my dreams and my pain jelled. I opened my eyes and watched the flames. They were unnaturally large and bright. The heat coming out of the fireplace was something like a furnace in hell. Something moved in the shadows by the easel.

"Nelson?" I asked the shape. It wasn't as crazy as it sounds. There was a time, not so long ago, my dead husband visited me and sent messages. He told me things would be fine and he even encouraged my affection for

Billy Blevins. I have accepted that the visitations are from my mind and not from the grave. It had to be a dream.

The shade straightened to stand beside the boat painting. For an instant I thought he would pick up a brush and go back to work. There was a knocking, then without seeming to move, the shadow stood at my door. It knocked at the glass.

I pulled the afghan around my shoulders.

The black form beat the glass door again and called, "Katrina."

I stood and tugged the cover tighter over my body. "Billy?"

"Katrina, open the door," Billy said, knocking again.

I clutched my afghan and opened the door without saying anything. Everything still felt like a dream. The fire was high and hot and I suddenly realized I was sweating.

"Are you okay?" Billy asked my back.

"No," I answered. Dreams make for honesty.

I dropped the cover and stood close to the fire. It was intense and I got dizzy standing so close.

"Why is it so hot in here?"

"I like it," I said. "It feels good. Maybe I can sweat the whiskey out of me for good."

"Have you been drinking tonight?"

I thought about that and again resorted to honesty. "I don't know."

Billy put his hands on my shoulders. His touch was careful, like he was approaching a dangerous animal. He urged me away from the fire. "Your skin is hot," he said. "You're bruised all over."

"Scars and bruises are the map of my life." More honesty.

"I don't believe that."

"Why?"

"Because I've seen the best of you and the worst. I've kissed your scars and never wished them away."

"Never?"

Billy wrapped his arms around me. He shook his head and his voice got low and soft. "Your scars aren't the map. They are just bits of bad road on a long drive."

"Do you always know what to say to everyone or just me?"

I woke up lying on the couch wrapped up in the afghan. The sun was throwing high angel beams through the windows. In the fireplace the fire had burned lower, but it had been fed. On the mantel were my badge and gun.

I didn't remember the pain until I tried to move off the couch. Everything, even my hair, hurt. Standing was agony. I might have stayed where I was, but there was a piece of paper under my service weapon. There was no believing my memory or the other things Billy left behind. I had to read his words.

It took at least a couple of minutes to limber up and shuffle the five feet to the mantel. It took another minute to calm my breath and focus my eyes.

The note read:

Katrina,

Once you read this note go back to bed, a real bed, and sleep the whole day. There were two witnesses who saw Sissy Fisher kick you and your reaction. That doesn't make it good or right. Sometimes we get away with what we shouldn't and pay hard for what was never our choice. I'm sorry that I never told you I was the medic who tended you in Afghanistan. Sorry can tear down walls or build them up. I'm not sure what this one will do. I have learned one thing, though: you are right about the difficulties of us working together and loving each other. Or me loving you, at least. I've never really known or understood your feelings. You do a better job keeping them buried than you do holding back the anger. I'll always be there to help with it as your friend and sheriff.

Bill

The most devastating thing to me was the name at the end. My Billy had stepped away and left me with only Bill. All the pain in my body echoed in my head. It was even worse when I realized the foul smell I was breathing in was coming from me.

* * * *

When Nelson built the house, he had an extra-large water heater installed. The shower always seemed to run hot forever. That day I used all the hot water and still lingered as it ran from tolerably warm to uncomfortably tepid.

In the shower I made a lot of decisions, but none of the important ones. The one thought that was clear to me was the lack of genuine police work I had been doing. Things happened, and I reacted rather than investigated. Everything had become personal. I was determined to change that.

When I stepped out, I didn't even bother toweling off before picking up my phone. It was time I backed up a bit and tried to pick up a trail I'd missed—make that ignored—earlier. I called a friend in the Greene County Sheriff's Department. Cops have a whole barter system of favor-trading. I would owe on this one, but my friend was willing to go to the hospital and check out Lawson's story about his father dying. I also asked him to check all the Springfield area hospitals and clinics for tongue injuries. Calls had been made, but sometimes a deputy showing up at the door gets more honesty. After that, I called into HQ and caught Calvin Walker working a desk.

"Why are you inside?" I asked.

"Tractor trailer ran off the road last night. I worked alone and got some frostbite."

"It was a busy night for everyone," I said.

"So I hear."

I wasn't sure exactly what I was hearing in his voice so I ignored it. "I need some paper files pulled."

"Whatever."

"Always a pleasure, Calvin. Do you have a pencil ready?"

"Just give me the list."

I told him what I needed.

"When do you need them?" he asked.

"ASAP. What, you have other plans?"

"I mean, when will you be in to look at them?"

"An hour or so, why?"

"I'll be here," he said, then disconnected.

I noticed he said he would be there, not the files.

The water still on my skin was making me cold, but I made another call. This one was to Uncle Orson asking him to trade trucks with me.

"Why?" he asked, sounding suspicious.

"I need another favor," I said.

"What else is new?"

"Would you get the back glass replaced in mine while you have it?"

"Let me get this straight." He went silent, but it was a grumpy kind of silence. "You want me to trade trucks with you on a cold, snowy day. Not only does your truck have no glass, you want me to get it repaired."

"It's pretty low on gas, too," I said. It was a tired joke, though I wasn't fully kidding.

Uncle Orson didn't laugh. He didn't say anything.

"What's wrong?" I asked.

"My truck is kind of a mess."

"A mess?"

"A mess. Dirty."

"How can it be dirty enough to be a problem?"

He was quiet again.

"Orson?"

"I'll be right over."

Uncle Orson disconnected. It was my morning for being hung up on. I went for a towel and made one more call.

There was a time I fought therapy every mental inch, but seeking help is one of the things it taught me. I was planning a drive into Springfield anyway, so I wanted to see if Dr. Regina Kurtz might have an opening. She did. Once the receptionist told me to come in, I allowed myself to acknowledge how important it was to me.

I was dressed and swallowing a handful of aspirin with coffee on an empty stomach when Uncle Orson came in the door without knocking.

"You look awful," he said, stamping snow off his boots.

"You couldn't do that outside?"

"That would just get more snow on the boots."

"Could you at least stay on the rug?"

He moved onto the rag rug and stomped again.

"Let me see your boots," I said.

He pulled up his pants legs.

"No." I pointed at his feet and shook my finger in a circle. "Your soles. Put them up."

He crossed one leg over the other with the bottom of his boot on display. There was mud clinging to the edges and packed under the heel rise. "Where'd the mud come from?"

"Your floors are so fancy they can't stand a little snow and dirt?"

"I was looking for something."

"What?" He put his foot down.

"They're smooth," I said. "Soaked through, too. You shouldn't wear leather soles in the snow."

"Why all the interest in my boots?"

"There were some prints at a crime scene I've been trying to understand."

"I wasn't there."

I put my coffee down and poured my uncle a cup without ever taking my eyes off him. "Where?"

"How long are you going to make me wait on that coffee?"

I waited a few more moments then handed the cup over. "Is your truck warm?"

"Warm but dirty."

* * * *

"Warm but dirty" was an understatement. Around the wheel wells were crusts of frozen mud. The sides were strewn with muck that had been cast by all four wheels spinning and digging hard. Uncle Orson had been doing some work he didn't want to talk about. I didn't want to talk about it either. I was too sore and tired and determined not to let another thing distract me from finding out who killed Rose Sharon.

Snow was falling again. It was a mix of dry, dusty flakes and crystalline pebbles that bounced off the windshield. What stuck melted in the heat of the defroster and froze at the window edges. By the time I reached the sheriff's office, my view of the world had become framed by a rim of ice. When I parked I lifted the wipers so they wouldn't stick.

The cold of the day was matched by the atmosphere inside the building. Everyone available was out. There was just Doreen at dispatch, with Calvin and another deputy on light duty. No one said anything when I entered.

We are a medium-sized department in a small-government leaning county. It shows in our budget. Resources tend to go to personnel and the vehicles we need to reach the citizens. Consequently, we have the computerization to do the job, but no files older than five years are digital. There was a stack of paper waiting on my desk.

There were the arrest jackets on E. Lawson and Levi Sharon. I had also asked for the investigator's report on the hit-and-run that killed the parents of Rose and Levi Sharon. That was where I started.

It was a thorough file. The descriptions were clear, with measured distances and speed estimates. There were photos of the crushed car showing the damage, its orientation and relation to the road. Some of the photos showed debris from the vehicles, including an amber signal light. The indicator was the old-fashioned kind that mounted on top of a fender rather than in the bodywork. The conclusion was a hit-and-run accident between the passenger car and an unknown truck.

After the accident material was the coroner's reports on Matthew and Cheryl Sharon. Motor vehicle trauma was listed as the cause of death. Both were wearing their seatbelts. Both had alcohol in their blood. His blood alcohol content was .03. Her BAC was .04. Those marks were well below the level of legal intoxication and seemed to suggest they each had a drink or two. The difference in BAC was probably due to body mass. They weren't drunk.

There was a matching set of notes from MHP. The highway patrol was listed as the active investigative agency and the case marked as ongoing.

If I had closed the file there, I would have missed the really important part. Buried behind everything were the handwritten notes from the deputy on scene—Calvin Walker. There were two things noted in neat, precise writing that were not in the form report. First, Calvin noted the color of the unknown vehicle as green, describing the paint as old and oxidized. Second, he made a guess at the kind of truck to look for. On a single line he had written the words *Log Truck* and underlined them twice.

I picked up the file and went over to where Calvin was splitting his time between paperwork and the phone. I noticed he was holding the handset as far as he could from his face. His ears and cheeks were bright red and slick with a salve. He frowned when he saw me, but when the call was ended he said, "What can I do for you, Detective?"

I held up the file. "You worked this accident."

He nodded. "I remember. T-bone hit-and-run in Merriam Woods. June of '07."

"It's a good file."

Calvin cocked his head like a dog hearing a strange sound.

"What?" I asked.

"You're not known for compliments."

"Is that your way of saying I'm a jerk?"

"I only use the soda pop language with ladies." He kept his gaze fixed on mine.

For once in my life I didn't take the bait and give someone the fight they wanted. "Yeah, I've never been very good at the lady thing."

Calvin looked away and seemed a little ashamed.

"It's never been your issue. Just my failing."

"What do you need?" The edge was gone from his voice.

"You have notes in the file that say you believed the unknown vehicle was oxidized green. And you underlined the words 'logging truck.'"

Calvin waved his hand downward, pointing at his desk. I noticed for the first time the tips were bandaged.

"Frostbite?" I asked as I set the file down facing him.

"It feels like a burn. Like I touched a hot stove." He used the flat of his hand to spread out the loose photos. "This one." He tapped the picture with a bandaged fingertip.

"What about it?"

"Look close."

I held up the photo and scanned it. Then I saw that in the crushed black metal of the car were streaks of pale color. "I see it," I said. "Green." I dropped the print back on the pile. "Why did you think it was a log truck?"

"For one thing, it hit hard. I imagine it had a lot of weight behind it. For another—" He pushed through the pictures again until he found one showing the gate the car had broken through in the crash. "That dirt road leads to land that was being selectively logged. Dirt driveway on the other side goes to an abandoned house with woods all around it. I went up the drive and found cut-off limbs and a bunch of fresh stumps. A log truck seemed like a good bet."

"I think so too."

I spent another hour reading the jackets and making calls. I added ten minutes to look at the other cases on my desk. Investigative cops usually have more cases than they can reasonably handle. In a department like ours we don't have the luxury of crime sections. I had files on my desk dealing with petty theft, vandalism, a liquor store holdup. I thought I could be forgiven for concentrating on murder.

"Can I ask you something?"

It was Calvin. I hadn't heard him walk up.

"You know, now that we're pals and all," he added.

"Always glad to help a pal," I said.

"There's a problem."

"Only one?" I laughed.

Calvin didn't join in. "I don't know what to do or how to fix it without making things worse."

"Tell me. I'll do what I can and I won't hold it against you."

Calvin looked away.

I thought he was checking the sheriff's office door. It was closed and the lights were off. "It's just us," I said. "Is it about him or me?"

Calvin shook his head. It looked heavy on his shoulders. "Neither," he said. He sat in the chair across from my desk. "Or maybe it is. That's part of the problem. Hooks have barbs."

"You're saying you're afraid of how things are connected."

"He's the sheriff's boy."

"Wait." I sat forward. "Who are we talking about?"

Calvin held up his hands showing the bandaged fingers, then pointed one at his face. "None of this had to happen."

"Calvin, I can't help but think you're taking a longer road than you need to. And I'm not keeping up."

"I feel like a snitch. If it wasn't for Bob…"

"Bob?" I was surprised. And I was a little concerned the conversation had become something I was not at all prepared for. "Deputy Rantz?" I couldn't help the narrowing of my eyes or the suspicion in my voice. "Is there something going on?"

"Going on?" He looked confused, then his face shifted to shock. "Hell no. She could be my daughter. I mean—that's—that kind of question is part of the problem."

"What part?"

"She's a good officer. She's smart, and she's the kind of young blood we need."

"I still don't get what you're saying."

"Bobbi Rantz deserves the chance to be a better deputy. Without having to put up with certain kinds of shit. The kind I think you know about."

"You're trying to protect her?"

"She shouldn't need protection. But she does."

I began to understand. I leaned back and settled into my chair without relaxing. Deputy Calvin Walker had a whole new shade of respect in my estimation. "Tom Dugan," I said.

"He was supposed to be there helping me last night. After that Branson show we were both put on patrol. I was on 65, he was assigned 160. The tractor trailer went off 65 close to the intersection. I called him in and he acknowledged. But he never showed."

"Did he say why not?"

"He doesn't have to. I know where he was. Same place he keeps disappearing to." Calvin looked at me like he expected understanding.

"You're going to have to fill in that blank for me."

"The place where the Rose girl was found."

Understanding burned through my chest like a swallow of kerosene. "The roadside shrine."

"He's obsessed. Always there. He shows off for the kids hanging around."

"I can see the problem for you. How's it affect Bob?"

"He's been calling her. Sending her text messages and pictures."

"Pictures?"

"Stuff about the dead girl. Pictures of the scene."

"Has she reported this to anyone?"

"She says he asks questions, makes comments. Everything he sends is supposed to look like one cop asking another for advice or collaboration."

"Bobbi doesn't think that's the reason."

"She knows it isn't."

I pinned him with my eyes. "Has it gone further?"

"Bob told me she's seen a cruiser near her house at odd times. She thinks it's him."

"And you?"

"I know it's him."

I nodded. "Me too."

"Are you going to do something about it?"

"You're damn right I am," I said. I pulled open a drawer and lifted a report sheet. I wrote the time and bullet-pointed the discussion we just had. I signed it and pushed it over to Calvin. "This won't come back on you, I promise. But we're going to make it official and on the record."

Calvin didn't look happy, but he signed under my name.

"Will Bobbi sign?" I asked.

"She will if she knows you're behind her."

"All the way." I took back the form. "One thing. What did you mean when you said he was the sheriff's boy? Billy's?"

"Yeah. You didn't know? Sheriff Blevins hired Tom on personally. Said he was doing a favor and asked me to make sure he did well."

"Favor for whom?"

"Hell if I know." Calvin rose. "But favors always turn out to be burdens in my experience."

That pretty much said it, I thought as I went to the copy machine. I made a copy for Calvin and two for myself. One of those I locked in my desk and the other I tucked into my jacket pocket. The original needed to go to Billy. He still wasn't in and I didn't want to put it in his mailbox or ask Doreen to deliver it. As I sat at my desk rereading the form, hoping Billy would show, my phone rang.

It was Deputy David Webb, my friend from Greene County.

"Did you find what I asked about?"

"I did and I didn't," he answered. "Lawson's father died in the hospital. But it was a month ago."

"Damn." My curse was directed at myself. "That puts a lie to his alibi and it puts the weight on me for not checking."

"It gets heavier."

"Of course it does. Give it to me."

"When I asked about Lawson, all the nurses remembered him. The big ugly guy, most of them called him. But I guess one nurse didn't find him so unattractive. Guess who didn't show up at work today."

"That doesn't sound like a coincidence."

"Not by a long shot. One of the nurses talked to me alone. She said she didn't want to get her friend in trouble. It sounded to me like that was exactly what she wanted. She claimed this nurse, named Jenifer Perry, fell in with Lawson while the father was dying. She also tells me that Perry took some supplies and left work early yesterday."

"What kind of supplies?"

"I figured you would want to know. They are checking the inventory now. I can call you back once we know. The nurses say her listed DMV address is out of date. I'm waiting on hospital HR for an updated residence. They are checking with lawyers."

"Tell them this is about her safety. Lawson is dangerous. Call my cell as soon as you know anything more. I'm out the door headed your way."

I hung up and gathered my effects to get on the road. The last thing I picked up was the original report form. I tucked it into an envelope, sealed it, and wrote *SHERIFF'S EYES ONLY*. Before I walked out I slipped it under his door.

Chapter 13

My borrowed truck's windows were crusted with sleet and powdered over with crisp snow. The air was so cold it felt sticky in my lungs as I breathed. Opening the door was a two-handed struggle. I started the engine and let it run a while before I tried scraping the windshield.

The weather had dimmed the ardor of the news media. There were still a few reporters around the SO but they were staying in their vehicles. Waiting for the engine to warm and loosen the ice, I tried to keep warm by kicking away chunks of frozen mud from the truck's body. I couldn't imagine what Orson had gotten into or why he had been out in this mess to begin with.

I pulled the scraper from under the seat and tackled the windshield. The spot directly above the vents was loose. A sharp rap broke the skin and let me get the plastic edge going. With my first hard thrust the ice flaked and flew up in a cold spray.

"That's cold work," someone said.

I looked up. One of the reporters was standing near the opposite fender. Her name was Erin Gray. She worked for the NBC affiliate in Springfield.

"How'd you sneak up on me, Erin?" I asked and kept on scraping.

"I didn't. You weren't paying attention." She pulled a microphone from her pocket and pointed it in my direction.

I chipped up a sharp corner of ice, then shoved the scraper blade as far as I could reach over the glass.

"May I talk to you?" she asked, stepping away from the flakes.

"Go right ahead."

"You know what I mean, Hurricane."

"Don't call me that."

"Would you do an on-camera interview with us?"

I stopped my work to look at her. Erin had interviewed me before, always about safe topics—safety of area tourists, the rise or fall of local drug activity. I was sure this request had nothing to do with softball news.

"Why would I do that?" I asked.

"You want to get your side out, don't you?"

"My side of what?"

"A triangle."

"Get out of here," I said.

Erin didn't flinch. She took her other hand from her coat pocket and held up a small recorder. "You should hear this."

She pressed the play button. Erin's voice came out. It sounded tinny from the small speaker but I could hear the words clearly.

"You've made some tough accusations against Bill Blevins," said Erin, "the sheriff of Taney County. What support do you have for them?"

Then came Sissy Fisher's voice. "I have Rose's journal."

"Is the sheriff mentioned in it by name?"

"In the journal Rose talked about her problems. She wrote about being afraid of being pregnant. She talked about the inspiration behind her song, 'You Took What Wasn't Yours.' And the fear she had that he would take more if things didn't change."

"How do you know she was talking about Bill Blevins?"

"The change she was looking for. Rose said that everything would be different once Billy was sheriff."

Erin clicked the recorder off. "Do you have any comment?"

"No."

"You have a relationship with the sheriff, don't you?" she pressed. "An intimate relationship."

My face must have glowed. I could feel the heat creeping up my throat to bloom on my cheeks. I wanted to climb over the truck hood and do Erin some damage. "Where's the camera?" I asked.

Erin didn't answer but her eyes did. She glanced over at the closest news van. Exhaust was smoking from the tailpipe. Half hidden by the vehicle but silhouetted by the vapor was a man sighting through the lens of a video camera.

"That's how you do it now?" I asked. "Pretend to ask permission but ambush?"

"Sissy Fisher has accused the sheriff," Erin said, speaking up louder. "Twice you've been in altercations with her. What are you trying to keep quiet?"

I resisted the urge to say, my gun. If I stuck around I might not have maintained that level of control. I climbed in the truck and drove off, sighting through the semi-cleared windshield.

Getting to the highway was a fight. The county roads were thick with new sleet. Falling temperatures had defeated the brine treatments. Potholes were standing with slush. Exposed asphalt was refreezing with black ice.

State Highway 65 wasn't much better. Northbound 160, the main corridor between Springfield and Branson, was being kept clear. I was able to pick up some speed. After a mile the remaining ice on my windshield broke free in a single sheet. It flew over the cab of the truck to shatter on the empty road.

I passed the spot where Calvin had been working the night before. Plowed furrows cut through the snow down to the dirt where the tractor trailer had gone off the highway. I couldn't help but think of Deputy Tom Dugan. He kept popping up in this investigation. Never in the middle but always around. I wondered if he was connected in any other way. Maybe before there was an actual investigation.

The back of the truck slipped and the bed began creeping to the right. I took my foot off the gas and steered into the skid. Once I corrected it, I remained at the slower speed and concentrated on the road.

* * * *

As I approached the town of Ozark, my phone rang. It was Deputy Webb. "What did you find out?" I asked.

"Several packs of gauze, a suture kit, and lidocaine are missing from inventory."

"Other drugs?"

"Those are locked away. It's not impossible she took some, but they are under a different inventory system. We don't know."

"It doesn't matter," I said. "If Jenifer Perry took the supplies to treat Lawson, she would have taken painkillers too. Once the lidocaine wears off, a sewn-up tongue is going to hurt."

"We have an updated address. Where are you?"

"Just passed Ozark."

"Not that far away," he said. Then he paused, I assumed making time and distance calculations in his head. "I'm sending units out, but weather is slowing everything down in town."

"Here, too. Just tell me where to go."

He gave me the address and contact information for Jenifer Perry. I called and got no answer. I didn't leave a message. Instead I hit the gas and passed a snowplow throwing billows of white to the side. At State Highway 60 I looped over to Campbell Avenue. North from there I made good time for a couple of miles, then turned off. That was where things slowed down.

Main city streets were plowed and treated. The side streets and suburban developments were mostly untouched. It took twenty minutes to go less than a mile off Campbell. Nurse Jenifer Perry lived in the neighborhood behind the giant Bass Pro Shop. Even in this weather that parking lot was clear and almost full of cars.

I parked and pulled out my phone. If Lawson was inside with the nurse I didn't want to knock on the door. I wanted the chance to get her out and away from him. There was no answer. The only number I'd been given was her cell phone. There was no house line listed.

I called again.

Everything felt ugly and wrong—the blowing snow, the low clouds that sat like a weight over the world, the small house with the unlatched storm door, me. I should have backup but that was a problem. My own department was too far away and stretched thin. The Greene County cops and Springfield city cops had their own problems. They would respond if I asked, but they would ask questions about Lawson I didn't want to answer. No law enforcement professional wants to admit to taking a beating at the hands of a suspect. Women officers are even more sensitive to it. In the boy's club, we all get judged by one set of standards. Those standards have little to do with the job and a lot to do with testosterone and upper-body strength. Going out of town and asking for help subduing someone who already kicked my ass was a sure way to make my life harder in the long run.

I got out of the truck. I pulled my service weapon and double-checked a round was chambered. Despite the cold and wind, I left my coat open to have access to the extra magazines, cuffs and telescoping baton on my belt. I'd learned my lesson with Lawson at the mill.

With my 9mm ready in a two-handed grip, I approached the house. I started at a window. Peeking through a torn screen and the frosted glass, I saw a front room lit only by the muted daylight. It was tidy except for the clutter of beer cans on the coffee table. I backed away from the front window and went to the one on the side of the house without crossing in front of either. The view there was a different angle on the same thing.

I ducked under and went to the next window and looked into the kitchen. Housekeeping had failed in there. The table was littered with more cans along with bloody wads of gauze. Dishes were stacked on the counter.

Ducking again, I moved to the rear of the house.

The yard was circled by a sagging chain-link fence. I leaned over it to glance around the corner. A loud slap of wood and rattling glass almost stopped my heart. I jerked my head back and gulped frigid air.

The door slammed again.

I darted my head out and sighted down the lap boards to the back door. It swung open, got caught in the wind, slammed closed once more.

The noise was a taunt. Each time the wind rose, the door whipped, cracking against the frame. Each time it did, my skin crawled. Challenging me to enter or warning me off, either way the door mocked my sense of courage. I hated the sound. Still, I moved forward with my weapon clenched in my two-handed grip.

The latch was broken; there was a retracted dead bolt. Someone had gone out and not set the lock behind them.

Or gone in, I reminded myself.

With a steadying breath I put a foot on the stairs. The two rising steps were rickety and moved when I added weight. I eased back and reseated my foot on the edge of the first step just in case it creaked. The second step I skipped.

The door led into the kitchen. There was trash on the floor that I hadn't seen from the window. There was blood, too. It stained the table and floor. It soaked bandages.

Someone was crying. A woman. The sound was faint. My history with the sound amplified it in my head. I wasn't alone in the freezing house. I took a moment to force myself to breathe normally. My hands got the message too. They relaxed, giving way grudgingly. My heart paid no attention. It raced in a thunderous pulse that echoed in my chest and ears.

The faint sound of pain got louder as I moved forward. I cleared the living room and stepped into the short hall. The first door was a bathroom. I pushed the door fully open and reached with my left hand to move the shower curtain.

Clear.

I reset my hands into the two-handed grip. The next door was standing wide open. It was a sewing room, cluttered and messy. There was no door on the closet.

Clear.

The last door was closed. The crying woman was inside.

I listened but heard only the sobbing. The knob was locked. At least it wouldn't turn easily. I wasn't going to rattle it.

Another breath. I noticed that I could see vapor.

The hall was narrow. I set my back against the wall and raised my right foot. I kicked out, planting my boot just beside the knob. The cheap interior door splintered and caved. I followed through with my shoulder and burst into the room, weapon front.

Jenifer Perry was alone. She was naked and bleeding from her brutalized face. There was more blood on the floor than her face could account for. When she saw me, she covered her face in the same mix of shame and terror I've seen in the faces of dozens of women. I've seen it in my own face.

"Is he gone?" I asked.

"I didn't mean to laugh." She wailed her explanation. "I helped him. I didn't want this."

"I know," I said. The words and my understanding felt small. "I'm calling for help." I stepped around Jenifer and crouched down to be close. She grabbed my arm and buried her bloody face. I kept my pistol pointed up at the door. Without looking away, I dialed 911 one-handed.

Springfield PD didn't have a female officer available. Jenifer wouldn't even look at a man so I stayed with her. I helped the female EMT do her evaluation and get Jenifer onto a gurney. She kept her hand in mine as the ambulance returned Jenifer to the same hospital she had stolen supplies from to help E. Lawson.

Jenifer was taken into surgery. She had suffered a fractured vertebra when Lawson threw her off the bed then kicked her in the back. I held her hand right up to the last set of hospital doors.

A patrol officer took me back to my truck. I didn't want to go back into the house, but the investigating detective had some questions. I did, too. I was allowed to take a look at Jenifer's phone log as I told the story of E. Lawson and his possible involvement in the murder of Rose Sharon. I tried to leave out the encounter between him and me at the mill. It didn't work. Any way I tried to put it together, the question of his wound came up.

The detective asked me again what I knew about Lawson's injury as I scribbled the number listed for E. in my notebook. Even after I closed the book I kept my head down.

Finally, I looked up. "Lawson is a monster. He uses his strength and size to hurt women." I handed over the phone. "He had me. He forced his tongue in my mouth. Half of it is still laying on the dirt floor of his sawmill. So you might say what happened here is at least partially my fault."

The detective stared. There was no telling if his shock was at me or my story. I didn't care anymore.

"If I had finished the job, he never would have been here to torment Jenifer Perry. She was trying to help him. She told me that she didn't mean to laugh."

I looked away from the eyes trying so hard to understand and make my story something reasonable, something to fit neatly into a report.

I looked instead at the bloody carpet where Jenifer had been lying when I broke her door open.

"That's all it took," I said. "A little laugh. It was probably when he tried to talk the first time."

"A man like that," the Springfield detective said, shaking his head. "No part of it was your fault or hers. And neither of you were the first. You can bet on that."

The image of Rose Sharon sparked in my mind. Then I heard her singing, "You Took What Wasn't Yours."

* * * *

Uncle Orson's truck idled at the curb. I waited for heat to begin flowing from the vents and stared at my phone. A first breath of warmth crawled from the dash. I dialed E. Lawson.

The phone on the other end rang twice before connecting. Nothing was said. The other phone waited. I had the feeling he knew who was calling.

"Did she hurt your feelings?" I asked.

The only response was a quiet huff of air.

I laughed. "You're a broken little bitch. Preying on small women and girls. You think you're a big, bad wolf. You're not. You're just another pathetic loser who thinks his big fist makes up for every other small thing in his life. Everything in your world is on fire, Lawson. And I'm the one holding the matches."

He said something. There was a wild, strangled sound on the line like a Pentecostal preacher channeling the holy spirit. No telling what it was, only that it was nothing I needed to hear. I broke the connection. Then I went into my settings and blocked his number. There is nothing a man like him hates more than a woman who refuses to listen.

I buckled in and put the truck in drive. The street that had been high and white was worn into a dirty slush by so much police traffic. My exit was much faster than my entrance. At Fort I turned north, heading to Sunshine Street. At the light I called the therapist's office. Dr. Kurtz herself answered. I told her what had happened.

"That's great news," she said.

I hesitated a moment as the confusion boiled in my head. "I think you and I are talking about two different things," I said.

"Yes and no," she answered. She had a way of being infuriatingly indirect sometimes.

"I don't—"

"You're handling it," she explained. "It wasn't that long ago you were in my office in a panic after your investigation led to a twenty-year-old sexual assault."

"That was a different situation," I said.

"It was a different woman," she hit back.

"Thank you."

"For what?"

Even though I was driving and on the phone, I shrugged. "For saying it."

"You're welcome," she said. "Now tell me why you needed to come in so urgently today."

"It's a long story," I said, trying to dismiss it.

"You've been in the news."

"That's part of it."

"What are the other parts?"

"A girl is dead. Her family is standing in the way of finding out the truth." Even as I said it, I heard the weakness in the statements.

"You don't come to me to talk about the job, Katrina."

It sounds silly, but one reason I allowed myself to trust Dr. Kurtz was the fact she never called me Hurricane. At the same time, trust was one of those issues I needed work on. "My therapy is a mandated condition of keeping my job."

"Screw your job," she said. "What happened?"

I didn't have the courage to hang up. I tried to wait her out in silence. It didn't work. After two minutes of letting her listen to me drive and breathe I finally confessed. "I'm going to kill a man."

Dr. Kurtz simply asked, "Who?"

I told her what had happened with E. Lawson at the mill and what he had done to Jenifer Perry.

"Sounds justified," she said.

"I hate my job."

"You've never said that before. The job was always the one thing you believed in."

"I still believe in it. I just hate it."

"What are you going to do about that?"

That was a question I didn't want to think about. I tried silence again. I believe what came next surprised me more than her. I broke the dead air by saying, "Billy is choosing his job over me."

She didn't miss a beat. Dr. Kurtz immediately asked, "Was it an honest choice or the only one he had?"

"What's that mean?"

"Sometimes we are hurt most when people in our lives make the only choice we leave them with."

"You're saying it's my fault?"

"I'm asking if you gave enough of yourself for him to keep holding on to." More silence.

"I don't know why I keep talking to you," I said.

"Sure you do." It was hard to argue with her confidence. "When your husband died, he left you wealthy. You kept the estate growing by letting lawyers handle everything."

"What's your point?"

"How much are you worth now?"

"I don't know."

"Yes, you do. Tell me."

I felt foolish and caught in a trap. "Close to five million," I admitted.

"And yet you hate your day job."

"You're the only one I hate right now."

"I get that." She actually chuckled. "You're a woman who likes strong men, military, police, but you hate bullies. You found one who was strong without being cruel."

"I married him."

"You married Nelson Solomon knowing that he was sick and dying."

"That's a hard way of putting it," I said.

"Truth is always hard, Katrina." It was her turn to use quiet. She didn't have the patience I did. "What kind of man is Billy Blevins?" she asked.

"Kind," I answered, angered by the admission.

"You told him you didn't think he was strong enough for the job of sheriff."

"Not in so many words."

"Copping out?" she asked. "That's not like you."

"Just get it out there," I said. "I'm tired of this dance."

"Don't do that," she said. "You're already the toughest woman I know. If you turn some of that courage inward, you'll turn some of the anger out."

"That easy?"

"Nothing is easy. But it's not impossible to have what you want. You just have to decide what it is and get out of your own way."

"I don't even know what we're talking about anymore."

"You can't get angry at people for not making the choices you want them to make when you don't even make the choices you want."

She got off the phone after that and I got on the highway. I hated therapy.

Chapter 14

Passing semis, pushing hard to make up time lost to weather, splashed my windshield with filthy ice. I was alone and disconnected in the silent cab of my truck. My thoughts make for poor company at the best of times so I called the SO and asked for Billy. I expected to go to voice mail.

He picked up saying, "I got a call from Springfield."

"I didn't think you would be in."

"Why wouldn't I be?"

"You've been out of touch lately."

"Just because I'm out of touch to you does not mean I'm not on the job."

I didn't want to argue. At the same time, I did. I wasn't sure about what, though.

Before I could think of what to say, Billy said, "Tell me about Springfield."

I did.

When I was finished Billy said, "Don't do that again."

"What?"

"Call a suspect to taunt him."

"I'm sorry," I said.

I heard a thump over the phone then a creak. It was easy to picture Billy dropping his feet off his desk and leaning forward. "What?" He sounded a little more stunned than he needed to. "For what?"

"I've made your job harder than it needs to be."

"No," he said. The smile in his voice was obvious. "You make everything more difficult."

I laughed, knowing it wasn't exactly a joke.

"You were on the news again today," Billy said. "We're a triangle, it seems."

"I'm sorry about that, too."

"Don't worry about it. I think things are blowing over."

"Wishful thinking," I said.

"Speaking of that. Stay away from Sissy Fisher. Stay away from the family altogether. Landis Tau was raising a stink about you talking to Donny without his lawyer present."

"There's something bigger going on here."

"Bigger than the murder of a girl?"

"Why did you rush to arrest Donny Fisher when you knew he wasn't the killer?"

"How do you know what I knew?" We played the silence game. Billy didn't last long at all. After a few seconds he said, "Yeah. I didn't think that one through very well, did I?"

"Probably not."

"I knew he was gay. And I knew he was close to Rose. I never suspected him. I was afraid he would become a target. Either for Levi, who has self-control issues and was always jealous, or for whoever killed her."

"Why didn't you try to bring him into protective custody?"

"That was the idea at first, but things have a way of escalating quickly around Sissy."

"I think there were two people with a history of stalking and abuse of women somehow entangled in Rose Sharon's life."

"Two?" I could almost feel Billy shaking his head. "You think E. Lawson is involved?"

"Yes."

"How?"

"I don't know. But I'm going back to his sawmill to have a look at something. Would you meet me there?"

"You said two."

"Rose asked you to hire Tom Dugan, didn't she?" I asked. It wasn't really a question.

"That's why the paper under the door."

"That, and he's been stalking Bobbi Rantz."

"Why am I hearing it from you?" There was hurt under the anger in his voice.

"Why did Rose ask you to hire him?"

"She said she would be leaving soon for Nashville. She wanted him to have something when she left."

"Or a reason not to follow?" I asked.

"You go to the sawmill. Call Chuck to come out if you want help. I have something to do."

"If you have trouble finding Dugan, look for him at Rose's murder scene."

"Got it," Billy said. That time there was resolve in his voice. It was a good sound.

* * * *

It was night and full dark when I pushed Uncle Orson's truck into 4x4 low. The path was visible only through the absence of trees. There were no tracks in the fresh and frozen-over snow. Even out there, ten crow miles, twenty road miles from Branson, the ground and clouds each glowed with trapped luminescence. Nelson would have loved the scene, darkness and light all in a black velvet texture.

I pushed through a door-high drift that filled the last bend. On the other side was the cleared valley with E. Lawson's sawmill in the middle. It had changed since I left it two days before. Even before my headlights hit it I could tell the mill had been burned. The bones of the shack were there. Thick oak posts that were probably old when my father and uncle went to Vietnam still stood. They were charred, but too massive to burn through before all the other fuel was exhausted. The result was a grim black skeleton with rusty iron organs draped in an ill-fitting shroud of white.

Around the burned building were rutted truck tracks too deep for the snow to hide. I followed them around and found the trailer and logs I had tried to burn. Like the timbers of the shack, the walnut was only scorched on the surface. The gas-oil mix I had doused them with never got the green wood hot enough to sustain a long blaze. The really interesting thing was that the trailer was not where I had left it.

Someone had hitched it up to a truck and dragged it about thirty feet. It appeared they were trying to add it to the bonfire of the mill. The plan was confounded by the only real damage my rage had done. All the tires on the trailer were burned away. The trailer was too heavy to pull with the wheel rims digging into the partially frozen ground. Mud and snow had been slung from four spinning wheels as a 4x4 truck had worked to get the load moving. That truck was the same one I was sitting in, there was no doubt.

Uncle Orson and, I was willing to bet, Clare Bolin had been out here last night. They had felt compelled to take revenge against Lawson. I tried to be angry about it. I couldn't. The only thing I did feel was the sense that my actions had put the choice in their hands. My anger was directed at myself.

What anger there was didn't last long. I was smiling, a little proud of the old men in my life, as I left the truck idling in the snow. Outside of the cab I felt exposed. I checked the seat of my weapon in the holster, then kept my right hand poised. With my left I pulled out my flashlight.

I worked my way through the snow. It was hard and fragile on the surface. Each step hesitated, then broke the cold skin. It took a careful minute to reach the open-front shed where the International Harvester was still sitting under its tarp. The old fabric was frozen to the contours of the ancient truck. I pulled. It cracked away like an insect's shed skin.

Underneath was exactly what I had believed I would find. The left fender of the faded green truck was crumpled. Jagged edges were mostly gone to rust, but in the edges where oxidized green remained were flaking streaks of black. On top of the fender was a mounting hole. One look at the right side told me it was for a round amber signal light.

I released my pistol butt to pull out my notebook. Two sheets of folded-over paper made improvised envelopes. I used the edge of one to tease off curls of black paint. I did the same with some flakes of green.

Once the paint evidence was tucked away I checked both ends of the truck for plates. There were none. I opened the driver's-side door of the cab. The air inside smelled of rot and age mixed with the urine and droppings of generations of field mice.

I was looking for anything that might give proof of ownership. I checked the dash. There was nothing. In the early 1950s, vehicle identification numbers were required on vehicles in the US. Placement wasn't mandated until later. I checked the door post and again, nothing. After that I moved around to the passenger side to check the glove box for registration papers or an inspection slip. There was only a rodent nest and a 1943 steel penny. I tucked the penny in my pocket for luck.

It worked. After about fifteen minutes of searching, I finally found a VIN plate. It was on the driver's side, riveted to the deck riser that holds the seat. I pulled out my notebook and copied the information.

A penny's worth of luck didn't last long. When I pushed the old door closed, a fading light caught my eye. It was coming from the cab of my idling truck.

My first thought was the dome light—someone had climbed in the truck and was waiting. I pulled my weapon and eased back deeper into the shadows to watch. Nothing happened and I didn't move for a few minutes. It was as if the world had gotten so cold that time froze.

The light came again. It was a rising glow that showed an empty cab. After another moment of confusion, I realized the phone I left sitting on the truck seat must be ringing.

* * * *

In the time I had been examining the dead green truck, I had missed eight calls. They were all from Clare.

"It's the sheriff," he said as soon as I called back.

"What happened to Billy?"

"No. Not Billy." Clare stopped.

As he was shifting mental gears I got there ahead of him. "You mean Chuck?"

"Yes. I keep forgetting he's not sheriff anymore."

"What about him, Clare?"

"It's bad," he said.

I felt the simple expression like a nail in my spine.

"Lawson was here," Clare went on. "He showed up at Moonshines looking for me."

"Because of the sawmill," I finished.

"He thought you did it. I don't think he believed that it was me and Orson. I didn't tell him about Orson anyway. I didn't get to say much of anything. He was on me like stink on a tumblebug."

"Are you okay?"

"Chuck was here. He never had a chance. He left his gun locked away because he was drinking. He got one good lick in then Lawson tore him up."

"Tore him up?"

"The ambulance left a bit ago. You should get to the hospital."

No details from Clare and no reassurance. It had to be bad for Chuck.

* * * *

Almost the entire Taney County Sheriff's Department was there when I arrived at the hospital. The parking lot was jammed. There were cars from Stone and Christian counties, as well as Branson PD. The news stations had also renewed their interest in us. Their vans and production trucks formed a perimeter through which everyone had to pass. There was so much activity that several officers had to be pressed into traffic duty. When I got inside, the lobby was packed. It smelled like old coffee and wet boots.

Calvin came out of the restricted doors that led to trauma treatment. He looked shaken. On his coat and disheveled shirt were blood. I caught his eye and he looked relieved. He tried to straighten his clothes then waved me over.

"He's in surgery," he said. Then he spoke up to the entire lobby. "He's got a broken sternum. His heart went into arrhythmia. They won't know until they get in if his heart is damaged."

"What exactly happened, Calvin?" I asked, keeping my voice low.

"I wasn't there."

I pointed to the blood staining his uniform shirt. "But?"

"I was the first deputy responding. That Lawson guy was already gone. Clarence Bolin said he was looking for you or someone to take your weight."

"I know. But what about Chuck?"

"The big guy, Lawson, I guess he walked into the bar at Moonshines and took hold of Mr. Bolin. One hit put him across the room. Bolin was on the floor and he wasn't getting up. Lawson lifted his foot up like he was aiming to stomp Bolin's throat. That's when ol' Chuck put his own boot in the back of Lawson's knee. The big guy went right down and Chuck Benson was waiting with a beer mug in his hand. He broke that thing right across the side of Lawson's head. It didn't do squat."

"He hit Chuck."

Calvin nodded. "He jumped up and grabbed Chuck by the shirtfront with both hands. Lawson lifted him up and tossed him into the glassware behind the bar. Clare said it all might have stopped there but Chuck didn't stay down."

"Of course not." I admired my former boss and, at the same time, felt a sense of inevitability about his choices. "What did he say to Lawson?"

"He said, 'Boy, your mama was a two-dollar punch and even she's ashamed of what you became.'"

"Chuck can curse a person better than anyone I know."

"That's when Lawson ran at him. He punched right across the bar and hit the old man in the heart."

"Where's Billy?"

"He's gone to fetch Miz Combs."

"Marion." I felt a deep sadness saying her name. Marion was a social worker for the county and an old friend of Chuck's. She helped him get over the loss of his wife a few years back. Recently, they had been helping each other to a new life. "I hadn't even thought of her."

The instant I said it I realized how true the statement was. There were many people I hadn't thought about. Clare said he didn't tell Lawson that it had been him and Uncle Orson who had burned down the mill. But they weren't why he was there. I had taunted him. He thought I had done everything. Lawson's revenge was striking out at the things and people in my life.

As sure as I knew anything, at that moment I knew that E. Lawson was going after Orson next.

"Are you okay?" Calvin asked.

I didn't try to answer. I didn't do anything to slow my run back to the truck.

The Ozarks is not a region of flat lands and straight roads. There is no easy, direct path from the hospital in Branson to Rockaway Beach where Orson's dock floated in the waters of Lake Taneycomo. The twisting roads, always a slow go, were made more dangerous by the impacted snow and the day's new sleet covering. I wished I was in my own truck. It had emergency lights. It was also built in this century. Orson's truck was strong and raised. It had more power but less control. Control was exactly what I needed at that moment.

Because of the truck I moved slower than I wanted to. It would have been easy to deny the restrictions of weather. But the moment was too important to give in to emotion any further than I already had. The slower pace forced me to think. I realized that I should have sent deputies with lights and sirens ahead of me. It wasn't too late.

Keeping my eyes on the road, I fumbled in my pocket to pull out my phone. I glanced once to orient my fingers and punched the emergency call icon.

I gave my ID and requested support and an ambulance at the dock. As soon as I spit out the words I broke the connection and dropped the phone on the seat. I didn't want to talk or explain.

To hell with it, I thought. Then I hit the gas hard. At the back of the truck the tires lost grip. The bed swayed to the side. I steered into it and kept going. The road dried out and the tires grabbed. I sped in the face of long odds. I could fail to get there or I could get there too late. Either way I would never forgive myself. Better to die trying.

The last sweeping bend into Rockaway Beach almost threw me. The truck slid. It was caught by the guardrail. I took the bounce and followed the bank down on the inside edge of the curve. I was dumped into the main road. It was dark even for a tourist town in the dead of winter. On the left side was the black gulf of the lake.

I looked ahead, expecting to see the string of clear white incandescent bulbs Uncle Orson kept burning all night, every night. They were dead, but something sparked.

I thought for a moment that it was moonlight reflected in the dark water. There was no moon, only thick clouds as black as grave dirt. Flames were shining on the water and breaking into a million reflections. Sunset colors shot through the waves, making a warning beacon that pointed right at the tail end of Orson's dock.

I twisted the steering wheel. The truck lost traction and I slid sideways across the left lane and into the parking lot that serviced the dock. I almost hit my own truck, which was parked close to the dock's long gangway.

Once out of the truck and running, I heard the clear sound of a rising boat engine. It was loud for only a moment. Distance quickly diminished it. At the same time, the calm waters let the sound skate to the far shore and back. The engine noise faded in intensity but not in clarity. I never saw the boat but its wake left a shimmering trail of reflected fire.

I slammed the bait shop door open. There were no lights on inside. Caught in the light of the fire was a horror-movie scene of gore and chaos. In the middle, the white case of a live bait well was streaked with an arc of blood that pointed like a neon sign to Orson. He was slumped over and soaking wet. His face was not his own. It was brutally pulped and swollen. He had been beaten and pushed under the water of the bait well.

I didn't approach. I couldn't move. My heart felt like a stone in my chest. My lungs were paralyzed and filled with dead air. I had no strength to even exhale.

Uncle Orson opened an eye.

I breathed.

He forced a drooping smile.

And I finally moved.

Orson lifted his right hand. It was still holding on to his weapon. It was an entrenching tool, a short, folding shovel. The E-tool had sat behind the counter since he came back from Vietnam. It must have been the only thing he could get his hands on.

I tried to take it from his hand, but he pulled away and used the tool to point out the window. The fire was growing.

It wasn't the dock burning. At least not yet. The flames were coming from the houseboat tied to the dock. It was my home away from home. Someone knew that.

"Lie back down," I said. "And give me this." I pulled the E-tool from Orson's hand and rushed out the back door. Heat was like a scalding wall. The boat was engulfed. Flame was reaching out and lapping at the wood of the dock. That wasn't the biggest concern. Beyond the slip the houseboat occupied were the gas pumps and tanks of the boat filling station.

I twisted the locking collar of the E-tool and angled the head ninety degrees. I used it like a hatchet to cut the mooring lines. There were gaff poles hanging on the wall of the bait shop. I grabbed one and used it to push the boat away from the dock. It took a lot to get the big boat moving, but once it started it got easier. When it was clear of the dock and I was sure it wouldn't drift back, I ran to the pumps and broke the glass panel that protected the fire extinguisher. The houseboat was a lost cause, but I was able to hit the places where the dock had caught fire.

Fire trucks were the first to arrive. They were followed quickly by an ambulance. I let the firemen take over killing the flames. There was nothing they could do about the boat but watch and make sure it didn't float back and become a hazard. I tried to help the EMTs with Uncle Orson. They made it clear I was only in the way.

Orson forced out a thick, phlegmy laugh and pointed to the big cooler in the corner. "Get everyone a soda," he said.

"No one wants a soda right now," I said, and regretted how angry I sounded. Uncle Orson managed to laugh again.

"It's not funny," I said, still sounding angry. "I'll take care of this, Orson. I'll get Lawson and make him pay."

"It wasn't Lawson," Orson said. His voice was a constricted croak.

"What?"

"Some young guy."

The EMT put an oxygen cup over Uncle Orson's nose and mouth.

I stepped away as they lifted him up on the backboard and lowered him onto a gurney. Levi Sharon was a friend of Billy's. It was possible that he knew how much time I spent on the houseboat.

I stayed where I was and watched my uncle be trundled out. They got him through the door and a deputy immediately came in. At first I didn't recognize Bob because I never see her in a regular duty uniform.

"Why are you here?" I asked.

"I was the closest," she answered. "All hands on deck these days."

"The deck has become a dangerous and unsteady place."

Bob looked at me with a curious expression. "What happened here?"

"When was the last time you saw Tom Dugan?"

All the curiosity dropped from her face to be replaced by a fuming sort of embarrassment. "Do you mean running into a colleague in the course of doing my job? Or do you mean—"

"Never mind." I stepped past her and pressed my face to the glass door. The EMTs were taking it easy down the gangway. I looked back at Bob and said, "I'm going to give you some bad advice." Then I walked back and ducked behind the counter. Kneeling down, I opened a drawer filled with junk, old coins, wire, some medals and a name tag that read Gunnery Sgt. Williams. The drawer stuck but I knew the combination. I lifted the front and jiggled. It worked free and dropped onto the floor. "And I'm going to give you an even worse option."

I reached back as far as I could into the drawer cavity and felt around. When I stood again I was holding a pistol. It was a J.C. Higgins .22 with a four-inch barrel and nine-round cylinder. I knew without looking that there were eight .22 longs loaded and the hammer sat on the empty chamber. I lifted it up to show Bob. "The grips are taped. No prints. And there is not a number to be found. They have all been ground out and too deep for recovery. Even if it had numbers, this gun is cold as moonlight."

"What are you saying?"

"Maybe it's just a backup." I held it out and waited. Bob took it by the handle then looked it over. "Maybe—if you feel you have no other choice—you use your service weapon. You do the job all the way. Don't wound and don't feel pity. And if he's not armed you leave this behind."

"A drop piece?"

"Some men like to make a show of challenging women. They use words that can sound innocent. They get too close and claim it is just an accident. To the outside observer, even to the woman, all the reasonable arguments create doubt. It is exactly what they want. They use your reasonableness and desire to avoid violence against you. Don't let it happen to you.

"Things aren't that bad," Bob said. She sounded like she was trying to convince herself as much as me.

"They never are—until."

"Until what?"

"Until they are." I grabbed up some keys from the counter and tossed them over too. "Make sure the firemen do their thing and lock things up after." I ran out the door and down the bouncing gangplank.

The ambulance had just buttoned up when I caught up. "Hang on!" I shouted at the EMT. "Open the door."

In the glare of the ambulance overheads Orson looked even worse. Both his eyes were swollen, his left worse than the right. A lot of the blood was coming from a ragged gash of scalp that was bunched and wadded with hair.

The woman sitting beside Uncle Orson was hanging a saline bag. She didn't look happy to see me. "We need to get him to the trauma center."

I ignored her. "Uncle Orson," I said. This time my voice was gentle. I was grateful for that. "Orson," I said, slightly louder.

His right eye opened slightly. His mouth twitched.

"I love you, Uncle Orson. You know that, don't you? I love you."

I swear he laughed. Then he reached up and shifted the oxygen cup sideways. "When was the last time you said that to anyone?" He was trying to grin through split lips as he reseated the mask. Then he said something that sounded like, "You need practice."

Chapter 15

There is no weight in this world that rests so heavy on the human spirit as the lifeless glare of hospital fluorescents at 3:00 a.m. Fatigue and harsh light burn away the pretenses of life. The realities, the fear—the terror for loved ones, guilt, and regret are always a late-night sepia stained with old coffee and futile tears.

I sat awake and alone. The cops had gone home or back to work. Marion was in with Chuck. She sat by his bed crocheting in the light spilling from an open door. She carried the night's weight much better than I.

Clare had been in for a short time. I had asked him to see to the cleanup at Moonshines and to check on the dock. The truth was, the only person I wanted there with me was Billy. He was busy with a job that had gotten a whole lot harder in the last few days.

Uncle Orson had lapsed into unconsciousness in the ambulance. They found a hematoma, a growing puddle of blood and fluid, putting pressure on his brain. The pressure had to be relieved surgically. The questions were, could they stop the bleeding and would the swelling go down?

While I waited for news I used my phone to write an email. In it I detailed the events of the day and the information I had gathered. I finished it off by noting the connection of E. Lawson to the Fisher family.

It is my belief that E. Lawson drove the truck that killed Matthew and Cheryl Sharon, the parents of Rose and Levi. Evidence also suggests Lawson was an unnamed conspirator in Levi Sharon's juvenile conviction for illegal logging. The fact that he has an ongoing history with the poaching of valuable trees suggests a continued connection between the two. A deeper connection between E. Lawson and the Fisher family must

be considered. Whether the connection is directly related to the murder
of Rose or tangential is the necessary focus of that investigation.

The fact that another party close to Rose Sharon, Deputy Tom Dugan, is
suspected of stalking one of his coworkers makes him an obvious suspect.
I suggest a deep search of Dugan's history with the goal of finding any
connections between him and Lawson.

I sent the memo off to Billy, then put my feet up on a bench that was
too short and too hard. I drifted off immediately.

Waking was slow. Before my eyes opened I inventoried the offenses
that sleep had brought to the surface. Every joint and muscle hurt. My feet,
which had been propped up on the bench arm, were tingling but otherwise
numb. My neck was cricked at a painful angle. Worst of all was the taste
of old dog and rot in my mouth.

I felt like I had been sleeping for years. It was about half an hour. When
my eyes finally opened, Billy and the surgeon were standing over me. Billy
was smiling; the doctor wasn't. He simply looked exhausted.

I tried to sit up and couldn't. "How's Orson?" I managed to ask.

Billy offered his hand. I took it and let myself be pulled upright. With
his other hand he pushed a steaming cup of coffee at me. It was the last
thing I needed, but I took it.

"Your uncle will get through this..." the doctor said.

"I sense a *but* waiting around the corner," I said.

"All the buts are a matter of wait and see." He took a deep breath. I
couldn't tell if it was part of his bedside manner, or if it was a man looking
at tough realities in the small hours. "He took a hard blow to the head and
the skull was fractured about here." He pointed to his own head behind
his left ear. "We won't know for a while the actual extent of the damage
to the brain. He might pull through just fine."

"That's a weak-sounding 'might,'" I said.

"You're right. Chances are that there will be some lingering effects.
Physical therapy may be required. There is a good chance of damage to his
hearing and eyesight. Those are lesser concerns when considered against
the potential cognitive issues."

"What issues?"

"Memory loss. Inability to recognize names or objects."

I looked him right in the eyes and didn't have any words to say.

The doctor nodded, as if I had said something obvious and sad. "Wait
and see," he said again. "There is no knowing until he is awake. Even
then, what we see may be temporary. Patience will be your greatest ally
in the next days."

"Patience has never been my strength."

He gave me another look. That one might have been pity. It might also have been goodbye. He nodded again and turned, saying nothing further.

Billy watched him go and said, "I hate doctors."

The statement hit me like a punch line. "What do you mean? You were an army medic. How can you hate doctors?"

He gave a small shrug and said, "Medics are mechanics who are proud of what they do. Doctors are the same, but they always seem vaguely ashamed of the repair work."

"He's just tired."

"Aren't we all?" Billy flopped down on the bench and stretched his legs out. "Sit with me."

"I've had enough sitting," I said, then I sat anyway. "I've had enough of a lot."

"I know that feeling." He pulled his phone from his coat pocket and held it up. "I got your email."

"I didn't expect you to read it tonight."

"Well, you're not the only one who's trying to get this job done."

"I know that—"

"There is no connection between E. Lawson and Tom Dugan."

"You're sure?"

"Sure enough."

"Have you—"

"I've looked." Billy wilted. "I've looked hard. I've talked to people who know them both. I pulled records. When I say I'm sure enough—I'm *sure enough.* It doesn't mean I'm happy about it. What it does mean is that it's my fault."

"How do you figure that?"

"I told you, Rose asked me to help Dugan out."

"So?"

"I should have caught it. I should have known she was trying to get away from him. I missed the signs."

"What signs?"

"Hell, I don't know. There had to be something."

"Because no one could hide something from you?"

"Because I should have known." Billy stared across the room. He wasn't seeing the cheap art prints of flowers or the neutral-tone wallpaper. He was looking at a moment and believing it could have been different.

"The world is never an easy place," I said. "People don't always say they need help. They don't always know. Rose may only have asked for help for a friend. She might have been trying to get an abuser out of her life. Anything in between. But there is no magic signal that the abused give. And the abusers are always masters at hiding their true selves. It's usually how they like to work, in plain sight. Safety in normalcy."

"But—"

"Save it." I shifted on the seat, then pulled his chin around to face me. I put my gaze right into his eyes. "If she was intimidated or abused, chances are she would never have opened up to you until it was too late. There comes a point when a woman mistrusts the motives and understanding of the best of men. It can be as devastating to be disbelieved, or given the—*logical explanation*—for what you know to be true, as it is to suffer the predator."

He looked away. Billy didn't want me to think it, but I was certain he was hiding his face.

"I would have believed her," he said.

I had no doubt of that. I didn't have any answer for him. I kept my mouth shut and let him have his feelings. Sometimes I think we rush too quickly to protect others from honest emotions.

We sat quietly for a minute. Billy didn't move any closer to me and I didn't reach out to him. We had put up a wall between us. I touched the scar that snaked out of my eyebrow and thought about that other wall in my life.

Funny how our lives pick up their own symbols, and how they come to define us. There were times I thought I never rolled out from under the shade of that mud wall in Iraq. It felt like all the blood in my body had drained out into the blowing dust. In those moments, I was sure my body had been left empty and naked in a foreign land, and all the rest of my life was a projection of might-have-beens on the sides of my grave.

That could have been the perfect moment to reject the feeling of isolation and reach out to the one good thing in my life. Timing has never been my best feature.

"Tomorrow," Billy said. He paused and appeared to be thinking something through. "Or later today, we're going to be a little more—" He waved his hands in front of himself like he was trying to find the perfect word in the air. "*Proactive.*"

"You look pleased with that word," I said.

"It's a good word. And about time." He got up from the bench.

"Where are you going?"

"I'm going to wake up Greg."

"Greg Sellers?"

"Yep. If the sheriff can't sleep, why should the prosecuting attorney?"

"What do you want him for?"

"So he can wake up the judge. I have some things to ask them both. Then we're going to have a talk with Hosea and Sissy Fisher." Billy seated his water-stained Stetson on his head and walked away.

I watched him all the way down the long hall until he turned for the exit. Then I watched a little longer.

* * * *

Uncle Orson still hadn't woken up and I hadn't slept any more when my phone rang. The sun was long up. You could see the slight brightening of the sky from the hospital windows. It did little to change the feeling of the endless hallways and fluorescent lights.

"Billy?" I said when I answered.

"I need you over here," he said.

"When?"

"Two hours."

"Why?"

"Proactive," was all he said. Then he hung up.

I checked in on Chuck. He was drinking juice and, I'm pretty sure, making romantic suggestions to Marion. She had a smiling blush. He had a crooked but still frisky grin.

"I guess you're going to be okay," I said.

"Better than okay," he said.

"How's that?"

"It's not every day you get that second chance."

Marion frowned at him and took the juice cup away. "Yes, it is," she said. "It's just not every day you take it."

Chuck looked at her, then over at me.

I expected an expletive.

Chuck turned back to Marion and said, "Well, shoot." He took her hand. "You always have a better way to look at things."

I smiled at them both and thought there's something to be said for being treated like a lady.

* * * *

Showered, changed, but at the short end of my rope, I walked into the SO. Billy caught me before I got very far. The door to his office was closed. "I need you to trust me," he said.

"About what?" I asked. "And who's waiting in there?"

"This won't be easy for you."

"What won't?"

"Shutting up and listening."

I looked at Billy. His face was grim, but I didn't see any anger.

"I'm going to say some things," he said.

"What—"

"Listen."

I did.

"We're going in there and I'm going to talk. I'm going to piss you off. I'm going to say things I shouldn't. If you can't hold yourself together, you can't be here. But it's better if you hear it."

"I trust you," I said. I meant it.

"Good." Billy turned.

I followed him into his office, where Sissy and Hosea Fisher were waiting with Landis Tau.

They were all seated. Billy stepped around his desk and sat. There was no other chair.

One of those kinds of meetings, I thought.

Landis gave me a pitying smile.

I returned one that, I hoped, communicated an it-is-what-it-is attitude. Then I leaned against the wall and waited.

Sissy kicked things off with a glower. "Does she need to be here?" she asked.

I wondered if her bandaged face hurt and couldn't help but smile.

That pissed her off even more. The look she gave me was a middle finger.

"I think so," Billy said. "The reason I asked you in was to give you my personal apology, that of the department, and Katrina's, for the difficulties that have come from our investigations."

Billy and Sissy looked at me at the same time. His expression was a warning. Hers was a self-satisfied victory lap.

I don't know what exactly my face said, but I'm sure it wasn't anything apologetic. I straightened my back and stood away from the wall.

Sissy must have thought I was coming after her. She uncrossed her legs, planting both feet on the tile, ready to jump.

I smiled again.

Billy repeated his apology, going into greater detail, but I wasn't listening anymore. My attention was welded to Sissy. More specifically, to her feet. She was wearing the same moccasins she had at the theater. They were rough-finished leather with beads in the fringe and silver conchas. Her jeans were tucked into them. I noticed wisps of rabbit fur sticking out through the lacings. The interesting thing was the absence of water stains. They were warm and waterproof. Not what you expect of pretty footwear.

"Isn't that *right*, Detective Williams?" Billy asked.

I looked up.

He was staring.

Sissy looked again. Then Hosea and finally Landis.

Billy added, "Your sincerest apologies."

He had asked for my trust. He had also warned me I wouldn't like it. He was right. I looked right at Sissy Fisher and said, "I am deeply sorry for the pain you and your family have suffered and for my part in it."

"It's about time," Sissy said. "Is she going to lose her job?"

"Consequences will be discussed and determined." Billy sounded very official.

It sounded, in fact, as if my job was on the line. I think Sissy believed him. I didn't.

"Again," I said, "I'm very sorry, and want to assure you that we are working hard to find Rose's murderer, and to track down Levi for the murder of Clark Beasley and for wounding Donny."

Sissy suddenly looked uncomfortable, and it wasn't with my apology. There was a shift in her eyes and body language when I said the name of the man Donny was with when Levi shot him.

Wanting to be sure, I asked, "Will Donny be able to attend the funeral of Mr. Beasley?"

Her response was quick. "No." She pulled her ranch coat closed and recrossed her legs. "They weren't that close," she said. "We will, of course, send flowers to the family." She looked up from her hunched position at Hosea, then back to Billy, as if he needed some clarification. "Clark had been with the Star Road Theater show for years. He was a wonderful musician."

"I know," Billy answered. "I knew him pretty well myself."

Sissy looked at the floor.

Sensing a weakness in his client, Landis jumped in. "What's the real issue here? I don't think you asked for a meeting to apologize. Not in the middle of a criminal investigation. What are you fishing for?"

Billy leaned back in his big padded chair. He looked at me with an expression as flat and bland as the Oklahoma turnpike.

I leaned back against the wall and waited.

Chapter 16

"There are developments," Billy said.

"In the case?" Landis asked. "Since when does the sheriff include civilians in an open investigation?" He looked over at me and back to Billy as if expecting to catch us sharing a secret code. He was sitting on the edge of the seat and his feet didn't touch the floor. He still had more class and dignity than his client.

Sissy said, "You found my daughter's killer?"

"Daughter?" I asked.

"Rose felt like my daughter."

"But Levi never felt like your son?"

She glared at me again.

I didn't give her the chance to say anything more. I asked Hosea, "What about you, Mr. Fisher?"

"None of 'em are mine. I just put the roof over us."

Sissy turned on her husband and flared like a cobra. "Stop it. That's not the kind of thing we're here to talk about."

Hosea looked defiant but wary.

Before the other man could say more, Landis pushed in again. "What *are* we here to talk about?"

"A second ago, I said developments," Billy answered. "You asked the obvious question, if those developments had anything to do with the case involving Rose's killing. The truth is that our investigations have gone wider. Her death is not the only case we're concerned about."

"I don't think anything you have to share is in our best interest to hear," Landis said.

"You're telling us Donny is no longer a suspect," Sissy said.

"Donny is not a suspect," Billy responded.

"We should go," Landis implored Sissy. "He's not doing you any favors."

"He's right," Billy said. "Beware of cops bearing gifts."

"I don't understand any of it." Hosea spoke like he was making a royal pronouncement. "But I think I want to hear."

Billy waited for any more objections, then went on speaking to Sissy. "We have two suspects."

She said nothing.

"You talked about Rose's diary and that she wrote about my election," he continued. "Rose asked me to hire a young man she was seeing."

"That's impossible."

"No. It's not. Secrets are a part of your household, aren't they?"

"I don't know what you mean."

"You didn't know she was involved with Tom Dugan. And that their relationship may have been abusive in some ways?"

"Then it sounds like you have your man. But you said *two* suspects. Or is the other someone a mystery to distract attention from you and the sheriff's department?"

"You know the other man, too. E. Lawson." Billy dropped the name like a shot across the bow, and it worked.

Hosea sat up straighter. In fact, he looked like a man ready for a fight.

Sissy looked down at her toes. "What makes you think I know any such man?"

"Too many coincidences," Billy answered. "He was the man stealing your trees, Mr. Fisher."

Hosea didn't look surprised.

"And, Lawson has a history of extorting local businesses."

"Not us." Sissy's denial was quick but quiet.

"Why not?"

This time her response was not so quick. "How should I know?"

"You're angling for connections that aren't there," Landis said. He slipped from the chair and stood up. He was barely a head taller than the sheriff's desk. "We're leaving."

"Hang on," Hosea held up his hand. Then he waggled his fingers as he thought something through. He looked at his wife. Then he looked at Billy. He looked at Landis, then back at Sissy before he asked, "You knew?"

Landis darted forward with both hands raised. "Not another word, Mr. Fisher."

The two of them, Hosea and Sissy Fisher, sat silent, but with the energy of a storm between them. Landis, already small, seemed even smaller as he stood between them. Each of them seemed to know something invisible had broken.

Landis clearly hoped the break was a crack. I know Billy wanted to make sure it was a crevasse. He asked, "Did things begin when Levi was helping E. Lawson steal the prime trees from your land?"

"Don't answer that!" Landis burst out.

"I don't think I will," Hosea said. He kept his gaze on the side of Sissy's face. "But not because you tell me so. In fact, you are really my wife's lawyer, aren't you?" He finally looked at Landis.

Landis stared up at the old man's face with diminishing hope. He didn't answer.

Hosea didn't wait. "I think I might need my own mouthpiece." He stood. "I think what's been in the dark is coming to the light. And ain't none of us going to like what we see."

I watched Billy's face as Hosea walked out the door. It showed nothing.

"I think you are an evil man," Sissy said. "You are using innuendo for revenge. It won't go unanswered or unpunished."

Landis dropped his head in apparent defeat. "Do you ever just stop talking, Sissy?" he asked, pinching the bridge of his nose. "Please, let's get out of here."

She didn't look at her lawyer. She didn't look at any of us. Sissy stood and marched out the open door. It was like she took a curse with her. We all breathed easier.

"Sheriff," Landis said, "I knew you were a dangerous man."

Billy accepted the compliment with a nod.

To me, Landis said, "I didn't know you had such restraint. When he offered an apology I thought you would pop. I wish you had." He walked out, and without looking back said, "I'm sure we'll be talking soon."

I shut the door behind him. "You certainly stirred that pot."

Billy didn't answer. He pulled a laptop from his desk and opened it as he leaned back to prop his feet on the open drawer.

"What are you doing?" I asked.

"Wait," he said. He punched away at the keys with two fingers, then right-clicked the touch pad like he'd done something important. Then he set the computer on the desk.

"For what?"

"I couldn't get a warrant. 'Not enough hard evidence,' I was told. What I could do was kick the woodpile and see what runs out."

"What's that supposed to mean?"

"Well, we can get call detail records without a warrant. Today I'm taking a little shortcut."

The laptop chimed.

"Looks like I've got mail already." Billy took his feet from the drawer and leaned in. "Instead of pulling the CDRs and digging through weeks of information, I thought we'd give them something to talk about. I asked a friend to keep an eye on Sissy Fisher's number. The note I just sent was to tell him to start. He just wrote back. She just made a call." He turned the computer around so the screen faced me, then asked, "Recognize that number?"

"She just called Lawson," I said.

"Yep." Billy put his feet back up. "I figure she cut her lawyer loose and did exactly what he told her not to do."

The laptop chimed again.

"Open it," Billy said.

"It lists the numbers and says, *Call Duration, 2:51.*"

"Getting harder for her to claim she doesn't know him." Billy looked pleased with himself.

Another chime.

"I wonder who that could be." He almost cackled with joy.

I opened the next email. "You had your friend logging Lawson's phone too."

"Yep."

"He just called an untagged number."

"A burner phone, I'm betting." Billy pulled out his own phone. "Read it to me." He added the number to his contact list as I did. "Now we wait again."

I sat in the chair Landis had been using.

"Thanks, by the way," Billy said.

"For what?"

"I asked you to trust me. You did. I know it wasn't fun or easy for you."

I laughed. "I've been censured by professionals. I didn't like bowing and scraping to that woman, though it did show me one thing you were wrong about."

"What's that?"

"Galoshes."

He shook his head and looked confused.

"At the murder scene," I reminded him. "We talked about the weird, featureless shoe prints. You said they had to be galoshes."

"Okay, I remember."

"They were moccasins."

"One more piece."

Another chime sounded from the laptop. I stood to open the email. "Lawson to the untagged number, 4:21."

Billy lifted his phone and hit the call button. "If this is who I think, we have all the pieces we need to make a vise and squeeze." He put the phone to his ear and listened. After a moment he said, "Hey Levi. We need to talk." He grinned at me like a boy who had just caught his first fish.

"Yeah," he nodded along to something Levi was saying. "What did Lawson tell you?" More nodding. "You know he's lying—no, I've never lied to you—

"No. He wants you to think Dugan killed her.

"He's using you. He's always been using you. Lawson wants you to get rid of Dugan so Dugan can take the blame and not be around to defend himself. Where would that leave you?

"I was trying to protect you. And protect other people from you.

"It's not bullshit, Levi.

"No.

"Come in and talk to me.

"I'm still your friend.

"Don't do that, Levi.

"There are always other ways."

As he talked, I could see the grin on Billy's face melt into a grim line. I hated to see him realize how far away his friend was from the man he remembered.

There was no goodbye. Billy put the phone down and told me, "We need to get Dugan in here."

"Do you think Levi knows where he is? Or even who he is?"

"He's seen him at the crime scene. The fence is like a garden of crepe paper flowers and saint candles."

"When you said 'all the pieces we need to squeeze,' what did you mean?"

"We gave Sissy information. She called and shared it with Lawson. Lawson shared it with Levi. I think we have a conspiracy."

"With what goal? How did killing Rose serve anyone?"

"I don't know," he said, staring again at his phone. "But put it with the paint you lifted and it goes way back."

* * * *

Billy set to work bringing in Deputy Tom Dugan. I headed back to the hospital. A phone call would have told me how Uncle Orson was doing. It wouldn't have shown me, and I wanted to see for myself. There was one other thing. What better place to hide? I was tired and sore. The bitter cold of the recent days seemed to have seeped into my body. Every feeling I had was somehow frozen, as if I would shatter at any moment. I wanted nothing more than to sit next to Uncle Orson in a darkened room, maybe put my feet up, steal some sleep, and be there when he woke.

Neither life nor duty takes time out for the things we want. My phone rang before I even got out of Forsyth. It was Hosea Fisher.

"You know about cuckoo birds?" he asked.

"How did you get this number, Mr. Fisher?"

"You gave it to me. That mornin'. You gave me your card and said to call you if I had more to say."

It had only been a couple of days since Rose Sharon was found dead. It seemed like a long lifetime. "I guess I did. So you have more to say?"

"Don't you listen?"

"Pardon?"

"Cuckoos and cuckolds, drunkards and fools. It's like we're all soiling the same nest and no one wants to talk about it."

My tired brain was reeling trying to make sense of the conversation. "You're not making any sense."

"Girl, I've found sense is what you make of it. Not hopin' or believing, but twisting it up and putting it in your pocket. Tangles."

Cops and crazies are like race car drivers on the same track at the same time, running two different races. We're bound to keep running into each other and trading paint. Whenever I have contact with the drug-addled and the mentally ill, I turn to two thoughts that help me make sense of the situation. First, I say to myself, *But for the grace of God...* And second, I ask myself the riddle from *Alice in Wonderland*: *Why is a raven like a writing desk?* One gives me patience; the other reminds me how I must have sounded more than once.

"Can we try again, Mr. Fisher? I think neither of us is speaking the other's language."

"What language are you talkin'? Because I'm telling you straight, and it ain't an easy thing to say someone else was warmin' your bed."

"Are you saying your wife had an affair?"

"Talkin' to you is about as easy as a chipped-tooth blow job, lady. Had. Is having. I'm the bird fooled by the cuckoo, raising chicks that ain't my own."

"You're not talking about the Sharon kids."

"I ain't."

"You're talking about Donny. He's Lawson's son."

"An' I've been feathering the nest all this time."

"Why are you telling me this now?"

"I ain't no kind of monster. You don't live so close to someone without gaining some affection. That girl was a good one. Even Donny was okay. The fact he was a queer burned his momma. I only wonder what it did to his real daddy." Hosea laughed. It sounded like a choking donkey. "I'm goin' to get me that lawyer like I said. Sissy's on her own."

He disconnected.

I didn't call back.

Chapter 17

At the hospital I went straight to Donny Fisher's room. He still had the tube in his throat but he looked stronger. The pad by his bed was tattered and well scribbled. At first he smiled, seeming glad to see me. Something passed over his face as I said hello.

"Your mother told you not to talk to me," I said.

Donny half smiled. At the same time he reached for the pad.

I stepped forward and handed it over.

He wrote, *And lawyer.*

"I understand."

He put his head down and wrote more. When he was finished Donny looked up and hesitated.

"You have a question?" I asked.

He held up the pad and it said, *You hit my mother. She has stitches.*

"Yes. It was wrong."

You don't sound sorry!

I couldn't hold my gaze on his face. I looked down and thought about what I wanted to say. He was right; I didn't sound sorry. "I'm not sure I am," I said, then lifted my eyes back to his.

Donny's head bobbed. He pursed his lips as if he was about to speak. He wrote, *She can be hard to get along with. Hard to like.*

"Yes."

I think everyone has thought about hitting her.

"Has anyone ever done it?"

Hit my mother?

"Yes."

Why?

"For any reason."

Donny shook his head and wrote in large letters, *Why are you asking?!*

"You mother is involved with some dangerous people."

Lawyer.

I stepped back with my hands up in surrender. "Okay. I understand. But you should know one of those dangerous people is your father."

Hosea has never hurt anyone.

"But he's not your father, is he?" I asked.

Billy wasn't the only one who could stir a pot. I expected a big reaction. Questions. Curses.

Donny Fisher laid the pad and pen in his lap and pointed to the door. He didn't look angry at all, simply despondent.

I paused, looking around the door at Donny, and said, "One other thing."

He looked at his lap and waved me away.

"Do you have moccasins?"

He looked up and raised his hand. That time when he pointed it was with his middle finger.

I got the message.

Walking to Orson's room, I called Billy.

"Are you getting a warrant for the Fishers' house?" I asked him.

"I'm taking what we have to the judge this afternoon," he said. "Why?"

"Amend the request on the moccasins. We don't want to limit it to Sissy's footwear. Add Donny's name and clothing to the warrant."

"You know something for sure?"

"No. But this is one seriously screwed-up family."

"We've got another problem," he said. The tension in his voice extended into the silence afterward.

"I'm listening."

"Tom Dugan went AWOL."

"What happened?"

"I talked to Calvin. He blew it."

"Calvin? How?"

I heard Billy's boots hitting his desk and the big chair squeak. He was still learning how to be comfortable in the office. "It's as much my fault. I got on the radio to call Dugan in."

"Nothing more suspicious than the sheriff calling you in personally."

"Dugan and Calvin were working an injury accident in Rockaway Beach. A car slid down that big hill on Larkspur and hit a mail truck. I guess it wasn't bad enough I called Dugan myself. Calvin had to tell him it was about time he got dealt with. I guess it escalated from there."

"Where's Dugan now?" I asked.

"He left the scene in his cruiser and hasn't been seen since." Billy sounded as tired as I felt.

"Where's Bobbi Rantz?"

"She's here at the SO. And I'm keeping her here."

"Okay. I'm going to check on Uncle Orson and Chuck. I'll come back in after that."

"Copy that," Billy said, then broke the line.

* * * *

Uncle Orson's room was dark and cool. The sounds of the hospital were muted and distant. It reminded me of a time I had been in a cave with Billy. That was another bad point in my life. He had taken me into the darkness to show me a little light.

I didn't say anything. Without talking to the nurses, I couldn't be sure if he was sleeping or unconscious. Not knowing was easier than facing hard realities at the moment. Instead of dragging the chair, I lifted it and brought it closer to the bed before sitting.

Orson's breathing was deep and steady. His face was slack, but still lined. His silvered hair still had tones of reddish brown. I noticed for the first time how thin it was getting on top. It was kind of shaggy. I stood to brush it back.

He didn't react at all.

I sat back down and instantly fell asleep.

When I woke it was because Clare Bolin was shaking my shoulder.

"I'm awake," I said, making sure he knew how bothered I was.

"I thought I'd find you here," he said.

I was slumping in the chair. I stretched and straightened my spine. "Where have you been? I thought you would be around here too."

"I was for a while this morning."

"How's he doing?" I looked at Orson.

"You haven't talked to the doctors?"

"I've been putting it off."

"You should have that talk. They won't share with me. Not family. But one of the nurses is an old student."

"And what did she say?" I asked. I didn't mean to sound annoyed that time but I did.

"He's doing well. The swelling is going down and easing the pressure."

"He looks like he's sleeping off a drunk."

"She said sleep's the best thing. He just needs time before we can see the truth of what will happen."

"Thanks, Clare. And thank her."

"I did." His smile was soft and inward looking.

"You have something to say?"

"E. Lawson did this?"

"Not directly," I said. "He hit you and Chuck in Moonshines. He used a guy named Levi Sharon to attack Orson."

"I've done some asking around."

I looked at Clare, trying to keep the anticipation off my face. "Yeah? Asking who, about what?"

"Asking people who would never talk to you about Lawson."

"Go on."

"Some folks say he's sometimes set up in a trailer deep in the woods off 160."

I sat up straighter. "Where on 160?"

"Between 176 and Silver Creek Road."

"The land owned by Hosea Fisher," I said, sure of myself.

"That's something that there's a little scandalous talk about."

"What?"

"Some people say Hosea owns the north side acreage. Some say his wife owns the land to the south."

"And the trailer Lawson likes to hole up in is parked south of Highway 160."

"You got it."

I pulled out my phone. Billy needed to know about that trailer and the land it sat on. It could be added to the warrant request.

"Something else you should know," Clare said.

I looked up from the phone. It was already ringing.

"I'm not the only one who's been asking around. A deputy named Dugan has been making noise."

The call connected and I filled Billy in. Clare slipped out while we were talking. After hanging up, I was alone with Uncle Orson and now wide awake. It was nice but seemed unproductive. On TV you always see people reading to unconscious patients. I didn't know if it helped. It couldn't hurt.

I wandered out to the nurses' station to look for something to read. The girl who had been a student of Clare's offered me a book from her purse. She also offered the disclaimer that it might not be my kind of book.

The next few hours were spent reading a sexy romance by Sierra Cartwright to Uncle Orson. It may not have been his kind of book. It was definitely mine. I probably would have kept reading until the happily ever after if not for the return of the nurse. She brought in a tray for me and a fresh saline bag for Orson.

I stared at the bland-looking plate of roast beef, mashed potatoes, and green beans, trying to remember the last time I had eaten. It didn't matter how bland it was. I ate without tasting. I may have eaten the whole meal without chewing.

After eating my uncle's dinner, I took the dishes and the book out to the nurses' station. The tray I stacked on the cart. The book I handed over to the grinning nurse.

"You liked it?" she asked.

"I hope you have it here tomorrow," I answered, echoing the smile. "My uncle really wants to know how it ends."

"I bet he does." She laughed.

My mood was much better leaving the hospital than it had been arriving. Uncle Orson would be okay. I was feeling sure of it. That's the thing about me and optimism. We have a gambler's relationship. The odds are always against a payout. Still, I always feel like this time is the one.

I lost again.

The midwinter sun was already down when I reached the exit. The sliding doors opened and let in a blast of air so strong and cold it brought tears to my eyes then froze them. I zipped my coat up tight and put my face down. From under the covered drop-off zone I heard a woman shouting. The wind covered the words, but not the fear.

Sissy Fisher was beside an idling truck, trying to pull her arm away from the grip of E. Lawson. The cheek wound and bruising I had given her was matched on the other side by a fresh swelling that promised a new black eye.

She shouted again. It turned into a scream as he twisted her arm in an effortless one-handed grip.

Lawson yelled back at her. The sound was wrong. Not simply taken by the wind, it was an incoherent babble of anger. When I remembered he was still dealing with a truncated and stitched tongue I felt gratified.

There wasn't any time to bask in the feeling. I went for my weapon.

He saw me. The evil delight in his face was colder than the weather.

To get to my gun I had to open my coat and reach my holster. I wasn't fast enough. Lawson pulled Sissy along as he strode forward. He was still ten feet away when I cleared my weapon. He threw Sissy like a sidearm pitcher.

She hit me hard. I heard the breath go out of both our lungs. Then I heard my pistol clattering on the walkway. I expected him to kick me while

I was down or to pull me up for a crushing punch. I prepared for that by pulling my knee to my chest. I was planning on putting my foot in his crotch. He surprised me and Sissy both by dragging her off me, keeping her dangling between us. I rolled and reached blindly for my gun. Then, for the second time, he used her for his weapon. He dropped her on my back.

I couldn't tell the next time if Sissy got herself out of the way or if Lawson did it. Her weight disappeared from me. The next moment he was pulling me up into a bear hug. His huge arms circled my torso. The ribs that were already damaged and painful literally crunched inside my body. The screaming I heard was my own.

"Stop," Sissy shouted from the ground. "You'll kill her."

Lawson grinned at the thought, only an inch from my face.

I reared back and slammed my head forward.

He saw me coming and lowered his own head. It was skull against skull, and his was much tougher than mine. I tried to slap my palms against his ears. I pulled his hair and I gouged at his eye.

Lawson laughed at me like I was nothing. His milky white eye was shimmering like quicksilver as my vision became fluid. I was afraid that the last sight of my life was going to be his crooked yellow teeth guarding the black hole of his mouth.

"Ust annoter itch," he said then laughed, squeezing tighter.

It was his attempt at calling me a bitch that saved me. His speech reminded me of the damaged tongue. While he laughed I shot my hand forward, shoving it as deep as I could into his mouth. I grabbed the nub of his tongue between my thumb and forefinger and squeezed with all the strength I could muster.

It was his turn to scream. When his grip loosened I fell. I kept hold of the tongue as long as I could. My gun was in sight when I hit the ground. It was only a few feet away. The crawl to reach it seemed endless. Each instant I expected to be lifted again.

I got the weapon in my hand and rolled over with it at the ready. I didn't plan on a warning or threat. If he had still been standing there I would have shot him.

I was alone.

Lawson was gone. His truck was already rolling away.

Sissy was also gone. With Lawson or into the hospital, I didn't know. At that moment I didn't care. The only thing I really cared about was getting to my feet. The trail of fresh blood leading to where Lawson's truck had been was a bonus.

Walking to Orson's truck was fresh punishment. Uncle Orson had gotten my window repaired, but in the chaos of the attack on him I hadn't traded vehicles. I regretted it. His was lifted, which required me to climb with a hand on the pillar support to get in. It hurt like hell.

Aside from that, Orson's old truck was horrible. It was great for plowing through snowbanks. For any kind of comfort, it was the wrong choice. The seats were sagging, the windows ill fitting, and worst of all, there was no radio.

I had no complaints about the engine. It started right up. The rumbling vibration was hard enough to be soothing. I left the lights off and turned the heater up high.

In the dark and the diminishing cold I became more aware of the pain in my body. Lawson had done more damage. The ribs that were bruised before, maybe hairline fractured, were certainly worse off. I consoled myself with the supposition that if they were broken, I wouldn't be walking or complaining so much.

Well, walking anyway.

The question came to me. *Is this what I want from my life?*

Since my rape at the hands of superior officers in Iraq I had been fighting. I fought the army for justice. I fought to keep a job that was itself a daily struggle. Every moment, I wrestled with sobriety and anger. Where was the happiness I was fighting for?

Could I even honestly tell myself I was fighting for anything? Even the breaths I took seemed to be simply in opposition to dying.

The truck was getting warm. I opened my coat to let the heat inside. The increasing temperature made me sag into the seat. My skin tingled. My eyelids were heavy. Sleep called. My body was dumping the adrenaline that had risen in the fight. The feeling was more pronounced because the recent days had been nothing but extreme highs and lows. There is a military cliché that says, sleep when you can because you never know when your next chance may be. A side to that cliché that most people don't understand is that after the stress and terror of combat, many soldiers want nothing more than sleep.

There was one other thing I wanted. Without thinking about it I reached over and opened the glove box. Inside there was a jar of clear liquid. It was moonshine, the real illegal deal. It was some of the last batch Clare had made before going straight and working for me.

I twisted the lid off. Unaged whiskey has no color and little smell. Both come from the wooden casks. That didn't stop me from raising the jar to my nose and breathing in the faint aroma. After that, I remember holding out the jar and looking into the liquid. I remember closing my eyes and asking myself if I really wanted to keep fighting.

Chapter 18

Dream, vision, or some other, secret reality—I never know which it is when the dead visit me. Usually it was my husband. For a long time, I would wake in the middle of the night to find him lying beside me. Sometimes he was as I imagined him to be before the chemicals of warfare began their slow destruction of his body. Other times he was a nightmare from the grave, sleeping with me, offering nothing but the cold of death.

That night he was simply a presence looking at me with sadness. He gave no advice or warnings. I didn't ask for any. We looked at each other. He faded from the seat beside me, his face replaced by Billy's.

Billy was outside the cab knocking on the window. He was smiling, happy to see me. There was concern, too. I reached over to pull the door lock and realized that my hand was empty. The jar of moonshine was on the floorboard. It was empty. The liquid was pooled on the mat. I felt cheated and grateful for it at the same time.

"Are you okay?" Billy asked as he climbed in.

"Why wouldn't I be?"

"You haven't answered your phone. We got a 911 call about a woman and a big man fighting in the drop-off zone. What happened?"

"You have pretty much the whole story. I walked out the door. Lawson and Sissy were there. I think he had been working her over a little bit. Then he saw me."

"Are you hurt?"

"Hurting," I said. "I don't think there is any real damage."

"Are you lying to me?"

I wanted to answer. I didn't. It's possible that I couldn't if I tried. For the first time, I was aware of how much I feared confessing weakness to Billy. He was a better person than I was. I had cursed his kindness as a liability on the job. It wasn't. My anger was. But I didn't want that taken away from me.

"I just wanted a drink." I said it like a dare.

"I don't believe you."

"Then you're a fool."

"You decided to have a drink? Or to pour it out?" He lifted his feet and put them down, making small splashes in the corn whiskey. "I know you, Katrina. And I know when you really decide to drink, you will."

I wiped my eyes with the sleeve of my coat and asked, "Did you get the warrants?"

"Yeah." Billy looked like he wanted to say something else.

I didn't let him. I asked, "When do we execute?"

He checked his watch and said, "Still a couple of hours. You were right about the trailer and land on the south side of 160. It is titled in the name of Sissy Harding. Her maiden name."

"Why start there?"

"The warrant says we're looking for evidence. We're really looking to catch Lawson and Levi. There is a good chance that's where they're hiding. And I figure they're most likely to be there at night."

Billy leaned his head against the passenger window and closed his eyes.

"What are you doing?"

"Grabbing a little nap. Join me?"

I looked the other way and rolled my eyes. When I turned back there was a fraction of a second where I wasn't sure who was in the truck with me, Billy Blevins or Nelson Solomon.

The next thing I knew Billy was sitting there with a steaming cup of coffee. The truck engine was dead. Cold was creeping back in.

"What happened?" I asked.

"I shut off the truck to save your gas."

"I was asleep?"

"You can call it that."

"Where'd you get coffee?"

Billy lifted a thermos from between his feet. "My truck. I come prepared."

"Always the difference between us."

"You're wrong about that. We're just prepared for different things." He handed me the plastic cup.

The heat was wonderful on my hands. I pressed it to my face.

"You should go home," he said. "Get some real sleep."

"Is that your way of telling me not to show up for the raid on the trailer?"

"Would you listen, if I did?"

"You would have to fire me to keep me away." The look on Billy's face made me regret saying it. He appeared to be giving termination serious thought. "I'll be fine. The coffee was all I needed."

He looked at his watch. Then he looked again and stared at it for too long. "I'm getting to the SO. I've pulled in everyone available to hit that trailer. Your time would be better spent staying here at the hospital."

"Uncle Orson doesn't need me at the moment."

"I was talking about checking in for a long stay of your own."

"Thanks for the coffee," I said.

Billy went to his departmental SUV and left. I waited for the coffee to warm me and put a little jolt in my heart. I could have waited forever it seemed. When I did go, I drove slowly. I felt worried. My mind was nothing but blowing brown dust. I touched the scar at my eyebrow.

I was still touching the scar when I pulled into the lot at the SO. I looked to be the last to arrive. There was a huddle of deputies around Billy. I left the truck running and joined the group.

"…one last thing," Billy said. He was speaking loud into the wind. "We have no evidence that either E. Lawson or Levi Sharon are on the property. That's why we're going in on the warrant to search for evidence. Don't let that make you complacent. Either or both of these men could be hiding in the trailer. They are dangerous."

"You couldn't say all this inside where it's warm?" Duck asked. "And I'm the CO. Why couldn't I stay in the jail, where even the prisoners get to be toasty and dry?"

"All hands," Billy said. "That includes corrections officers, Duck."

Calvin came out of the SO building and scanned the parking lot. "Hey," he called. Not quite loud enough.

The group was already shuffling off to their vehicles.

"Hang on," I shouted.

Everyone stopped.

"What's Calvin want?" I pointed to him. He was waving his arms and running over.

"We have radios, you know," Duck said. A few of the guys laughed.

"Where's Bob?" Calvin asked.

No one laughed. We all looked around.

"Did she know what time we were gathering?" Billy asked.

"You know she did. You told her yourself," Calvin answered.

"Did you—"

"I called." Calvin cut Billy off. "Home and cell."

"Maybe her unit got stuck in the snow," Duck suggested.

Billy lifted his hand radio and said, "Dispatch—from sheriff."

"Go ahead, Sheriff."

"Do you have a 20 on Deputy Rantz?"

"Negative. The board lists her as off until 2100."

Without needing to, Billy looked at his watch.

I was already running to my truck when he said, "Calvin, you ride with me."

Duck yelled, "I'll go with Hurricane!"

"You'd better hurry up then!" I called back.

Duck was a big, slow man. If he wasn't a friend, I would have left him. At least he had a radio. Billy's voice came over it, calm and forceful. Three units were responding. I wondered if that included us.

Dispatch was reading out Bobbi Rantz's address before we got out of the parking lot. She lived in Forsyth, so we were on her street in minutes.

"We have a 911 report of shots fired at the address," dispatch said when we were three hundred yards away.

Bob lived in a small frame house in a line of similar houses all painted some shade of white. They were packed close together but erratically located. In the piled and filthy snow, they looked like ragged teeth in a diseased mouth.

Billy had taken the lead, running fast with lights and siren. Duck and I came up second. Uncle Orson's old truck didn't inspire a lot of confidence on slick roads. It was in its element, though, when I reached the house and kept going through the drifts to stop in Bob's yard.

Piled snow flew like the froth of rough seas. Through the spray I noticed a Ford truck parked on the street two doors down. I kept my eyes on the truck as the air cleared. It was the same one Levi had been driving when he confronted me at the Star Road Theater. Beyond it, parked in a vacant lot and barely visible behind still-green junipers, was a Taney County Sheriff's Department cruiser.

We all piled out of our vehicles and I called out, "It's not just Dugan!" Everyone looked and I pointed out the truck and cruiser down the street. "Levi Sharon is here. Probably inside."

Another two cruisers pulled up. Billy pointed to the deputies and shouted, "You!" He shifted the aim of his finger to the gathering groups of people on both sides of the house. "Get those people back." He turned to Calvin. "Get more people here. Set up a command post and take over site control. Back my SUV across the street, park it by that tree. That'll be the CP. Duck!" Billy pointed again. "Go around back. Keep under cover." Duck went as fast as he could. His pace almost qualified as a run.

Billy joined me, keeping Uncle Orson's truck between us and the front of Bob's house.

"If Bob was okay, she'd be outside by now," I said.

Billy nodded in agreement. It seemed like flakes were falling off his Stetson. They weren't. It was snowing again. We both looked to the sky. As if on cue, the air stilled. Flakes, fat and wet, dropped in slow motion. They immediately began to pile up.

I started to say something. It was going to be about the situation. I wanted it to be about the job at hand. I said, "I wish you would put a rain cover on your hat."

The surprise in his face was worth the foolish feeling I suffered. He didn't quite smile. He didn't say anything, either. But he understood the comment probably more than I did. He turned his attention back to the front door of Bob's house.

"I'll get one," he said. Then he shouted, "Levi—Dugan—whichever one of you is standing—you need to come out!"

The front door swung in. The opening was empty and dark.

"Who's there?" Billy called out.

"Who you think?" Levi shouted back.

"Levi, is Deputy Rantz all right?"

"The girl is fine. She ain't happy."

"Why don't you send her out? Then we can talk."

"We're talking now. And if she's out, there's nothing stopping you from coming in."

"How about if I make you a promise?" Billy asked.

"Most times that'd be enough." Levi's shout carried a sad weight.

"This time?"

"It's snowing again."

Billy looked at me. Then he let his head hang. He moved to the edge of the truck hood. That left his upper body exposed. "Yes, it is. Pretty hard."

"I like the snow. Remember how we talked about the trees and the seasons we missed in Iraq?"

"I remember."

"I missed the snow."

"Levi!" Billy barked the name. "We need to talk in a way to move things forward."

"There's only so far forward we can go, Big Billy."

"Don't talk like that."

"It's a truth and an inevitability. All things come to this point."

"There doesn't have to be an ending. Not here."

The shadowed doorway remained silent.

"Tell me what's been going on in there, Levi," Billy said, stepping to the bumper of the truck. That left him fully exposed. His weapon was pointed into the piling snow. He held it in a relaxed one-handed grip.

My grip was two-handed and tense.

An anguished screech came from the house. Then Tom Dugan came into view. He flopped forward, his left shoulder propped against the doorframe. He sagged on one leg. Blood was running from his pants. He had been shot either in the hip or high on the thigh. It was hard to tell.

"This is the bastard that killed Rose," Levi shouted from behind Dugan.

"No, he isn't," Billy answered. He turned to look at where he had staged Calvin.

I followed the direction of his glance and saw that there was already an ambulance waiting. Calvin was sending other deputies out to circle the house. I was impressed and proud of him. I resolved to let him know.

"Your cops are screwed up, Billy," Levi called. "They're killing girls and attacking each other."

"Ask yourself who sent you after Dugan," Billy said. He wasn't shouting anymore. "Then ask yourself the last time Lawson had your interests at heart."

Billy was several inches in front of the truck. The snow showed gouged trails where he was scooting through it rather than stepping.

"Lawson's as bad as they come," Levi said. "That don't make him wrong."

"You okay, Dugan?"

"Hell no, I'm not okay." His voice was a loud whine. "She shot me."

"Seems to me you brought that on yourself, pardner," Billy said.

"That's bullshit. I just came here to talk to Bobbi. That's all, talk."

"I'm betting you came uninvited." Billy kept creeping forward.

I lifted my weapon and sighted over Dugan's right shoulder. I tried not to think about actually trying the shot if Levi raised a gun on Billy.

"Just to talk!" Dugan wailed his justification. "I left my weapon in the car. I came to talk to her."

A loud, derisive laugh came from behind Dugan. Then Levi said, "He keeps saying that."

Dugan squealed like a kicked pig.

"Don't you?" Levi asked him. "That leg sure hurts, don't it?" To Billy he said, "This piece of shit keeps crying about all the ways he's misunderstood. He moans about how he left his gun behind. When I got here he was on the floor and this was beside him."

A small, familiar pistol came out the door. It bounced once on the covered porch and landed in the new snow on the top step.

"It's not mine!" Dugan pleaded.

"I don't care," Billy said. His voice had a crystal edge. It was as cold as lost grace. He was almost halfway to the porch and had never yet lifted his feet.

I looked to the left and saw more deputies had arrived. Calvin was working the radio and using hand signals to fan them out around the house. Two were crouch-walking behind me to get to the left side. Wind kicked up and the falling snow whipped up into a froth. When I looked again, Billy was veiled. The house and the black hole of the open door appeared to have receded into a fog. I saw movement in the opening but could make no sense out of it.

I took a few steps, moving out from behind the truck and around to flank Billy.

"Let him go," Billy said.

I doubted that his voice would carry to the house, he spoke so quietly. It carried. Levi answered. "I'm doin' your job for you."

"You're doing Lawson's scut work."

"You don't know what you're talking about."

"I know a lot more than you, Levi." Billy shuffle-stepped a few more inches. "You're carrying the weight for things that happened a long time ago. It's time to put it down before it kills you."

"Get me out of here!" Dugan shouted out, seemingly to no one in particular.

"Shut up," Billy told him.

"Yeah, shut up," Levi echoed. He punctuated the command by snapping Dugan's head against the doorframe.

"How about it, Levi?" Billy asked. "Come on out and learn the truth."

"I've gone my whole life and never knew a true thing except Rose. You gonna give me her back?"

"I can tell you who took her away. And it wasn't that shitbird you got there."

"You don't know what I saw, Billy. I watched this guy. He was hanging out where Rose was killed. He put pictures from the scene on the internet. Pictures of her. Kids there were treating him like a hero. I saw him dialing his phone and getting madder and madder each time he didn't get who he wanted. Guys like him—you pretty much know what they're mad at. It's always a woman. I followed him here. He cut the back screen and pried the door open."

"I just wanted to talk to her," Dugan said again. "I deserve that, don't I? To talk. Explain."

I sidled forward to keep Billy at an angle and to keep the door in view. Without looking, I was sure the deputies were moving in as well. The wind was making the snow an opaque screen between us and the doorway.

"You don't want to talk to anyone here about what you deserve, Dugan," Billy said. "Keep quiet."

"I looked in the window back there," Levi said. "This guy likes to do his talking with his fists. I went in to help. The girl had already shot him."

"And that'll go in your favor. If you come out now."

"You think I'm going to let him go?"

Wind swirled the snow and for a moment I had a clear view of Levi leering over Dugan's shoulder. He didn't appear to be the same defeated man I had seen before. He was radiating an energy. It was something dark and resolute.

"I think you want your sister's killer to face justice."

Levi's face twisted into a grin that had no happiness in it. He put his mouth to Dugan's ear. Then his pistol snaked up Dugan's exposed arm. Levi put the barrel of the gun an inch in front of his sneering lips and pressed it to the other man's head.

"He's going to," Levi said.

"I told Lawson about Dugan," Billy said.

Levi and Dugan both looked stunned.

"It was a trap," Billy continued. "We suspected them both, so I told Sissy Fisher about Dugan. We monitored her phone number. She called Lawson, and a minute later he called you."

"I don't believe you."

"Think about it, Levi. I called you just a few minutes later, didn't I? How did I get the number? Why would Lawson tell you Dugan killed your sister after that, except to get you to take him off the board? How easy would it be to frame Dugan with him dead? He already looks guilty."

"I've known Lawson since—"

"Since Sissy Fisher sent you away. Since she started grooming Rose to be the next big country star. Since E. Lawson drove a truck into your parents' car."

Billy was only about ten feet from the bottom porch step. He had his gun pointed at the ground and his free hand hanging open. He looked like a man in supplication.

"Don't let them win it all," Billy said. "Please."

The light that I had seen in Levi's face a moment ago was gone. His eyes were tired spaces where nothing but loss resided. "Even if they lose I can't win," he said like he was apologizing to someone. "I've never won."

I realized too late what that meant.

Billy, I think, knew all along what was going to happen. He raised his weapon at the same time Levi pushed Dugan out ahead of him.

When Dugan toppled down the stairs, my shot was still blocked by the doorframe. I wanted more than anything at that moment to save Billy from killing his friend.

Levi raised his pistol toward Billy.

Billy didn't shoot. He was ready, but didn't seem to believe Levi would kill him. He was right. Levi didn't fire.

From where I was I could see only the gun and Levi's extended arms. I moved toward Billy to open up my target. Levi must have caught a glimpse or maybe he knew I was there all along. He stepped through the door and pivoted, aiming his pistol at me.

Billy fired two rounds. They both hit center mass.

Chapter 19

What light there had been in Levi's eyes collapsed into nothing. It wasn't darkness. It was simply absence. He was dead.

I slogged forward through the still-deepening snow. Dugan was trying to rise. I shoved him aside. "Stay there. Don't move. Don't speak." I kicked the small revolver I had given to Bob into the snow and out of his reach. I did the same with Levi's weapon on my way into the house.

"Bob!" I called.

"In here," she answered.

I found her in the kitchen cuffed to the refrigerator. "Are you okay?"

"I'm fine. It sounds like I'm the only one."

"Yeah," I agreed. "Nothing fine about any of this." I put the key into her cuffs.

"Thanks," Bob said.

Calvin came running in with his weapon still in his hand. He stopped at the kitchen and looked around like a man wishing there was someone left to shoot. "Are you okay?"

"I'm good," Bob answered. She looked at me again and said, "*Thank you.*"

I didn't say anything.

"The EMTs loaded Dugan up." Calvin pointed back over his shoulder with his thumb. "Sheriff Blevins cuffed him."

Outside, I picked my way around Levi's body and the blood in the snow. The falling flakes were already obscuring the fresh crimson.

"Bob's okay," I told him.

"I know."

"How could you?"

"If she wasn't, Levi would have said something or gotten her help."

"I guess he would have at that."

We stood in the cold wind and showering flakes without speaking while the deputies and medical personnel did their work. The coroner's van arrived and I issued directions without leaving Billy's side.

Calvin came over and asked, "What about the warrant on Sissy Fisher's mobile home, Sheriff?"

"I think we've had enough for one night," Billy answered. "Regroup and re-plan tomorrow."

Calvin looked a question at me.

I kept my face as blank as I could.

Calvin left without saying anything more.

The scene cleared. Duck took Dugan's cruiser back to the SO. A tow truck operator was called in to take Levi's truck to impound. Calvin took Bob away in her car to stay with friends. The house was secured and the doors blocked by crime scene tape. The neighbors all wandered back to their houses. I still stood with Billy.

The brim of his hat was piled with new powder. I brushed it off.

"What are you going to do about Orson?" he asked me.

I didn't understand. The question was so untethered to the moment I didn't even ask what he meant.

"You need to look into his insurance situation. I doubt he has anything but VA benefits."

"I think you might be right about that," I said. "Why are you bringing it up now?"

"I've always thought the best way to stop worrying about the dead is to make sure the living are taken care of." Billy turned and without saying anything more walked back to his SUV. He started the engine, then sat there for a few moments as if waiting for something.

It wasn't until he put his emergency lights on and drove away that I realized I'd missed a chance to fix some things for both of us.

* * * *

I was in Kirbyville on my way back to the hospital when I changed my mind. Or, I thought about changing it. First, I pulled over to find the number, then called. It took a couple of transfers to get to the nurses' station outside Orson's room. When I connected it was the same nurse who had lent me the book. After I told her who I was, I asked why she was still there.

"Working a double," she said. "Gotta pay those bills."

"I've been thinking about that," I said. I ignored the pang of guilt that reminded me I had not thought at all about it until Billy had asked. "I'm going to need to talk to someone about my uncle's insurance and bills."

"Accounting won't be open until 8:00 a.m. They can help."

"I'm a little out of my depth here," I admitted.

"Take your time," she said. "These are the worst circumstances for making important decisions. You want the best for your family, but other people will be looking at costs. It will be up to you to keep a clear head and fight for him."

"I'll make sure he gets the best of everything."

"I hope you can." There was an ominous sincerity in what she said.

"I'm sorry I haven't asked before. What's your name?"

"Julia."

"If my uncle was awake you would have told me by now, wouldn't you, Julia?"

"Yes."

"May I ask a favor?"

"I've already read a chapter to him," she said, her voice much brighter. "I should be able to get another one in before I go."

"Thank you," I said. "It sounds like he's in good hands."

I tucked my phone away and spun the back tires into a U-turn. Taney is a large rural county cut through with lakes and few bridges. Forward or back was about the same distance on the big loop of 76, 65, and 160 highways. Turning around and going back through Forsyth allowed me to take a detour back to Rockaway Beach and Orson's dock.

I went there to trade trucks. My big GMC was covered with snow and still more was falling. It took a few minutes to get it warm and the piled flakes swept from the windshield. Once that work was done I looked out over the black hole of Lake Taneycomo. Something was missing. It took a moment but I realized it was the dock itself. I had never seen it dark at night. Uncle Orson always kept the string of clear bulbs burning—the dock looked like a party waiting for fishermen returning home even at the latest hour. Darkness never looked so mournful to me.

I went to the gangway and unlocked the gate. There were no prints in the snow. No one was fishing in that weather. The bait shop door was locked too. I let myself in and hit the lights.

It was my plan to turn on the strings of lights that illuminated the outside of the dock and boat slips then leave. I couldn't. Too much needed to be done. Blood still stained the floor. I scrubbed it briefly then resolved to buy some paint.

Other chores were easier. Floaters needed seining out of the live bait wells. A rack of sugary snacks, mostly MoonPies, Twinkies, and Cherry Mash, was spilled. A bucket of unboxed crankbaits had been dumped, too. The floor between the swimming bait and worm cooler was littered with little treble-hooked booby traps.

When things were tolerable, I headed for the door, then stopped. I thought about a drink and was surprised that it wasn't a longing for whiskey. The old soda cooler was chugging away. That's where I went.

I grabbed an orange soda, then hesitated. I put my hand back in and pulled out a grape and a root beer. The orange I opened. I stuck the other two bottles into my coat pocket and headed back to the truck.

* * * *

With nothing more than hope and a hunch I found Billy. He was parked in the bare-tree overgrowth off the trail that led into Sissy Fisher's land. I followed tracks in the snow to where he turned off. In the headlights I could see smooth snow ahead. I killed the lights and turned.

Billy's SUV was stopped in a tangle of grapevine and on top of a bent-over hedge apple. I parked right behind him, then carried the two sodas to his passenger door like a neighbor coming to visit.

The door was unlocked. Billy didn't look at me as I sat. He did look when I held up the bottles of pop.

"Kind of cold for that, isn't it?" he asked.

"No one's going to force you."

"Give me the root beer." He looked at the lid when I handed the bottle over. "Did you bring an opener?"

"No reason to. You always have one with you."

"Always so sure of everything?" He reached to his hip and pulled a multi-tool from the case on his belt.

I held up my bottle as he unfolded the tool and turned out the blade with the opener. Billy popped my top then his own.

"Just you," I answered.

"Am I so predictable?"

"Yes."

He laughed. It seemed to be more at himself than at what I'd said. It wasn't a happy sound. "I guess that's how you knew where I'd be."

"You're not like me."

"What's that supposed to mean?"

"If I'd shot an old friend...I would be drinking. Or wrapped up in fighting the urge."

"And me?"

"You're one of those healthy, mentally sound guys. You don't mope or drink. I knew you would be out—somehow finding a way to work your way forward."

"I sound pretty boring."

"Sometimes."

He laughed again. It was a soft chuckle more in his body than his voice. He lifted the root beer in toast. We clinked our bottles.

"Can you even see anything from here?" I asked once he took a drink.

"Depends on the wind and how thick the snow is." He pointed out the windshield. "Mostly you can see the black shape of the trailer."

I peered out, searching the darkness for something blacker within it. There was a long rectangle at the bottom of the hill in a clearing. "What are you waiting for?"

Billy shrugged. "Lights, I guess. Then I thought I'd see who was there."

"Anyone coming in would see your tire tracks."

"Mine would have been gone soon. It's yours they'll see."

I took a drink of my grape soda without answering.

Billy laughed again. That time it was genuine and at my expense. "No worries. There is another track into where the trailer sits. It's had more traffic. I think that's the primary driveway."

"You think you're pretty smart, don't you?"

Billy laughed again. Before it turned too sad he stopped and said, "If I was smart, I would have handled this whole thing differently. More people would be alive and unhurt."

"I'm not sure how much smart has to do with it," I said. "Bad things happen."

"They do. Bad things. Bad people. Bad—really damn bad decisions."

I didn't have anything to say to that. What could I say and what good would it do? We both remained quiet. The chill got deeper in the vehicle, boosted by the mood and cold sodas.

"Screw it," Billy finally said. He turned his root beer up and drank the whole thing down. When the bottle was empty he set it aside and opened the door. "Let's go."

"Where?"

"Where do you think?" He got out. "Are you coming?" Billy took off, tromping through the snow and denuded woods right toward the black spot at the bottom of the hill.

I followed.

The dark shape resolved into a mobile home as we got closer. It was an older single-wide with a built-on bump out. The skirting was haphazard. The roof was penetrated by a stovepipe. There was no smoke.

"What do you think?" Billy asked when we stopped at the edge of the clearing.

"I think it's a bad idea."

"We have a warrant."

"Got that in your pocket, do you?"

"I can get it here if we need it."

"Just saying, 'if we need it,' shows we're not here to serve a warrant and execute a lawful search."

"Since when are you a stickler for the rules?"

"What I am isn't the point."

"Fair enough." Billy strode forward. His feet kicked mounds of snow as he went straight for the trailer. He stopped at the bottom of the loose cinder blocks that served as stairs.

All the prints on the steps were filled in by new snow. No one had come through the front door that night.

"What do you want to do?" I asked when I caught up.

Billy pulled his weapon and climbed the stack of bricks.

I pulled my 9mm. I held it two-handed and pointed at the ground, ready to go when he breached.

He didn't. Billy hesitated, examining the door, its knob and the opening. There was no storm door. Snow was drifted over the threshold. He knelt and brushed away the drift. "Look at this."

I climbed up to the porch for a better view.

Billy stood and used the toe of his boot to point at something sticking out from the base of the door.

"What is it?" I asked. In the dark I couldn't see much except a shiny spot on the white aluminum skin of the door.

"It's the end of a bolt. Someone drilled it out and mounted something to the bottom of the door."

"A security chain?"

"Down there?" Billy holstered his weapon. Then he pulled the multi-tool from his belt. "Whatever it is can't be good," he said as he shaped the tool into pliers. He used the pointed end to grip the nut securing the bolt, and turned. It didn't take much. The nut came loose. Billy finished screwing it free with his fingers. Once it was clear he held up the nut and a small washer for me to look at. "New," he said. "No rust."

"How can you see that?"

"I can feel it." He opened up his tool and pulled a long, thin punch blade. Putting the tip of the blade to the end of the bolt, he pushed. When he was satisfied the hole was clear, he stood and swapped the tool for his pistol. "Ready?" he asked.

He didn't wait for an answer. Billy gripped the knob and turned. It was unlocked. He led with his weapon and used his toe to ease the door open. "Have your flashlight?"

"The wonder tool doesn't have a flashlight?" I pulled mine out, holding it with my left hand. My right hand gripped my pistol and sat crossed over my left wrist. The light was blue-white, cold as the air in the filthy trailer.

"Down here." Billy pointed to the floor.

There was an eyebolt lying on the tattered shag carpet. Still linked to it was a hook, onto which was tied a thick monofilament line.

"See the hook?" Billy said. "When leaving, you can hold the door open just enough to put it over the eyebolt. When you come back, you can get your finger in enough to unhook it. But if you don't know it's there…"

We both entered the room with small, careful steps. Once we were inside, the flashlight beam found the other end of the fishing line. It was tied to a bit of emery paper that was tented over a bundle of stick matches and made tight with a rubber band. The matches were stuck in the mouth of a five-gallon gas can and secured with electrical tape.

"A booby trap," I said.

"Or an evidence cleaner," Billy said. "Maybe both. Open the door and the paper is pulled away. The rubber band makes sure it stays tight and gives enough friction to strike the match heads. That gas would go up pretty quick."

I shone my flashlight around the room. The paneling sagged. The furniture, what there was of it, came from another century. There was a couch and a chair covered in gold velour. They faced an ancient Zenith console TV with foil-wrapped rabbit ears. The kitchen was avocado-green appliances and orange wallpaper.

"Or maybe they just didn't want anyone seeing the '70s decor."

I kept looking through the dark trailer. In case the switches might be booby-trapped too, and to keep from warning anyone approaching, we left the lights off. Billy cut the matches from the neck of the gas can then tossed it out into the snow.

The bathroom was beige and moldy. I bypassed it and went for the two bedrooms at the back. The smaller one was filled with old tools, mostly chainsaws and axes. The master held an unmade bed. Two things stood out. Hanging over the edge of the sagging mattress was a lacy and expensive-looking bra. Draped over the bedpost was a necklace of silver squash flowers. I didn't think it was much of a jump to assign ownership of both to Sissy Fisher.

"Anything?" Billy asked from over my shoulder.

"Sissy's been here," I said.

"She owns the place."

"Ownership isn't the issue." I cast the flashlight beam around the walls and on the floor. There were piles of glossy magazines from the state tourism board and Branson chamber of commerce. There was one country music magazine lying open to a profile of Rose Sharon. It had a headline that proclaimed, "Going Places." "Do you think it could be as simple as Sissy being jealous of Rose's success?"

"No," Billy answered. "I don't think there's anything simple or even sensible about any of this."

Chapter 20

We closed the trailer door, then slogged over our own tracks back to Billy's waiting SUV.

When the engine was running and the heater turned all the way up, Billy said, "No point in staying here, I guess."

"I know where Lawson is," I said.

"You do?"

"Ever since I saw Sissy's bra hanging on his bed."

"I don't follow."

"You remember how angry Hosea Fisher was in your office?"

"Angry. Not entirely surprised."

"Not at all, I'm thinking." I rubbed my hands together over the vent. "He wanted his own lawyer. Do you think he's staying in the same house with Sissy now?"

"I wouldn't be."

"How do you want to handle it?" I asked. "Get everyone back together and storm the house? Or the two of us?"

Billy stared out the windshield. It seemed he was considering my question. But when he turned to me he said, "I'm sorry."

"For what?"

"I should have told you from the first, it was me with you in the back of that Humvee."

That was the last thing I expected or wanted to hear at the moment. "Is this the time for that conversation?"

"What do you think, I'm going to get mushy and you're going to miss your chance at Lawson? Or would you rather I never talk about it at all?"

"Mushy?"

"You know what I mean."

I looked at my hands. "Yes—I do."

"We've been a part of each other's lives for a while now."

"You've saved my life in more ways than one."

"You're a woman worth fighting for."

"That's—" I turned back to look at him. Billy's bare gaze was waiting. Caught in his eyes, I hesitated. Then I looked out the window, expecting to see the snow. There was only my own reflection in the glass. "That's probably the best thing anyone's ever said to me."

"No, it's not."

"Why?"

"Because I don't think I have that kind of fight left in me."

"Oh," was all I could think to say. My mind teetered. Billy was the one person not an old man who I was truly connected to. He was my tether to the real world and a literal lifeline. I had seen myself swimming away from him, but never imagined he would be taken out of my grasp. "What's changed?"

"Nothing. That's the problem, isn't it?"

Neither of us said anything for a moment, then Billy opened his door. "I've got to…" He thumbed back, pointing into the darkness. "Too much coffee and soda."

He climbed from the SUV and closed the door. I could see him in the mirror walking off toward my truck. I closed my eyes and concentrated on breathing without crying.

I can't say how long it was before the door opened, but Billy had changed his attitude. "Alright," he said, settling into the seat. "You want to do this?"

"The only thing I really want to do is sleep for a week, then wake up to find these few days were a bad dream."

"You don't have to go," he said. "I can handle things alone."

"You're not getting rid of me that easy."

"I never thought I would." His eyes looked a little manic. I thought he was going to laugh.

"Are you sure you're in the right frame of mind?" I asked.

"No putting off a bad job," he answered. "I'll lead the way with my lights on. Think you can keep up?"

"I can keep up." I opened my door and dropped into the snow. "Are you sure you're up to this? It's been a long few days."

"It has been." Billy's eyes settled. He smiled and it was that warm, genuine smile that I always counted on. "You better get going. I'm not going to wait on you." He dropped the transmission into reverse.

I shut the door and went to my own truck.

As soon as I cleared the back of the SUV, Billy started backing up. He twisted the wheel and all four tires gripped. They churned the snow, driving the vehicle over small trees. After being in the darkness so long, his brake and back-up lights seemed like fireworks bursting too close.

As I climbed into my own cab, Billy turned on his emergency light bar. The skeletons danced with their shadows on bone-white snow.

I started my truck.

Billy was already behind me, cutting his wheels sharply to back onto the invisible path of dirt.

In my rearview mirror I could see the SUV's white back-up lights go out. The vehicle rolled a few feet forward and stopped.

I didn't wait for the heat. I popped the GMC's transmission into reverse and pressed the gas. The truck moved, but at an awkward angle. It fought my steering. I stopped and tried again with the same result. Hitting the gas harder only made the problem worse.

I got out of the truck to see if I could find a problem. Billy drove away up the path to the highway. Through the trees I saw his lights, rotating red and blue and flashing white strobes, diminish. They were quickly gone.

I pulled out my flashlight. My right front tire was almost flat.

I crouched and looked closer. The cap was off the valve stem.

Billy.

I couldn't find a hole. The stem was intact. He'd simply let the air out. I imagined him thinking I would have to call for help or wrestle for an hour changing the tire in the snow. I had another idea. In the compartment behind the back seat I kept emergency supplies. It took a few minutes to dig through the flares and chains and stand-up reflectors. In the very back, of course, was what I needed. Flat fixers are cans of compressed air with a sticky sealant to plug tire leaks. I had a two-pack.

It took both cans and fifteen, cold, angry minutes, but I got the tire to a drivable pressure.

On the slick, snow-packed asphalt I realized that "drivable" was a generous assessment. I gave so much of my attention to keeping the truck traveling straight that I neglected to call into dispatch. Billy needed backup.

I finally thought to call it in when the county blacktop gave way to the suburban roads that wound through the Fishers' neighborhood. Those streets were untreated and thick with drifts. There was no doubting the new tire tracks in the snow were Billy's. I navigated by staying in his path and pulled out my phone. My hands were still stiff and cold from working to fill my tire. The touch screen wouldn't even respond until I put a fingertip in my mouth to warm it. When it did respond, I punched the emergency button. When the 911 operator picked up, I told her to send all available units. As an additional thought, I told her to wake Calvin Walker and get him back on duty and out here.

I dropped the phone in the seat and concentrated on staying in Billy's tracks.

I hadn't stopped being angry. Maybe I had begun to understand. Billy had always walked a fine line between protecting me from my own worst impulses and supporting my best ones. More than anyone, he understood the line was blurry in my eyes. He would never have shamed me by ordering me away or telling me to my face that I couldn't handle Lawson.

I decided I wouldn't shame him by kicking his ass in public. It would be a private exercise.

Anger and resentment went out the window when I rounded the last bend. Billy's SUV was parked at a sharp angle cutting across the yard and driveway. The emergency lights rotated in a garish blue-red wash that colored the white night. The clear strobes were bright shots of light that froze every movement into a jerky old-movie stutter.

Caught, center frame, in brutal combat were E. Lawson and Billy. Standing on the porch, clutching at a thin gown, was Sissy.

The most startling part of the entire scene was the change in Sissy Fisher. She looked smaller without her costumes. The bruises on her face and bare arms diminished her as well.

I slid to a stop in the yard, my headlights focused like hot spots on Sissy. Her hands were clutched tightly under her breasts and where they pulled the fabric tight, more contusions showed through the thin white cloth.

For the first time I felt sorry for Sissy Fisher. But the only way to help her was to get Lawson into custody.

Billy was doing a good job. But it hadn't started that way. The fact that Billy wasn't holding the bigger man at gunpoint was the obvious problem. Billy's weapon wasn't on his belt either. Lawson had caught him by surprise and disarmed him.

I was not at the same disadvantage.

I pulled my 9mm as I climbed down from the truck. I stalked through the snow, leading with it in both hands. Using my best command voice I shouted, "Lawson! Stop where you are. Down on the ground."

He stopped.

That was the moment it was clear that Billy wasn't doing as well as I thought.

Lawson's huge right hand was still gripping Billy by the trapezius. His left was fisted and poised to strike.

Billy was looking ragged. His breath was coming in deep gulps through his bloody mouth. His left arm was dangling with an extra bend in the middle of the forearm. Despite Lawson's notice of my weapon, the force of the grip on Billy's shoulder didn't look to be letting up.

Billy grimaced silently as he was forced lower.

"Release him! Step away!" I commanded.

Lawson opened his fisted left hand and lowered it. At the same time, he grinned as if the fight was all in fun.

"Step away!" I commanded again.

His hand slid down Billy's shoulder and arm.

"Don't!" Billy tried to pull his arm away. He didn't make it.

Lawson clenched Billy's injured arm in crowbar-like fingers and lifted. Billy looked as if he needed to scream. He didn't.

With Billy's body blocking my shot, Lawson grinned even wider. "A broken arm is a painful thing," he gloated.

I raised my aim. Lawson was too big to hide entirely behind Billy. "A bullet between the eyes isn't," I said. "But it's a terminal thing."

Lawson's expression faltered. Then his grin returned.

Billy shouted, "Behind—"

He was cut off by the cracking sound of a small-caliber shot. The bullet came so close to the side of my face I heard the buzzing flight and felt a tingling heat.

I turned.

Sissy was holding a small automatic. It was still aimed at me.

I fired a single shot that burst through the bony chest above her right breast. She fell back, then bounced against the door before she tumbled forward. The last drop was slow—as if gravity didn't work the same on her.

"Katrina!" Billy shouted another warning.

It was too late. Lawson hit my back like a windshield hits a june bug. My weapon flew. My face plowed a furrow in the frozen powder.

I got up, scrambling for my pistol. I found it. I turned in a crouch, hoping the 9mm would function. Billy was already staggering toward me. Sissy was in the snow gasping for lost breath. My truck was on the road, its taillights fading.

Lawson was getting away.

"Get my kit," Billy shouted. He dragged himself past me and to Sissy.

I slogged to the SUV, still dizzy with the new kinds of pain invading every bone.

"Go after him," Billy said when I dropped the kit beside Sissy.

She was looking cyanotic. Her breath was quick and shallow, like she was stealing each one from the air. When she exhaled, the vapor puffed in little clots of wind that lost their heat almost instantly.

Billy jerked the med kit open and grabbed what he needed without looking.

"Are you sure?" I asked.

"What can you do here? Backup and an ambulance are coming. Take the SUV."

"Can you help Sissy?"

"She's bleeding into the pleural cavity. Her lungs can't expand properly. I have to drain the blood."

"I can—"

"What? Put in a chest tube?" He looked up at me, just for a second. Just long enough for me to know he had his part under control. And he trusted me to handle mine. "Go."

I didn't wait to be talked out of it. I did stop at the vehicle's open door to clear my weapon.

Chapter 21

Lawson's fresh tracks slalomed in the unplowed road. They led the same direction I had come in until the county highway. There they turned south. For a few miles I sped faster than I knew him to be able. Every so often I saw the lights of my big GMC ahead. I was closing the gap.

Around one bend there was a flashing of yellow emergency lights. Headlights pointed from a ditch into the sky. A tow truck was off the road. I didn't think it was an accident.

I stopped to ask the driver what had happened.

"I was forced off by some son of a bitch in a pickup," he shouted over his engine and mine. "He did it on purpose. Came right at me."

"Are you alright?"

"I'm fine," he said. "We'll see about the truck. You after that guy?"

"Damn right I am," I answered, then drove on.

I used the vehicle radio to call in my position and where to find the tow truck operator. I asked for anyone not helping Billy to back me up. On a night with a deep winter weather hazard, that didn't leave many.

The road constricted as I got farther from the main towns. I followed the erratic tire trenches left in the snow until I met a snowplow coming the other way on the top of a hill. I gave way to let it pass. When I started moving again, the tracks I had followed were mostly eradicated.

I knew there was an unmarked farm road ahead. If I was trying to evade someone it was the way I would go.

I slowed.

The plow had mounded slush over the road entrance. Beyond it there were tracks.

I knew where this road led and I assumed Lawson did too. I knew for a fact he'd been there before.

Sure enough, at the next intersection he'd turned right. That set him on the same hilly road that went directly in front of where Rose Sharon had been murdered.

People tend to romanticize crime. It's a way of giving reason to the unexplainable. Most of us can't fathom the black morass required to allow a soul to kill or brutalize. We want there to be rules even for those who show no connection to humanity.

I knew better through experience. I never for a moment thought that Lawson was on that road due to any deep psychological relationship with Rose's death. It was much simpler than that. The hills and valleys of the road were dangerous at the best of times. In nighttime snow, it was like a bobsled track lined with trees.

The first hill had an easy rise that I took at a slowing coast. On the other side I saw a raked skid that slipped over into the ditch before straightening out. Lawson had lost speed and all the advantage he thought he'd gained by ignoring caution. I could see his taillights sinking over the next rise.

I pushed hard again, knowing that the SUV with four good tires had the edge over the truck with a front end out of balance.

The next hill was steeper on both sides. The rise was sharp and the top was narrow. I wasn't going fast enough to catch air, but the SUV did lose traction. The steering went loose and the back end came around to the right.

I slid down the hill sideways.

At least I stayed on the road. Ahead of me, on the up side of the valley, Lawson was grinding his tires in the ditch. All four of them were spitting snow and mud.

I turned the wheel to no effect. I let off the gas and waited. Eventually some magic formula of traction and speed was reached. The SUV righted and I hit the gas again.

I hit it hard.

This time when I topped the hill I was going dangerously fast. I caught up to Lawson. My headlights illuminated him in the truck cab, furiously working at the wheel for control.

He got it, or got enough. We didn't collide. No thanks to either of us. We both went sideways. The vehicles spun around an invisible point of gravity until we were alongside each other skidding to the bottom.

Both of us were pointed more to the fencerows than the road. I saw the GMC shudder with effort and all the tires again spinning rooster tails of snow. He twisted the wheel my direction. I thought he was trying to ram me.

He missed.

My tires slid off the slick pavement and onto the dirt shoulder. The change pulled me around and toward the ditch. At the same time, the power he was applying spun Lawson's back end around. He ended up facing the right direction and running up hill.

I ended up facing backward and sinking into the ditch. There wasn't even time to curse. I dropped the SUV into 4x4 low and punched it. It grabbed traction and lurched forward. I kept the gas down and whipped the wheel over.

The transmission groaned unhappily as I kept the pressure up. When I was facing the right way I stopped long enough to move up to 4x4 hi. My foot was on the floor still when I hit the hilltop. I jerked it away when my hood dropped forward on the deep hill and I saw my truck at the bottom. It was stopped sideways. It had slid into a deep drift. Snow was piled up to the window on the far side.

Lawson couldn't get out his door. He had climbed over the seat and out the passenger side. The door was still standing open.

I got the SUV stopped without hitting my own truck. It wasn't pretty.

The radio squawked. Dispatch asked my 20.

I gave my position and warned them about the jam-up. Before getting out of the SUV, I pulled my weapon. Once more I checked it. When I stepped out, I left my coat open so I could get to the extra magazines and my telescoping baton if I needed to.

All night long the wind had been sharp as broken glass. It died. The air cleared of the crystalline specks that had been swirling.

The lights on my truck were still on. I left the light bar on the sheriff's vehicle going as well. I stood in a dancing pool of light that made the darkness beyond seem that much deeper.

I walked with my weapon extended, taking a long circle around the front of my truck. There was nothing on the far side but footprints.

I followed them up the hill.

Lawson had gone straight up the center of the road. I edged over to the shoulder. Under the snow, dirt gave a better grip for my boots.

I knew it was a good choice when, near the top of the hill, I saw where he had fallen. There was a muddle of prints where he had struggled to his feet.

I approached the top, trying to recall how many of the hills we had passed. *Is this the last one? Is there one more?* I paused to take a breath. It was like breathing razor blades. Below me, the lights on the vehicles made an almost cheerful scene.

I didn't linger.

It was the final rise. At the top I could see the gentle straightaway slope. And in the distance were the lights of parked cars.

It had never occurred to me that the barbed wire memorial for Rose Sharon would have visitors in this weather.

A shadow moved between the distant lights and my eyes. Lawson.

I would have run if I could. My body refused the order and my lungs laughed at the thought. So I marched, high-stepping slow but steady. I could only hope that Lawson was as tired as I was.

It seemed futile. The man was a beast.

As I approached I heard voices. One bellowed and cursed. The others were meek objections. Kids.

Someone, a girl, screamed. In pain or terror, I couldn't tell. It didn't matter. I broke through my own body's resistance and ran. It was still more of a high-step jog. It got me there as Lawson was folding himself into the same little beat-up car I had first seen the day this all began.

"Stop!" I commanded. The force of the word tore at my cold throat. "Get out of the car! You kids move away."

The young people complied, moving away from the car and closer to the paper flowers and saint candles. Lawson didn't. He shoved the key in the car's ignition and twisted.

The starter gave one feeble turn then died.

I would have smiled if I had it in me.

Lawson got out of the car. He looked over at the knot of kids huddled around the shrine.

"Run!" I screamed at them. "Don't let him get close to you."

They scattered into the surrounding darkness. Some made it to cars that had working batteries.

E. Lawson and I stood alone by the memorial. He looked it over, then spat.

"I never understood shit like this," he said. His speech was still a mess, but I understood the words. It helped if I didn't look at his mouth. "A pile of trash by the road. It's supposed to mean something? It's supposed to make anyone feel better for being dead?"

"You're under arrest," I said.

He raised his hands. "Then come put the cuffs on me." His smile was a challenge and a dismissal.

"On the ground, hands behind your back."

"I don't think so."

"I didn't either."

He took a small step forward.

"You need to stay where you are." I didn't command. I didn't even try to make it a warning. It was simply information.

"What are you going to do?" he asked. "Shoot an unarmed man?" He stepped again.

"Yes," I said.

He hesitated. "I believe you would."

"I'd just as soon you didn't believe me. Come on ahead."

"You're a wild one. Frozen inside—deeper than all this weather. Harder than heartwood." Lawson eased forward again.

"You're coming," I said. "Good."

"I don't think you're the killer you claim." He stepped. "I think you're just another frigid bitch in a cold, cold world."

"I'm glad to hear that."

"I called you a bitch—you're glad to hear it?" Another step. His arms sagged slightly.

"I'm glad you think I'm not a killer."

"Why?"

"It means you're going to try."

"Oh?" Lawson looked around like he was playing Simon Legree on ice. "Try what?"

He was a cartoon villain with one note. All his power was muscle and threat. He could no more put together intricate thoughts than a spider could spin an atom bomb.

"Sissy was in charge all along, wasn't she?" I asked.

"She was in charge every time I beat her down like a dog. She was in charge every time I took her into my bed and spread her legs." He lowered his arms a fraction more.

"She was afraid of you. I don't doubt that. But she made the plans. She had the needs that you fulfilled."

"Fuck you."

"How long has she been using you?"

"You don't know anything."

"How did you feel when she went home to a husband who gave her a nice house and glamorous job?"

"How did he feel? How do you think he felt when she went home with my marks and my smell on her? Do you think he ever imagined her on her knees? What do you think—"

"Did she ever tell you Donny was yours?"

"Not true. The little faggot was his."

"She took a DNA test. Donny is your son."

"You're lying." Lawson's hands were down and clenched by his sides. He crouched with one foot back, ready to spring.

"That's gotta dig like barbed wire in your head," I said. "She used you to build her little musical troop and didn't even tell you one was your own son."

I kept watching Lawson, holding my 9mm in the two-handed grip. My stance was open with my feet set wide. My finger was on the trigger, already applying a few ounces of pressure. I was ready.

Lawson dropped his hands. He stood straight, then turned his head to the left so he was looking at me with the one good eye. It was narrow with suspicion. "All that can't be." He sounded as if he was trying to convince himself more than me.

"Think about it, Lawson. Whose idea was it to kill Matthew and Cheryl Sharon? Who sent Levi to you and kept the girl for herself?"

"Those were things I did for her. To make her happy. She wanted her own kind of Partridge Family like on TV."

"What did you get out of it?"

"Sissy was mine—is mine." His voice had lost its strength. Lawson's one clear eye filled with doubt. "It was about stickin' it to Hosea. Taking his trees and his precious money."

"Think about it, Lawson. You spent a lifetime killing for her—running her errands—and you never even knew what it was all about."

"See, that's where you're wrong." Lawson nodded his head, then reached up to push the blowing hair out of his face. "It was over. And it was me she wanted to be with. I was taking a lot of trees. She was taking cash from Hosea and the theater. We were running off and doin' it together."

"Why was it over?"

"The boy and the girl. Both of 'em screwed us."

"What are you talking about?"

"Sissy had papers made up for a whole Rose and Donny show. Then the girl started pullin' away and gettin' too big. Sissy told Donny to fix it."

"Fix it?"

"Fuck her. Beat her. Marry her. Whatever it took."

The words were hot coals poured down my throat. My chest caught fire. My gut boiled. "Donny?"

"I swear to God the boy cried more than the bitch did."

"Donny is gay."

"What do you think Sissy was trying to fix?" He looked at me with new intensity.

I got the weird feeling he was seeing me through the ruined lens of his clouded left eye.

"Why did she kill Rose?"

"The girl was already singin' about it. How long till she was talkin'? She was friendly with the new sheriff. She had to go."

My arms were shaking. My spread legs were trembling. It wasn't the time or the cold. Lawson looked like he might actually be spent.

It was possible I could talk him into cuffs if I kept taking it easy.

To hell with that.

"Get on your knees!" I commanded.

Instantly, Lawson clenched his hands into sledgehammer-size fists. He crouched again, ready to strike.

Good.

"Down! Put your hands behind your back."

"I don't take orders from a bitch."

"Then one of us has a problem."

Lawson lunged. He charged like a one-man stampede.

I let him come.

He kicked snow into the clear air. When he was close enough, I saw death and understanding in his eye.

I emptied my magazine into his chest.

E. Lawson was already dead when his body fell on top of me. I rolled with the fall so he didn't pin me in bloody snow. But I didn't get up until Calvin Walker arrived. He offered his hand and helped me pull my legs from under Lawson.

Because of the blocked road, deputies had taken the long way around to reach us. Calvin apologized for the time it took. I told him everything was all right. Then asked if he had a lighter.

He dug a book of matches out of his pocket and handed them over.

I made my way through the tramped snow and crowd of deputies' vehicles to the small shrine lined up along the barbed wire.

Two of the glass saint candles had gone out. I lit each one and replaced them in the snowdrift.

Epilogue

Sissy Fisher survived. She lived to wish she hadn't. Landis Tau did a great job trying to push all responsibility onto E. Lawson. It simply didn't fit. The worst part of it was the obligatory parading of her abuse at the hands of the man she manipulated for years. Maybe what she did was defense against a bad situation she had gotten into. Maybe it was part of her plan all along. Deeper truths often get lost in facts. And the facts were that she had coordinated a nightmare life for three young people all to satisfy some weird fantasy of a family band and record deal.

In the end, it was her own son and his guilt that burned down all the excuses. Sissy was sentenced to spend the rest of her life up in Chillicothe. She was lucky to get the new prison. Not so lucky to be slender and pretty and the famous, rich bitch who murdered a girl many of the inmates identified with. Donny admitted to his part, which included raping Rose. He served five and got out on good behavior. The wound in his throat made sure he never sang again.

Tom Dugan testified as well. He had been harassing and stalking Rose. He turned out to have known what Donny did. He used a young girl's shame and pain to pressure her into sleeping with him. That was a record he would never be able to hide from.

Chuck Benson made it out of the hospital in a few days. Billy made his assistant sheriff position permanent. Mostly I think to keep him out of trouble. I suggested to them that Deputy Calvin Walker needed more responsibility in the department. Billy bumped him up to fill our open detective position.

Clare fixed the damage to the bar and Moonshines quietly reopened after a month.

Uncle Orson didn't bounce back as quickly as we hoped. It took him a week to wake up. It took another several weeks for him to walk. Insurance would have been an issue if Orson didn't have a rich niece. I paid his bills and hired Julia Grieves away to be his personal nurse. Her job turned out to be reading to him as much as nursing him.

Levi and Rose were buried together at a small cemetery in Hollister. A plot for her had been donated at a larger cemetery in the Branson city limits. Billy was the one who pushed hardest to keep them together. The service was held at the Ozarks Star Road Theater. It was attended by a famous Nashville artist who already had a huge hit with her version of Rose's song. Tears flowed freely when Billy took the stage and played his guitar to accompany her. Together they sang:

There's a pew in the church where I carved your name
It was a prayer written out and cast away
The liberties you've taken are the heart of pain
Now there's nothing left that you can say
Now there's nothing left that you can say
Hearts gave way to hands and rage
And your rage turned my blue eyes black
I wrote it all out and I burned the page
But your promises kept coming back
Bad promises keep coming back

You came and stole what was mine to give
You took a shot at my open heart
I tried to keep a secret place for love to live
But you broke me down and took it all apart
When you took what wasn't yours
You took what wasn't yours

You had to show me what it means to be a man
But you couldn't stand in the light
With a lie on your lips and harm in your hand
You said love was a thief in the night
You make love like a thief in the night

There's a place on my heart where you carved your name

It's a spot that's gone cold and dead
The promises you made have been all in vain
Life is nothing more than the tears I've shed
Let me show you all the tears I've shed

You came and stole what was mine to give
You took a shot at my open heart
I tried to keep a secret place for love to live
But you broke me down and took it all apart
When you took what wasn't yours
You took what wasn't yours

* * * *

It was a clear day and almost warm when I was restored to duty. The snow was gone and the blue skies were reflected in the lake waters. Spring was a real possibility in the world. I had used the time off to get Uncle Orson the care he needed and to do a lot of thinking. There were so many questions I had avoided for years. They couldn't be ignored any longer. The only thing Orson had was the dock and bait shop. He couldn't do all that work alone and I couldn't see taking it away from him.

There were other issues—other questions. I had options.

What do I want?

Who ever heard of a cop with a multimillion-dollar bank account?

Money has nothing to do with it, does it? For me, the answer came in the form of a debt to be paid.

Deputy David Webb called in his favor a month after he'd helped me locate Jenifer Perry. By then I was already like a coyote in a trap, ready to chew my own leg off to get back to some kind of active work. David didn't have to ask me twice.

He was tracking a boy named Gary Wingo who David believed was in Taney county. He called me because the boy's parents refused to cooperate. The school had called for a safety check when Gary stopped showing up and the parents turned belligerent. David needed me to quietly check the Leviticus Camp. Its real name was The Leviticus Sanctuary—The Rule and Rod of God. The walled and gated property was a dozen acres of Christian reeducation with a history of blindsiding kids and locking them away to pray away, or if that didn't work, exorcise away the gay.

It was a touchy issue. It was hard to call it an abduction because the parents were aware; they had even paid for it. On the other hand, Gary was seventeen and openly gay. He had obviously not chosen gay "conversion therapy." I found him, but there wasn't a lot I could do for him as a cop. I knew someone who could do something. And I kind of figured that Landis Tau owed me, too.

Landis and his Midwest Center for Civil Rights jumped right in on Gary's side. So did I. I volunteered to act as investigator on the case and found something no one else had mentioned. Gary was a member of a Buddhist temple near his home in Springfield.

The parents' lawyers cited religious freedom to justify their treatment of Gary. Landis used the same argument to get him released.

Landis and I helped a boy, took a stand for civil rights, and no one got shot or beaten. Gary and his parents even reconciled. I had a lot to think about when Landis asked me to become the full-time investigator for the Center at half my cop pay.

I parked the GMC in the SO's lot and went inside. People smiled and called me over. Some congratulated me on my return to duty. I waved but walked straight to Billy's closed door. I went in without knocking.

Billy was behind his desk. Calvin and Chuck were sitting in the visitors' chairs. All three looked at me like I was crazy. Then Billy smiled.

It was a great smile.

"Get out," I said to the other men.

"What the hell?" Chuck asked.

He had more to say but I said again, "Out."

"Katrina..." Billy said.

I pointed at him. "We have things to talk about." I pointed to the other two. "Get out. This is important."

They went, with confused looks, then hesitated right outside the door. I shut it in their faces.

"What's going on?" Billy asked.

I stepped up to the edge of his desk.

Billy watched me for a second, then said, "You look good." He smiled that perfect smile again.

"The bruises are almost gone. But I still ache like an arthritic old woman."

"You're not that old." He let his smile spread into a grin.

I pulled out my badge and service weapon and dropped them on his desk. "I know what I want."

"What's that?"

It was my turn to smile. I didn't even go around the desk. I put a knee up and crawled on top of it. Papers fell. My badge tumbled to the floor. I kissed him. It was the most honest, genuine kiss of my life.

When it broke, I took a breath and said, "I resign."

Acknowledgments

This is my fourth book about Katrina Williams. I have to admit that it is as much about the region she calls home, the Missouri Ozarks, as it is about her. None of the books would exist without the place or the towns mentioned: Branson, Forsyth, Rockaway Beach, Nixa, and Springfield. They are part of my past and remain with me always. Even though I have fictionalized them, and in many ways depicted them as I remember rather than as they are, I hope I have done them justice.

The Katrina Williams series would not exist without the great people at Lyrical Press, who have worked to make me better and get my books in as many hands as possible. Special thanks go to my editor, Martin Biro.

If you enjoyed *A Killing Secret*, be sure not to miss the previous Katrina Williams novels, including

Sheriff's detective Katrina "Hurricane" Williams confronts deep-rooted hate and greed in the Missouri Ozarks in this riveting police procedural...

What at first appears to be a brush fire in some undeveloped bottom land yields the charred remains of a young African-American man. As sheriff's detective Katrina Williams conducts her inspection of the crime scene, she discovers broken headstones and disturbed open graves in a forgotten cemetery.

As Katrina attempts to sort out a complex backwoods criminal network involving the Aryan Brotherhood, meth dealers, and the Ozarks Nightriders motorcycle gang, she is confronted by the sudden appearance of a person out of her own past who may be involved. And what seems like a clear-cut case of racially motivated murder is further complicated by rumors of hidden silver and dark family histories. To uncover the ugly truth, Katrina will need to dig up past crimes and shameful secrets that certain people would kill to keep buried . . .

A Lyrical Underground e-book on sale now.
Keep reading for a special look!

Chapter 1

Burning is not the best way to dispose of a body. It's hard to get a fire hot enough, long enough, to burn through the layers of fat, muscle, and bone to destroy all the evidence you need gone. It doesn't smell very good either.

Before it ever got to me, the situation had worked through a few preliminary steps. First, the pair of teens who discovered the fire debated calling it in. They had been parking and fooling around in a secluded spot off a rutted dirt track—usually used by fishermen going to the lake. I imagine it was a tough debate among hormones, responsibility, and fear of angry parents. They told me later they would have let the blaze go if the boy's father hadn't been a volunteer fireman.

After a brutally stormy spring, the summer had been hot and dry. Over recent weeks, the Ozarks had fallen into a deep drought. Lake levels were way down, crops were withering, and small fires were whipped into big ones by even the smallest breeze. The boy had been lectured about it so many times, it was impossible for him to pretend ignorance.

After the kids called 911 to report what they believed was a trash fire, deputies and the fire department were dispatched. The boy's father showed up on the pumper. I understand there was a parenting opportunity that involved a little tough love.

That opportunity was probably lost when the embers were raked out and doused. In the center of the smoking pile was a charred lump everyone assumed was a log. When it was hit with direct pressure, the log split open. Under the black surface was pink meat and steaming flesh. That was when they called me.

My phone rang a few minutes shy of two a.m. Late Saturday night—or early Sunday morning—depending on how pedantic you are about that sort of thing. I'm not at all, at least not at that hour. I was in bed, and not yet sleeping because it wasn't my bed.

Every call to my phone rings the same tone except one, the Taney County Sheriff's Department. I knew it was a work call even without the tone. Real life always intrudes whenever I find a bit of peace in my life.

"This is Katrina," I said softly into the phone.

"Who're you whisperin' for?" our jailer asked. He laughed like he actually knew something. It was a thick, rheumy cackle that made me picture the soggy cigar in his jowled face.

I was actually relieved. If he was calling, I might be able to stay in bed. "What do you want, Duck?" His name was Donald Duques, earning him the permanent sobriquet, Donald Duck—always shortened to simply Duck. He laughed again and I became unpleasantly aware of being naked.

"Got a body," he interjected between wet hacks of laughter.

"What?" Given who he was and the old school Ozarks diction, I can be forgiven for thinking he was commenting about my appearance.

I was about to give him some choice thoughts on his manners when he said again, "We got a body. Out on the west side shore of Bull Shoals by Kissee Mills."

Detective Billy Blevins shifted in the sheets behind me. His arm moved against my bare thigh and hip. I was distracted by the warm contact. "What?"

Duck laughed again. "What'd I catch you doin'? Work can't hold your attention?"

"Why are you calling me?"

"I told you—"

"Why you, Duck?"

"Oh," he swallowed the laugh. "Gettin' a little overtime. Workin' weekend overnights on dispatch."

"Then stick to the job at hand, would you? What's the call?"

"Couple 'a kids called in a fire. Calvin called for a detective when the fire department found a body in the brush heap."

"Where?" I stood and broke contact with Billy's arm. My skin immediately regretted the loss.

"That undeveloped bottom land, down the fishing trail that goes off of Hole Road."

"Who's there?"

Duck told me the names of deputies on scene and I started searching for my underthings. They were close by on the floor. Finding them made me think of losing them. I smiled.

"I'll be half an hour," I informed Duck.

"From your place?" He sounded surprised.

"Half an hour," I repeated and broke the connection.

Moonlight through a high window illuminated Billy lying in the sheets. It was a nice sight. I was amazed—and alternately delighted and terrified—by that development in my life. Not as amazed; however, as I was that he'd never woken while I talked on the phone and dressed. Maybe I was projecting. My own sleep was fragile and filled with ghosts. Billy seemed to have the ability to sleep without demons.

He and I had circled each other for years. We were deployed to Iraq at the same time. In the worst moment of my life, Billy appeared for the first time. I don't even know if the memory is real. Everything else about that time is solid and undeniable. I was raped and brutalized by two superior officers. They left me for dead in the blowing brown dust that eddied behind a mud wall. Grain by grain, the dun-colored wind piled a grave on top of me. I pulled myself from the dirt, staggered then crawled to a road. Insurgents found me first. They would have shot me like a rabid dog in a ditch if an Army patrol hadn't shown up. All of that is true. And it's true that a young medic, a corporal, cleaned and stabilized me in the back of a rushing Humvee. There's a little piece of that, the piece I believe but don't know: Billy Blevins was that medic. He's never said and I'm afraid to ask. But I believe.

There were so many reasons why we never should have gotten to this point. I hated giving up any moment of lying naked with him.

Still. . . I'm a cop and the real world was calling.

I kissed Billy and bundled up my clothes. I needed to change. I didn't have anything at his place. Two minutes later, I was outside in my underwear. I held my good clothes and shoes as I opened my truck. You don't dress up for a late night call—in the woods—to investigate a burned body. I tossed the date clothes in the crew seat, then pulled out my old jeans and worst pair of boots. When you've been a rural cop for a while, you're never without disposable clothing. Even though Billy's house was remote and screened by a thick growth of trees, I felt exposed dressing in his drive. I refused to go back in the house. It would be too hard to keep from waking Billy—and that would make me late. I covered quickly.

The night was clear. The day had been so hot that not all of the heat had yet escaped into the bare sky. Before I climbed into the big GMC, I took one more glance at the diamond sky. It always made me think of Bob Dylan.

With the stop for gas and coffee, it took a bit more than thirty minutes to arrive on scene. By then I was wishing I had woken Billy and made him come with me. When I thought about explaining that to the on-duty deputies, I let the wish go out the open truck window.

Deep night in the Ozarks woods was lit up like a Spielberg movie about friendly aliens. Emergency lights and strobes were circling and flashing through a screen of brush and trees. I followed the light show to a rutted mud track between old posts where a gate had once been.

We're a mostly rural county, even on a Saturday night things can be pretty dull after one a.m. Four Sheriff's department cruisers and three fire vehicles were on scene when I parked between scrub oaks. The path was about seventy yards from where the shore line of Bull Shoals Lake was supposed to be. "Supposed to be," because the drought had pushed the shore out another few yards. On higher ground beyond the fence was a housing development adjacent to farm land. Down by the shoreline, it was overgrown and thick with underbrush. The fence row that paralleled the dirt path was clotted with under growth and hedge apple trees. The ground between the lake and the barbed wire fence was private land that had not been redeveloped after the White River was damned. It was freshly cleared, all low weeds burned brown. I could tell the land had been worked before. Around the clearing, there were no original or even second growth trees. All the foliage, oak, and hawthorn—mixed in with hedge apple and coils of grapevine—was no older than I was.

All the activity, the reason I had been called, was centered about a circle, close to the north edge of the clearing.

I was pleased to see that deputies had already put crime scene tape around the burned circle. They illuminated the circle with headlights and spots. I wasn't so pleased to see that one of the volunteer firemen was inside the perimeter.

"Calvin," I shouted at Calvin Walker then pointed to the man within the tape. Calvin is not my biggest fan.

"He's got to make sure the fire is completely dead," he shouted back, "What do you want me to do?"

"I want you to get him out of there unless it's on fire right now," I answered sharply. I wasn't a huge fan of Calvin Walker either.

Calvin went to talk to the fireman. I had another deputy bring me the kids. We had barely gotten started when Calvin shouted again, "Hurricane."

The girl turned from her boyfriend to look me in the face for the first time. "You're her," she said. "Hurricane."

"I'm Detective Katrina Williams."

"But you're the one they call 'Hurricane Katrina'." She had a look of big eyed wonderment. "You kick ass."

"Hurricane!" Calvin shouted with more force.

"You guys stay here," I told the pair, "we have more to go over."

"Check this out," Calvin said as I ducked under the tape. He was standing with the fireman who was leaning on a rake. "This is Cherry," Calvin indicated the fireman. He was an older man, but not as old as he appeared at first. Sometimes life hangs on people in a way that leaves no room for denying the years. His body was lean and hard looking; but in the white wash of headlights and spots, his skin—even that tracked by old blue ink—was thin looking.

"Cherry? Really?" I had to ask.

He gave me a tired look of acceptance, but didn't offer his hand. "Cherry Dando," he said. He examined me with the kind of curiosity that I'd almost gotten used to. "I know you."

"I get that a lot." Shifting my attention back to Calvin I asked, "What have you got?"

"Check it out," Calvin said again pointing into the char on the ground. Everything was black.

"Check what out?"

"Show her," Calvin said to Cherry.

Cherry Dando looked like that was the last thing he wanted to do. He pursed his lips then sucked in his cheeks like he was hoping to find an excuse hidden in his mouth. He didn't. So he reached his rake out and touched the tines down alongside a bit of black shape on burned grass.

I knelt. It wasn't the only shape in the ashes that didn't look like bits of wood. Fishing in my pocket I came up empty. "Either of you have a flashlight?" I asked.

Calvin hit the bone with light. After a second Dando added his. The shape was a scapula, a shoulder bone.

I looked up, then pointed to the larger, black-on-black, shape in the center of the burn circle. Calvin and the fireman turned their lights. The body was intact. It had carbonized on the outside but there were no pieces missing. In the beams of the flashlight it was still steaming.

"There," I said, pointing to the ground under the body. More bones littered the ash. As we swept the burn area with flashlights, we spotted two sets of teeth in lower jaws.

"You think there's any chance this fire could have burned two bodies to the bone and left one intact?" I asked Cherry Dando.

"I look like an expert?"

"Then what are you doing here?"

Dando sucked in his cheeks again. He looked like a man holding something back. "Nope." He sounded more resigned to the answer than confident in it.

"Why?" I pressed.

He sighed. It was the put-upon sound of a kid asked to do a chore with no handy excuse. "See the dark circle?" He outlined the pattern with his flashlight. "It was piled with dry brush. There aren't any big logs at all. Not enough fuel for a long burn. Someone poured gas on a brush pile, set it, and left it."

As soon as he said it, I noticed the scent of gasoline in the air.

"What about around there?" I pointed to the burned area that wasn't as dark.

Dando used his flashlight again to draw out the shape on the ground. It was more of a smudge than a circle. "That's where it caught the grass. If the night was windy, it would'a been a mess—that's for sure."

"Was he alive when it started?" Calvin asked.

"That's for you folks to find out," Dando answered. He turned his head and spit over the tape and didn't turn back.

"Lord, I hope not," Calvin said with genuine feeling in his voice. I was a little less bothered by him.

"Tape up a new perimeter," I said. "Push things out twenty feet that way and this side, all the way out to the truck path. Set up parking over there," I pointed to another clear area on the other side of the road ruts. "I already woke the scene tech as I made the drive. Call him back, tell him to tow the big light rig with him." I turned to Dando. "We'll need you to stick around a while to keep an eye on things. Outside the tape."

He shrugged without looking at me then ducked under the tape.

"Can I keep that?" When he looked I pointed to the rake in Dando's hand.

He stared down at his hand or the tines of the rake—I couldn't tell. He seemed to be giving the request a lot of thought. "I'll need it back."

"I promise."

He put it on the ground and pushed the handle over like he didn't want to get too close to me. Without another word or look, he walked to the firetruck.

I leaned the rake against a scraggly oak, then pulled out my phone to call Chief Benson.

* * * *

An orange-red sun bloomed in the east—giving new life to bleary eyes. Our crime scene was populated with a couple of dozen people by then. The coroner's van was there and waiting with open doors to take in the remains. To one side, Sheriff Benson, Chuck to his friends, was glad-handing with Riley Yates. Riley was one of the sheriff's friends. Almost everyone in the county was. Riley was also a reporter. In that role, he didn't seem so happy with the sheriff. I've heard that conversation before. Being friends didn't mean the sheriff was unprofessional about his job.

With the rising light, I was able to get into my own investigation routine. I retrieved a pencil and pad out of my truck and set to sketching. Photos catch the objective reality of the scene. But I find that, sometimes, the truth of things isn't so objective. It was an old habit that got stronger when I met my husband. Nelson Solomon had been a Marine, and after that a successful artist. When he died, he left me richer in many ways—not the least of which was a better eye for the small parts of a big picture.

I stood by the oak I had leaned the rake against and put the main shapes into the sketch. There was the tape perimeter, three trees, and the push bumper on a cruiser around which the tape was looped. Around the outer edges were tall grasses and weeds. They were all brown and friable from the drought. In the center was a black circle of ash and char. In the middle of that, like a bull's eye in hell, was the burned man's body.

I worked quickly. People were waiting for me to release them to their jobs. Using the side of the soft lead, I made broad shades to fill in the burn circle. With my thumb, I smeared the lines out—smoothing and feathering them from black to grey to almost not there. After that, I used the point and a light touch to draw in the bones.

It wasn't until I had the bones in and compared my sketch to the reality that I noticed what was missing. In the ash were the clear furrows where the rake tines had been pulled. There was something else. Sticks and bits of bark—unconsumed by the fire—were raked out and evenly spread. The bones were scattered widely and—in some cases—covered by ash. They had been given particular attention.

I glanced over and took a look at Fireman Dando—who was standing beside the pumper truck talking with his squad mates. In the rising light, I noticed, for the first time, the close crop of his hair and the corded muscle that I had taken earlier for frail thinness. His thin skin showed the sinew, and the tattoos on his arms highlighted each sharp angle. Even from where I was, it was easy to see the body art was not of the highest quality. It was the kind of old and faded ink you see on retired vets.

To justify my continued staring, I kept sketching the layout of the larger scene. I added Dando at his truck and resolved to hit him with a few pointed questions.

While I drew my notes, a truck barreled up the dirt track. It was an old Dodge, lifted with knobby tires and pipes run out to stacks poking over the top of the cab. The engine snarled. When it passed the fire pumper, but before getting to the spaced out cop cars, the truck slid to a grinding halt. Dust billowed up from the skid and breezed in from the draft. Dangling from the back of the hitch were two huge hex nuts on a chain—truck nuts. Classy.

The driver bounded from the cab before the truck even finished its dieseling death. "You got no right," he shouted. "This is private property. You got no right to be here." He was a big man, wide and strong-looking. His long stride ate up the ground.

Dando bolted forward and tried to slow him down. I saw the two of them exchange quiet, stressed words to no effect. The angry man pushed the fireman aside and kept right on coming.

At the same time the deputies, the sheriff, and I paced in to converge with him.

"Don't think I don't know what's going on," he shouted as soon as he picked the sheriff out.

Sheriff Benson met him with upheld hands and a stoic face. "Settle down now, Johnson."

"Settle down my ass." Johnson shot back instantly. "You're on my property. I want to see a warrant."

Johnson towered above the sheriff. He must have been six-five without the additional inch of heel under his lacer boots. Not just tall; the man was broad. His shoulders, thick with muscle, were as wide as an ax handle was long. He had a faded red beard shot through with grey. It dangled to his chest and was the most striking thing about the impressive man, until I got close enough to see his eyes. They were blue—the color of deep and ancient ice. Johnson looked like Odin stripped from the old, Norse stories. And he was an angry god.

"We don't need a warrant for this," the sheriff said. He was making an effort to sound reasonable. "It's a crime scene."

"Who says?"

"The body someone tried to burn on a brush pile," I said.

"It still don't give you the right—"

"It gives us every right, Mr. Johnson."

"Mr. Johnson?" he looked at Sheriff Benson with an incredulous expression. "Where the hell are you getting cops these days, Chuck?" To me he said, "Keep your dyke mouth closed a minute. I'm talking to the boss."

The sheriff got a look on his face that I always took as license. It wasn't exactly permission for the kind of anger that's defined my career in the department—so much as it was an acceptance of inevitability. He took a small step back—the kind that said whatever happened was not his responsibility. "Hurricane," he said, putting a little extra emphasis on the nickname. "This is Johnson Rath. All around pain in the ass."

"Chuck Benson, all around king of the great society," Johnson spit back.

"I'm a Republican, Johnson. You know that."

"You're a pissant." Johnson pointed a thick finger at the sheriff. "And a traitor." He jabbed the digit into the sheriff's chest. It was what I was waiting for. Any contact with a police officer in the performance of his duty can be construed as assault. The laws are pretty broad and always work in favor of the officer. Johnson's finger made contact just to the heart side of center. The force of it shoved the sheriff back on his heels.

I reached with both hands. With my right, I grabbed Johnson's finger and twisted. I opened my left hand and slapped it, palm up, into his elbow and pushed up.

He was surprised, but strong. His arm bent around, following the force of my hold. His head turned. His cold gaze set on my eyes. From there, it was like a terrible arm wrestling contest. Johnson didn't fight, he simply resisted. The more force I applied, the more he tensed against it. Other than that, he showed no sign that I was bothering him at all.

If I had grabbed his wrist rather than his finger, I'm not sure I could have held him. As it was, the finger was a perfect grip and gave me painful leverage.

Johnson spit without taking his gaze from my eyes. "You sure you want this, little girl?" he asked.

"Talk and insults the best you got?" I asked back. I wasn't feeling as sure as I had a moment before though.

"Think you can hold me? How long?"

"At least until your finger breaks, asshole."

He nodded over his shoulder, almost smiling.

In my hands, I felt him shift and tense. I applied more pressure.

His almost-smile broke into a knowing smirk.

The finger I was holding twisted against my efforts. To keep my hold I had to push harder and force the digit backwards.

Johnson's glacier-blue eyes were locked with mine when I felt the bone break. Nothing changed in his expression. I was startled that it had gone that far. The snap caused me to let go.

He took the opportunity to turn in and bring his other hand high and fisted at my face. I blocked with my upper arm and shoulder, still the knuckles slipped past and caught me above the ear. I went with it, lowering my head and bending at the waist. I came around pulling my telescoping baton. It was too late.

Johnson was already crumbling to his knees as a bright gouge of blood opened on his temple.

The sheriff held his revolver casually by his thigh. The barrel of the brushed nickel .357 was streaked with blood. "Subtlety is wasted on a man like Johnson." He showed me the gun and the blood on it. "Sometimes the old ways are the best." He turned to the deputies standing gape-mouthed. "Cuff him, Calvin. Take him in to cool off a bit."

When they were taking him to a car, the sheriff turned to me and said, "Your temper is going to get you into trouble one day."

"My temper? You're the one who pistol-whipped him."

"I couldn't let him land that haymaker."

"Well, thanks for that. Who is that guy?"

"I can tell you that," Riley Yates said. I hadn't seen him approach.

"Yeah," Sheriff Benson nodded. "Riley can tell you better than I can. And without calling the man a goddamned sack of shit."

The sheriff was a good man, but kind of rough with his language. I always took it as a compliment that he restrained himself for *ladies,* but he let it fly around me. Charles Benson had never made me believe that I was anything less than any other cop in his eyes. It was something I always appreciated.

"What's the story?" I asked Riley. I nodded at the sheriff's back as he went back to his car. He wiped his pistol on his pants leg before he holstered the weapon.

"I'm surprised you haven't heard that one," Riley said. He pointed to the burned circle behind the tape. "Quid pro quo?"

"You know I can't tell you anything more than the sheriff would."

"You owe me a little more."

I hit him with a look. No one likes to be pushed, especially by a friend. Besides, he was right. I owed him. Riley used information I gave him several months back to write a story exposing a group of CIA and private mercenaries who were trafficking arms and women to pay for nation-building by Kurdish separatists. His writing probably made it impossible for the government to retaliate.

"I know I do," I answered. "But. . ."

"Don't sweat it Hurricane. I don't expect anything that you can't share. Maybe you can share a little differently than your boss?"

"Fair enough," I said. "And don't call me Hurricane."

"I think you're way past fighting that."

"Sometimes I wonder if every woman named Katrina has to deal with that hurricane every day."

"It sticks to you because it fits so well."

"Yeah. Thanks." I needed a change of subject. "Tell me about this Johnson thing."

Riley nodded. It looked to be in part agreement, and in part a physical effort to shake loose the memories. "That was a long time ago. It was 1978 or '79."

"Sock hops and soda pop."

"Not *that* long ago. But we still played records with needles, and it was a big deal when gas soared over a buck a gallon."

"Quaint."

"The past always is if you didn't live through it. There was a lot going on. One of those things was the rise of the religious, end-of-the-world, white power, gun nuts, militia guys."

"Like Waco and Ruby Ridge?"

"Nothing like those. Both situations were tragedies that could have been handled with patience and communication. Just because you want to be left alone doesn't mean you're a danger to anyone else. These guys were different—are different."

"These guys?"

"The New American Covenant–The Word and the Sword. That entire mouthful was what they called themselves. They wanted a separate nation right in the middle of this one. One with their own rules, of course."

"Old Testament rules, I'm guessing."

"Old Testament—without the messy Jewish connection. All Aryan and racially pure. They had a big compound across the line in Arkansas. But they liked to come into Missouri to raise money. Robbery. Extortion. Drugs."

"And Johnson Rath was one of them?"

"Johnson was the biggest, baddest, and angriest of them all. He was a founding member of the Ozarks Nightriders. He's still connected to them but has a whole host of new friends. None of them very nice. "

"So what happened between him and the sheriff?"

"Chuck was a brand new sheriff. He'd barely won the election and he lost the next one. He probably wouldn't have even been there if he didn't feel he needed the exposure. It was over in Rockaway Beach. The town still had the resort thing going on, fishing lodges, go carts, arcades. It was Saturday night on a Memorial Day weekend. Hundreds of people filled the streets. Every dock had a band or a juke box going. Nights like that are gone now. Part of the reason was Johnson Rath."

Riley paused. I couldn't tell if he was remembering or wishing.

"Anyway, like I said, Chuck was working the sidewalk crowds, shaking hands, making sure everyone knew his name. Johnson Rath was in the middle of the street where things were thickest. Drinking—probably drunk. He was the kind of man who never had to look for trouble because he brought it with him wherever he went. A kid named Earl Turner walked right into that trouble."

"They had a history?"

Riley shook his head, a firm negative. The thought and memory came after. He looked around like the past would sneak up if he wasn't careful.

"It was a sad and shameful night."

"You were there?"

"It was a big deal. Summer was in the air. A decade was ending. Things seemed bright. It was a good time to celebrate. A lot of us who lived around here were there. A lot of names you would know. Your Uncle Orson was there for part of it. The end."

"What happened?"

"The streets were crowded. People had beer and hard liquor in plastic cups and no one cared. It was like Mardi Gras down in New Orleans— except for one thing. All the faces you saw were white. It was something you didn't think about until you had to."

"Earl Turner?"

Riley nodded, then let his gaze lock with mine. "The one black man in the crowd. He was walking with a white girl when they bumped into Johnson." Riley broke eye contact with me, then turned to stare at the sheriff standing over by his car. Sheriff Benson was cleaning his gun with a rag. He looked like he was whistling. "It was like something out of a movie. Like a silent bomb went off in the middle of the crowd. All at the same time, everyone knew to back away. Johnson stood alone with Turner."

"I imagine Earl had to know he was in trouble. Hate has a way of burning its cues into your head."

"They fought?"

"No. Turner was a skinny, twenty-year-old kid. Johnson was a man with the muscles of a bull. It was ugly and brutal. It wasn't a fight. It was a massacre. There was no stopping Johnson. Not that anyone tried. I saw it from a balcony. I even took a picture that was never put into any paper."

"The sheriff?"

"Sheriff Chuck Benson pushed his way through the bodies. I'm sure he thought that he was coming to break up a drunken fight. What he found was Johnson standing over Turner. The kid was trying to scream. All the wind and pain were locked in his lungs. He was on the asphalt with Johnson's foot on his ribs. His arm was in Johnson's hands. Johnson was twisting it—not like you did with his finger.

"Johnson had the arm twisted out of the shoulder socket. No joint should bend like that. His muscles and tendons had to be stretched past breaking. If Johnson had put any more pressure on the arm, skin would have ripped. That arm was about to come off when Chuck ran in.

"It changed everything for him."

"How?" I looked over at the sheriff. His weapon was clean and put away. He looked to be doing a crossword puzzle.

"Until that moment, Johnson and Chuck were friends."

Meet the Author

Robert Dunn is the author of the Katrina Williams series, the acclaimed crime novel, *Dead Man's Badge*, as well as the supernatural thrillers *The Red Highway* and *The Harrowing*. He can be found on Facebook at https://www.facebook.com/RobertEDunnAuthor on Twitter at @WritingDead or on Instagram as @redunnauthor.

BODY OF PROOF

Katrina Williams left the Army ten years ago disillusioned and damaged. Now a sheriff's detective at home in the Missouri Ozarks, Katrina is living her life one case at a time—between mandated therapy sessions—until she learns that she's a suspect in a military investigation with ties to her painful past.

The disappearance of a local girl is far from the routine distraction, however. Brutally murdered, the girl's corpse is found by a bottlegger whose information leads Katrina into a tangled web of teenagers, moonshiners, motorcycle clubs, and a fellow veteran battling illness and his own personal demons. Unraveling each thread will take time Katrina might not have as the Army investigator turns his searchlight on the devastating incident that ended her military career. Now Katrina will need to dig deep for the truth—before she's found buried . . .

DREDGING UP THE TRUTH

Still recovering from tragedy and grieving a devastating loss, Iraq war veteran and sheriff's detective Katrina Williams copes the only way she knows how—by immersing herself in work. A body's just been pulled from the lake with a fish haul, but what seems like a straightforward murder case over the poaching of paddlefish for domestic caviar quickly becomes murkier than the depths of the lake.

Soon a second body is found—an illegal Peruvian refugee woman linked to a charismatic tent revival preacher. But as Katrina tries to investigate the enigmatic evangelist, she is blocked by antagonistic FBI agents and Army CID personnel. When more young female refugees disappear, she must partner with deputy Billy Blevins, who stirs mixed feelings in her, to connect the lake murder to the refugees. Katrina is no stranger to darkness, but cold-blooded conspirators plan to make sure she'll never again see the light of day . . .

www.ingramcontent.com/pod-product-compliance
Lightning Source LLC
Chambersburg PA
CBHW050530260626
47157CB00004B/1537